MW00795174

Beowulf

Beowulf

Poem, Poet and Hero

Heather O'Donoghue

BLOOMSBURY ACADEMIC

LONDON • NEW YORK • OXFORD • NEW DELHI • SYDNEY

BLOOMSBURY ACADEMIC
Bloomsbury Publishing Plc
50 Bedford Square, London, WC1B 3DP, UK
1385 Broadway, New York, NY 10018, USA
29 Earlsfort Terrace, Dublin 2, Ireland

BLOOMSBURY, BLOOMSBURY ACADEMIC and the Diana logo are
trademarks of Bloomsbury Publishing Plc

First published in Great Britain 2024

Cover image: Hildebrand, Gabriel, Historiska museet/SHM (CC BY 4.0)

A catalogue record for this book is available from the British Library.

A catalog record for this book is available from the Library of Congress.

ISBN: HB: 978-1-7883-1288-2
          ePDF: 978-1-3502-1271-8
          eBook: 978-1-3502-1272-5

Typeset by Integra Software Services Pvt. Ltd.
Printed and bound in Great Britain

To find out more about our authors and books visit www.bloomsbury.com
and sign up for our newsletters.

for Joseph O'Donoghue

Contents

Introduction

Beowulf is an Anglo-Saxon poem over three thousand lines long about the adventures of its eponymous Scandinavian hero, Beowulf the Geat. Beowulf fights three monsters: towards the beginning of his career as a freelance hero, he kills the man-eating troll, Grendel, and Grendel's even more formidable mother; and at the end of his life – and the poem – when Beowulf has been ruling his own kingdom for fifty years, he takes on a magnificent dragon which has been ravaging his people. These extraordinary events are related against a backdrop of early Scandinavian legendary history. Grendel and his mother are presented as the scourge of the Danish king Hrothgar. Beowulf arrives in Danish territory from his native Geatland – probably imagined as being in southern Sweden – to rid Hrothgar's kingdom of the monsters, but though triumphant in this endeavour, he is powerless to avert the bloodshed and violence which awaits the Danish royal house in the narrative future of the poem to which the poet alludes darkly from time to time. Fifty years later, back home in Geatland, Beowulf dies fighting the dragon, and in a complex set of flashbacks, the poet sets out the long history of the hostilities between the more northerly Swedes and the Geats, thus loading the mourning at Beowulf's funeral with the grim prospect of renewed attacks on a now leaderless people. And throughout his narrative, the poet makes reference – sometimes in the narrative voice, sometimes through stories sung or told by other figures in the poem – to characters and events which throw light on the main substance of the poem: good kings and bad kings, betrayals and allegiances, victories and defeats, treasures and curses.

Beowulf is a literary masterpiece. The poet presents an unforgettable picture of an imagined heroic society, a past which glitters dangerously, both materially and ethically. The poem is by turns thrilling and reflective, crudely violent and delicately emotional. Dark and desolate landscapes are contrasted with bright human communities, and deep, disabling griefs with sudden outbursts of joy. These changes of mood and tone are held together in tension through verbal artistry of the very highest quality. Against an unceasing flow of poetic compounds and synonyms, and an inexorable and yet flexible metre, ideas, images and states of mind echo throughout the poem, and throughout the many stories the poet tells. But at the poem's heart is the fundamental issue of what it is to live a good life, and combat the forces of evil, a dilemma refracted multiple times in different places and historical periods, and amongst different peoples.

However, there has been more specialist scholarship on *Beowulf* than critical appreciation of its literary qualities, and readership of the poem in its original language has necessarily been limited. Translations are, in essence, different texts, and the better the translation, the more different the text. Inevitably, the poetic textures of the original are obscured to some degree. The poem's reputation as a great work of literature has been more often asserted than illustrated, and of course amongst what you might call professional people of letters, the status of *Beowulf* as a formidable text for undergraduates to translate (too often wryly treated by them as it were a sort of punishment or penitential exercise for some unspecified crime) has dominated its reception. Many more people remember Woody Allen's jocular advice not to take any university courses that make you read *Beowulf* than have ever had any contact with the poem itself, and years ago, Brigid Brophy, in her iconoclastic literary history *Fifty Works of English Literature We Could Do Without*, began – inevitably – with *Beowulf*. More recently, screen versions of *Beowulf* have introduced it to a popular audience, but have introduced what? Not an immaculately crafted work of literature and an exploration of the human condition, but a series of sensational encounters between a superman hero and a trio of undeniably terrifying monsters. Incidentally, scholars have over the years privately – and not so privately – diagnosed a similar duality in the poem, solemnly regretful that the poet wasted time and energy on imaginary enemies, and relegated what they would prefer to read about – the shadowy histories of Scandinavian royal houses – to the background, or the outer edges of the poem. But as we shall see, the poet has woven the monster fights inextricably into the politics and history of the poem, and a proper appreciation of that must see these links as well as recognizing the evident contrasts in the substance of the material.

It is certainly true that *Beowulf* has presented specialist scholars with a host of difficult and sometimes, one suspects, unanswerable questions. To the best of my knowledge, only one scholar has publicly and explicitly stated that they have read the poem for pleasure (although that doesn't necessarily mean that others haven't enjoyed the subject of their research, just that they haven't felt the need actually to say so). Of course, the language of *Beowulf* is the primary barrier to wider readership. Old English is evidently and demonstrably an earlier form of English, but as so many English undergraduates have found, it's not something one can read without considerable effort, practice and skill, and furthermore, the *Beowulf*-poet's elaborately complex poetic diction and unfixed syntax makes the language a challenge even by the standards of other Anglo-Saxon texts. But *Beowulf* is a mysterious poem in many other less obvious respects. For example, it is preserved in only one manuscript, in a volume which narrowly escaped destruction when the library in which it was housed – the grimly appropriately named Ashburnham House – caught fire in 1731. The edges of the pages are charred and crumbly, and sometimes unreadable. As it happened, an Icelander had both commissioned, and himself undertook to make, a copy of the text some years earlier. He had some knowledge of the original language; the man he commissioned did not. Who, then, would you say made the more accurate copy? Scholars are still arguing. It is evident from certain mistakes in the existing text (some words repeated; others missed out; some nonsense words apparently created from a misreading of original letter forms) that the poem we have was copied from a written exemplar. But can we be sure that the poem's two medieval scribes were otherwise unimpeachably accurate? Might they have interfered in the text, either by accident or design? What right have modern scholars to question or emend their work?

The date of the poem is perhaps the most contentious issue amongst scholars. One of the characters – Beowulf's lord, the King of the Geats, Hygelac – can (probably) be identified as an actual historical figure who lived in the sixth century. And the manuscript itself can be dated to the turn of the eleventh century, perhaps as late as 1016, when the Danish king Canute came to the throne of England. But no-one can be sure just when, in the five centuries between those two dates, *Beowulf* might have been composed. It's the equivalent of not being able to tell whether a poem was written by Shakespeare or Seamus Heaney. None of the usual dating criteria work, mainly because there is so little else to compare the poem with. Even if we could date the language of the poem, that wouldn't necessarily give us a date of composition – poetry can be notoriously archaic in its diction and syntax. You only have to look at Keats' rich Shakespearianisms, or the obsolete, old-fashioned language of bad contemporary verse, with its use of contractions ('Tis'); archaisms ('ere'); inversions ('ladies fair'); or periphrastic past tenses ('as she did say'), presumably used either to sound traditional and therefore venerable, or in a desperate attempt to fit the chosen metre. And further, *Beowulf* may not even have a date of composition, as such: the text could be simply one record of an oral poem, the latest version of a poem which had been constantly evolving, or one which had been preserved and passed down in oral tradition.

Impressive efforts have been made by scholars to identify a time and place in Anglo-Saxon England, a set of kingdoms sporadically and then chronically plagued by Viking raids and Danish invasions, in which a long poem about illustrious Scandinavians might find favour, or seem politically relevant. The poet evidently knew the Bible (at the very least, the Old Testament) as many allusions make clear, but what's not clear is whether the way the poem depicts pre-Christian Scandinavians indicates a securely Christian author and audience, or whether it's a brave early attempt to reconcile old and new belief systems. Comparisons between archaeological finds and the poet's descriptions of material objects, such as weapons, or rituals such as funerals, are beset by the same problems as linguistic criteria: the poet may be describing ancient artefacts or rites, known either first hand, perhaps as heirlooms, or as part of some cultural memory, or indeed from older literary texts. And in any case, the poem is set not in Anglo-Saxon England, but in early medieval Scandinavia, an imagined landscape and society perhaps unfamiliar to both author and audience, and not necessarily a historically authentic recreation. As ever, all such attempts at dating the poem founder because there's so little in the way of archaeology, literature or history to set the poem against. And this brings us to the key mystery of the poem: nothing else like it has survived, even presuming something like it had ever existed. There is nothing so long, nothing so ambitious or wide-ranging – nothing, in fact, remotely as impressive as *Beowulf*, although much shorter and sometimes fragmentary lyric poems in Old English have been rightly admired and enjoyed. But no mention whatever of a poem anything at all like *Beowulf* has ever been found, anywhere. The great Anglo-Saxon scholar Alcuin, who graced the Frankish court of the Emperor Charlemagne in the ninth century, wrote a letter to a bishop in England bemoaning what he regarded as the inappropriate enjoyment of secular, heroic literature read out at the monastic dinner table. 'Quid enim Hinieldus cum Christo?', he complained – what, then, has Ingeld to do with Christ? The name Ingeld is mentioned once in Beowulf, in an allusion to the bloody future facing the Danish royal house. And that's it. It's a tenuous connexion: one passing reference to a figure whose name is mentioned once in *Beowulf*. The rest is silence.

This book will very much *not* be concerned with the knotty problems and pervasive uncertainties outlined above. I shall confine myself to the text as we have it, imperfect and fraying around the edges as it is. I shall certainly not be discussing any of the scholarly debates over dating or authorship or palaeography. Of course, this will entail some big assumptions: most obviously, the assumption of a single, supremely talented poet who succeeded in producing a magnificent epic poem. I shall also make some executive and often silent decisions about doubtful manuscript readings which scholars have rightly regarded as significant for our understanding of the poem, but have been unable to agree on, or provide definitive answers as to how to make the best sense of them. There will not be any footnotes. In the best editions of the poem, there is more footnote material than poetic text, by far, not to mention glossaries, commentaries, textual notes and manuscript variants. I've spent my working life using, respecting and admiring such volumes, but this is not the place for their distinctive contribution to our – and my own – understanding of *Beowulf*. I won't translate or anglicize proper names, apart from substituting 'th' for the equivalent Old English characters, for the reason that I prefer it that way, although I recognize that how to pronounce some Anglo-Saxon names is not self-evident. Similarly, I shall mostly quote in the original, with literal translations in the body of my text, even though the spelling of Old English is hardly ever a good indication of how it might have been pronounced, or how it might relate to modern English. Finally, I concede – though cannot help – the fact that my own reading of the poem is rooted in my own historical circumstances. I hope that my knowledge of the Anglo-Saxon period will prevent the most glaring misreadings, but part of the point of a book like this is that there should be room for an appreciation of the poem which does not depend on specialist knowledge.

I shall begin with a detailed analysis of the opening of *Beowulf*, an opening which showcases the poet's characteristic skills, for the beginnings of long poems are always stuffed with significance and designed for maximum impact and attention grab. The rest of the book falls into three parts. The first will be an account of the poem's imagined world, in both its material and ethical aspects, moving on to look at its depiction of that world's inhabitants – its human characters and its monsters. This constitutes, as it were, the substance of the poem. The second part will show how this substance is dispensed to us: focusing on the overlapping roles of poet, narrator and an imagined reciter of songs (the Anglo-Saxon *scop*) I will try to convey the poetic art of the poem; its narrator's confident but complex interaction of past and future in its many stories; and the refractive contribution of the poems and songs recited within the body of the text. Finally, as a sort of epilogue, I will consider what various post-medieval audiences have made of the poem, and why. Those who already know the poem well in its original form may be curious to see how it stands up to what is essentially little more than a very close reading. Others, who will, I hope, turn from this book to one of the many translations of the poem, will at least have some idea of how that translation relates to and compares with the original poem it was founded upon. But I suppose my great hope is that some readers may even be inspired to read for the first time this extraordinary poem in its original – or at least, singularly surviving – form.

Beowulf begins

Beowulf begins with a bang. The poet, or narrator, playing the part of a *scop*, or Anglo-Saxon court poet, calls an audience to attention as if this text were a record – the script, as it were – of a recital. The *scop* and the poem's first word is 'Hwæt!', which may be either an onomatopoeic rendering of the clatter of the Anglo-Saxon equivalent of a gavel, or the anticipatory twang of a lyre; or a conventional verbal call to attention, which one translator represented as 'What ho!' – this now seems risibly dated, but it conveys rather well the sound and peremptory quality of the original. Seamus Heaney's celebrated translation picks up the self-conscious and traditional authority of the Northern Irish storyteller – 'So' – indicating the significance and solemnity of the substance to follow.

Exactly what the poet-narrator is introducing is to some degree unclear. Much of the punctuation in post-medieval editions of *Beowulf* is not in the manuscript, so that the precise interrelationship of the poetic half-lines, which roughly equate to brief clauses or parts of clauses in modern syntax and most often contain only two stressed syllables, is unfixed, and may give rise to more than one precise meaning. The words themselves are tightly knit together in alliterative patterns. While each half-line typically contains only three or four individual words, so that the general impression is of a laconic, trimmed-down style, the characteristic poetic practice of the *Beowulf*-poet – and, indeed, as widely seen throughout Old English literature – is to set out, twice or more, the same subject in different words – a technique known as variation. All this is much easier to illustrate than to describe, analyse or explain (to employ variation myself here).

Thus, the first six half-lines of the poem are:

Hwæt,		Hwæt!	
we Gar-Dena	in gear-dagum	we of [the] Spear-Danes	in yore-days
þeod-cyninga	þrym gefrunon	of people-kings [the] glory [have] heard
hu þa æþelingas	ellen fremedon.	how those princes bravery furthered.

This literal translation doesn't do much for clarity of meaning, but the shape of the paired half-lines is immediately obvious, and also the way the lack of 'small words' – for instance, definite and indefinite articles – creates an emphatic, laconic style. We should note, too, the pared-down effect created by a striking density of compound words – Spear-Danes, yore-days, people-kings. At the same time, we can experience the freedom in the way the half-lines might be fitted together: have we all heard about the Spear-Danes, and about the glory of people-kings or have we heard about the glory of the people-kings of the Spear-Danes? And without the word 'the' (which I've added in square brackets in my translation) do we expect to be told about the specific glory of these people, or about glory in general? And are Spear-Danes, people-kings and princes all different terms for the same subject – an example of variation? Or have we got two subjects: the kings who were glorious, and a younger generation of princes who furthered bravery? Is performing brave deeds the same as, or a necessary prelude to, accruing glory?

But in spite of all this possible and indeed rich ambiguity, we can see how precisely and economically the alliteration binds words together: *þrym* (glory) is the attribute of *þeodcyningas* (people-kings); *ellen* (bravery) is furthered by *æþelingas* (princes). And immediately following the opening 'Hwæt!' we have the intricate echoing of the first two compound words: *Gar-Denas* and *geardagum* – terms which also sum up the subject of the poem's opening: Spear-Danes in days of yore.

It is clear from the outset that this is being represented as a shared, a collective enterprise: what is to be related is purported and presumably assumed to be material familiar to both poet and audience, with the bracing, unambiguous inclusivity of very second word – the 'we' who have heard about the glory of the Spear-Danes in days of yore. On the other hand, can we now hear a 'but' coming? *Beowulf* as a whole is very far from a simple celebration of the martial glory of ancient Danes. Rather, the main body of the poem shows Hrothgar, the Danish king, beset by a monster he is powerless to control, in spite of all that glory and greatness and deeds of bravery. Furthermore, in spite of Beowulf's victory over Grendel and his avenging, nameless mother, the future for the Danish royal house looks very bleak. And by the end of the poem, the future of Beowulf's own kingdom is terminally threatened. So perhaps this resounding opening to the poem implies a subtext: 'We all know about how great the Danes were, and about brave deeds performed by young princelings, but this is going to be a different sort of story.'

But all this is still in the future – the future of the rest of the purported recitation and the future of the storyworld it describes. For the moment, the poet dwells on the glorious past of the Spear-Danes and leaves as yet unspoken what was to come – and also, what came before. The poet's history of the Danes begins with their king Scyld Scefing, whose military and political success is figured by the statement that he deprived many peoples of their mead-benches. Political and military autonomy is perhaps unexpectedly represented as the freedom to enjoy communal celebrations – mead-drinking and feasting – and in conquering neighbouring tribes, Scyld Scefing has deprived them of this. It's a curiously oblique way of describing battles and violence, but it clearly foreshadows Grendel's attacks, which caused the Danes to abandon their great hall, Heorot.

Given that attack is the best form of defence, Scyld's name, which is related to the modern English word 'shield', and gives rise in the poem to the name of the Danish dynasty, the so-called Scyldings, is suspiciously appropriate. His apparent patronymic – 'Scefing' – is more difficult to account for. On the face of it, a figure such as Scyld, who mysteriously and almost magically appeared amongst the Danes when they most needed a great leader, would have no known father, and indeed we learn that Scyld was a foundling, like the biblical Moses, or Oedipus. The first element of the name Scefing seems to denote a sheaf, so whether *scef* refers to an attribute or an ancestor, Scyld Scefing would seem to embody the two fundamental aspects of early kingship, the defence and fertility of the realm. He is starting to look like a mythic progenitor of the Danish royal house.

The possibility of a mythic dimension is furthered in two very different ways. There are numerous (and all slightly different) accounts in early medieval chronicles of a strange ritual apparently used to determine claims of kingship and/or land. The earliest, from the tenth century, involves a foundling called Scef, who is washed up on the shore of an island named as Scaney, and becomes its king. A century later, one Sceldius (specified as 'the son of Sceaf') is similarly washed up, but this time with a handful of corn at his head, and on an island called Scandza. He too comes to rule his adopted land. And in a thirteenth-century chronicle, the monks of Abingdon monastery, in Oxfordshire, are described as performing a curious ritual in order to lay claim to land for their home foundation: they placed a handful of corn on a boat-shaped shield, together with a lighted candle, and set it afloat on the river Thames. Wherever the shield touched the riverbank was held to indicate rightful monastic land, and most remarkably, at Gifteleia (modern-day Iffley) the floating shield touched a meadow called 'Beri' which, in wet weather, was cut off from the mainland and became an island. Of course, land claims – now as well as then – are and were the subject of all sorts of improbable justifications. But the similarities here are very striking, especially the arrival over water to an island, which is, after all, how the Anglo-Saxons figured their own prehistory. The old form of the name of Iffley seems to indicate that although the chronicle may long post-date *Beowulf*, it may well be based on very early traditions. The original monastic site where Timoleague Friary, in Co. Cork, Ireland, now stands, is said to have been determined by a very similar ritual.

The second reason to suppose some mythic basis to the story of Scyld Scefing comes from the poem itself. We have already seen that details of whom King Scyld fought, and where, and when, are completely absent, subsumed under the euphemistic metaphor of the deprivation of mead benches. But Scyld's rise to power in Denmark is recounted in unmistakeably agricultural terms: he *weox under wolcnum* – 'waxed under [the] welkin' – that is, grew tall beneath the sky. This coming to fruition is redolent of growing plants, arable crops ripening in the open air, ultimately to be gathered into sheaves, perhaps. Next, the poet suddenly pulls back from such agricultural terminology and praises Scyld in more conventional terms: for making neighbouring tribes consent to his rule and pay him tribute. All this makes for a good king! But Scyld is then credited with providing his subjects with one final, sustaining dynastic gift: a son, Beow, whose name is related to the word for barley (as is the name of the island in the Thames at Iffley that the monks laid claim to when their floating sacrifice washed up against it). Beow (which the scribe, probably mistakenly and certainly confusingly, copied out as 'Beowulf') is also introduced in quasi-agricultural terms: his *blæd wide sprang*. *Sprang* is the past tense of the verb *springan*, just as in Modern English the past tense of 'to spring' is 'sprang', and it is used elsewhere in Old English as a verb describing the growth of plants, to spring up. And what sprang widely was Beow's *blæd* – on one level, his glory, or prosperity, but on another – and elsewhere in Old English – his fruits, or riches, as in 'the fruits of the earth'. Beow is implicitly associated with the new spring growth of crops.

Just as Scyld's seizure and control of his neighbours' meadbenches anticipate the poem's account of the fight against Grendel for control of the Danes' great hall, Heorot, so Beow's career foreshadows Beowulf's own achievements: commanding the loyalty of his retainers, giving out treasure and performing celebrated deeds of bravery. The poet in this way combines the mythic and the plausibly historical or legendary. But the account of the end of Scyld's life strongly reinforces a mythic pattern. Scyld, as we have seen, arrives from an unknown starting point on to the shore of the Danish kingdom. When his predestined date for departing this life arrives, his body is laid in a ship riding at anchor, together with heaps of treasure. The fine vessel is loaded with more rich armour and valuable objects than the poet has ever heard of. All this treasure is to travel with Scyld's body, to depart on a long journey into the keeping of the ocean, as the poet puts it. With a rather mind-boggling exercise of what seems to be traditional understatement, we are told that Scyld certainly didn't depart this life with fewer accompaniments than he arrived with, a destitute foundling – that is, he departed with a very great deal more. The poet concludes this account of Scyld's strange funeral with a mystery: no-one, not even the wise men of the royal court, knows where or by whom this precious cargo was received.

The symmetry of Scyld's arrival and departure across the sea, from an unknown setting-off point to an unknowable destination, clearly traces a familiar cyclic movement. Might the poet be making an unstated allusion to the diurnal, quotidian journey of the sun, with its similarly unknowable progress from setting to rising, glowing brightly as it descends to the horizon? And like the sun, the ship is *utfus* – 'eager to go' – just as the sun seems to increase the pace of its setting as it nears the western horizon. Is there, in addition, something seasonal about these timings, which reinforces the organic terminology, given that the other adjective applied to the boat is *isig* – 'icy' – with its suggestion of winter after harvest time? Or might we simply have a metaphor for human life itself, from the ineffable non-existence before our birth to the undiscovered and unreturnable-from bourn of death? Whatever we conclude – or feel – Scyld's reign is manifestly not simply a linear period of historical (or even legendary) human rule. And his secret and separate autonomy is emphasized by the fact that he himself sets out the terms of his funeral: like the seed of plant, its blossoming and dying is contained in itself.

I put forward all these possibilities in order to suggest the richness of *Beowulf*, how well it responds to a very close reading, rather than to suggest that the poem is full of unanswerable questions. Every section of the poem is susceptible to equally close readings, although, as I have said, beginnings are always a special case. I need to raise one final issue, showcased in the poem's opening, but at issue throughout. The poet states quite baldly that the birth of Scyld's son Beow was a gift 'sent from God', as a comfort to the Danish people who had suffered so terribly from being leaderless before the miraculous (and I use this word advisedly) advent of Scyld Scefing. Succession (as the Norse gods, whose tragedy was that their great hope Baldr met an untimely and unavengable death, could tell you) is everything. We should bear this in mind when we learn how Hrothgar plans to counteract the vulnerable youth of his own sons and the threat presented by his nephew Hrothulf; what the entailment of Beowulf's childlessness might be; and how Beowulf's grandfather Hrethel reacted to the death of his eldest son.

But who or what is being evoked by the term 'God' (the same word in Old English and Modern English)? It is often pointed out that the poet makes numerous references to the Old Testament, but never mentions anything pertaining to the New – there is no Christ, no apostles or Blessed Virgin, anywhere in the poem. Is the poet's 'God' an anonymous deity, an over-arching abstraction serving both Christian and pre-Christian purposes? The poet's vocabulary is no help – the word for 'lord/Lord' in Old English is *Frea* – clearly cognate with the name of the Old Norse (and pagan) god Freyr, but we can't be certain which tradition did the borrowing. Was the name of the pre-Christian god adopted by early Christians to be applied to Jesus Christ? Or were they both separately developed from an early respectful word for a reverenced being? The poet of *Beowulf* uses compound words for deities such as *Lif-Frea* ('Lord of life'), or the doublet *wuldres Wealdend* ('Ruler of glory') but close as they are to Christian usage, they remain tantalizingly unspecific. At base, the issue is whether the terminology reflects, at the risk of anachronism, the poet's own post-pagan beliefs and culture, or whether a diplomatic attempt is being made to suggest that the Danes in the poem, whilst manifestly not specifically Christian, are not totally alien to Christianity, even in their paganism. Whatever sense we have of this, the poem is suffused with a powerful, all-purpose piety, an unswerving recognition of a higher being watching over the affairs of mankind, whoever they might be.

Although, as I have said, the whole poem would repay similar detailed analysis and comment, I will not treat all three thousand or so lines in the same way. Having given, I hope, a preview of the poem's mystery and richness, I will instead move on to give some sort of sense of the world in which this poet has set the action, a world at once both alien and familiar, peopled by human characters who sometimes remind us of ourselves – at our best as well as our worst – although sometimes acting in unfathomable and apparently outlandish ways, and a world also inhabited by patently outlandish monsters.

1

The Storyworld

(i) The setting

The geography of *Beowulf* is vague, to say the least. In the poem, Hrothgar is represented as the king of the Danes – the *Gar-Denas* – but in early times, southern Sweden was under Danish rule. Beowulf is the nephew of the Geatish king Hygelac, travelling across the sea from his homeland – which has no certain historical basis at all – to offer help to Hrothgar. In the poem's future, an attack from the Scylfing people, who are associated with northern Sweden, is dreaded by those Geats who live on after Beowulf's death at the hands of the dragon. The whole action of the poem, past present and future, takes place within the bounds of what is now Denmark and Sweden. But there are no names in this Anglo-Saxon poem which might anchor the action to a particular geographical location. The poem's setting is a Scandinavia of the mind, an unspecific Northern European landscape as likely to have been created from the poet's experience of Anglo-Saxon England as from any first-hand knowledge of Scandinavia. There are no towns, or harbours, no distinctive topographical features which might identify actual places. Such place names as there are, are generic: *Hrefnesholt* (Raven's Wood); *Hronesnæsse* (perhaps, Whale's Ness). The Victorian scholar Daniel Haigh claimed that he recognized topographical features on the north-east coast of England, and in the Tees Valley, as the sites described in the poem; others have made quite different suggestions.

The landscape is impressionistically described, a blurred and shifting mass of lakes, misty moors, mountains, streams and, above all, cliffs. This is a landscape dominated by the sea, and the cliffs which demarcate it from the land. The poem is full of synonyms for the sea. Beowulf and his men first arrive by sea, and his people, the Geats, are repeatedly referred to as seamen. It may well be that Anglo-Saxons stereotyped medieval Scandinavians as a sea-going people, just as we do today, defined above all by their ships. As we have seen, Scyld Scefing's last mysterious journey is across the sea. And the stock phrase to indicate an immeasurable, dividing expanse is *be sæm tweonum* (between two seas), although it's not clear which two seas this might refer to, if any in particular. Where we might say, 'he was, to Hrothgar, the dearest man on earth', the poet says 'the dearest man between the two seas'. The land is defined and circumscribed by what it is not. The sea is always there, on the edge, beneath a cliff, and then stretching further than one can see. And when the Danes in Heorot are listening to the story of creation, a tale from the far distant past, the human world is imagined as a bright plain surrounded by water.

Dry land in the poem is itself unrelentingly wet. As well as lakes and streams, there are fens and marshes, watercourses running underground, and a sinister pool – Grendel's mere – where a wind stirs waves on the surface which are whipped up to meet the descending mists. The natural world, on sea and on land, is the home of monsters, and human civilization has barely made a mark on it. Journeys by sea, which must surely, in actuality, have been supremely dangerous undertakings, are represented in *Beowulf* as swift and uneventful. This is partly the result of human ingenuity: the Geats are celebrated sailors, and their boats are a triumph of organic engineering, shown lightly riding the waves, skimming over an alien environment. In fact, these boats are given, through the poet's art, a life of their own; although humanly constructed, once they take shape, they assume the living properties of flesh and blood steeds. We have already seen how Scyld Scefing's funeral boat – with perhaps unfitting gusto – seems *utfus* (eager to depart), like a highly strung horse straining at a leash. Beowulf's boat is *famiheals* (foamy-necked) on the journey from Geatland to the Danish kingdom, like a horse ridden hard, foam-flecked with exertion, although the poet follows this up with a contrasting simile: the boat is *fugle gelicost* (most like a bird), as if what was needed was the evocation of the bulk and power of horse tempered by the effortless glide of a sea-bird. I will discuss the poet's use of kennings and compound words in more detail later on in the book, but this is perhaps the moment to draw attention to a very particular group of kennings, or metaphorical circumlocutions, in which boats are figured as if they were the living inhabitants of the sea, not crafted contraptions. Equally and in a way, oppositely, we also find in *Beowulf* the kenning *swan-rad* (swan-road). The sea is precisely not a road, not in any sense a human creation, and can only be forcibly designated as such via the swan element, in that from a swan's perspective the sea is as ordinary an environment as a path over dry land is for a human. These sorts of poetic formulae are familiar throughout Old English and Old Norse poetry. The effects they create are multiple, as I will explain in due course; here, we are led to recognize the sea as an alien environment for humans, mastered – to some extent – by ship-building skills which paradoxically recreate the product of human ingenuity as a living creature.

On land, the natural world outside Heorot is not homely and picturesque, but menacing: another unaccountable and uncivilized wilderness. A good example is the celebrated description of the strange and unnatural surroundings which are home to Grendel and his mother. These monsters are said to inhabit a secret land of wolf-slopes and windswept headlands, where a mountain stream – perhaps a waterfall – falls through the mists of headlands and then mysteriously disappears under the ground. A mere is overhung with frost-covered woods which cast deep shadows over the surface of the water, and it is said to be bottomless. Further, this place defies the laws of nature. A hunted deer would rather face its pursuers and certain death than plunge into the water and escape by swimming. And at night, the mere is home to an extraordinary and perverse phenomenon: the water burns.

This is hardly a realistic description of an actual landscape; it is hard to create a coherent image in one's mind of the topography. All its features are designed to dismay and repel an audience. In fact, some of the elements here – especially the burning water – are paralleled in literary sources from elsewhere which depict conceptions of the entrance to Hell. Again, then, this is a landscape of the mind, a world outside Heorot which consists of an assemblage of everything that is threatening and inimical to human civilization.

Throughout the poem, we hear nothing of villages, settlements or farms; the terrain outside Hrothgar's great hall, Heorot, may not all be as intensely alien as Grendel's mere, but it is largely uncultivated, unmapped and barely traversed. When the poet tells us that because of the depredations of Grendel, the great hall is deserted, we have no idea of where the Danes can have taken refuge. When, after the unexpected revenge attack of Grendel's mother, we are told that Beowulf was not in Heorot, but had been given lodging elsewhere, it comes as a surprise, and even something of a puzzle, because we have had no clear sense that there were habitable buildings outside Heorot, beyond a couple of shadowy references to the fortified strongholds past Danish leaders are credited with controlling. Crucially, Heorot itself is not imagined as a place where people live. It is a vast, communal space, an arena for the exercise and enjoyment of the characteristic values of the heroic society we are gradually being introduced to: gift-giving; speech-making; drinking together. All told, it is a place for bonding. And in the end, it is a structure symbolic of Hrothgar's power, the power to make an emphatic statement of human domination of the natural world. This is why Grendel's attacks have been so devastating, and why the burning of Heorot, hinted at as part of the poem's future, carries such symbolic weight.

Heorot is a new building when the poem opens. It is a human construction of immense ambition. It is to be the crowning glory of Hrothgar's glittering reign, which has been marked by military victory and the springing up of a whole new generation of brave and loyal retainers. Hrothgar summons an international workforce to raise it – it is telling that he has the wide-reaching authority to command such a thing. Like the time-honoured glory of the Danes with which the poem opens, Heorot will be something that everyone will have heard of. And indeed, we have all heard of the glory that was Heorot, although perhaps more for the infamous tragedy of its ruination by fire, than for its youthful grandeur, just as, in Scandinavian tradition, the Danish royal house was remembered not for its glory, but for bloodshed and betrayal.

Beyond the superlatives of its size and the treasures inside it, we are told rather little about the architecture of Heorot. In fact, it is when Beowulf's fight with Grendel causes the building some serious damage that we learn more about its construction. We already know that it is made of wood, because of its susceptibility to fire, and Beowulf's heavily armed Geatish company causes its wooden floor to resound when they march in. There is frequent – if rather unspecific – reference to gold decoration. But with Grendel's attack, there is more detail, as if the poet needed to visualize and convey more clearly the circumstances of the encounter. The doors, for example, are fastened with iron bars, and the walls cunningly braced with iron; the floor is decorated, and mead-benches are anchored to it. The whole structure is solid, able to withstand the destructive force of the fighting between hero and monster. But perhaps we learn most about Heorot from its name, and one detail of its decoration. The poet describes Heorot – The Hart – as *heah ond horngeap* (high and horn-gabled – this may mean that stylized antlers were attached to the gable ends of the hall, or, perhaps more likely, that the hall's roof terminated in antler-like projections). It could be that the element *horn* simply indicates breadth, so that Heorot is wide-gabled. But the association of hart and horn is surely no coincidence, and picks up the image of the powerful, antlered stag which would rather be torn to pieces by hounds than save its life by swimming in Grendel's mere. Heorot is – just like the foamy-necked longships – a man-made model of a living creature: a great stag, standing tall, with spreading antlers.

The construction of Heorot, a massive monument, is recalled at the very beginning of *Beowulf*. But its destruction is mentioned almost in the same breath. There are only two other man-made structures described in the poem, both monumental in their way, and they are designed as secure holding places not for the living, but for the dead. They are stone edifices, and thus impregnable to fire and, it appears, to the ravages of time. Both are introduced at the end of the poem, and both, like Heorot, are filled with treasure. But whilst treasure in Heorot is always on the move, given and received, bright golden currency flowing through the hall and carrying with it the gratitude of both giver and receiver, the hoards in the two burial mounds at the end of the poem are fraught with sinister associations: they are corroded and dulled from lack of use; believed to be under a curse; and most bleakly, as the poet declares, the treasure is *eldum swa unnyt | swa hit æror wæs* (to people in those days as useless as it used to be before). (One tiny point: in quotations from the original, as here, I am using the symbol for a poetic line-break – | – between every half-line, to mark not just the break between each pair of half-lines, but also (again as here) the space between half-lines, the caesura.)

Like Scyld Scefing himself, all that gold has been returned to the dark place it came from. At best, such hoards remain under the earth, inert and unpolished, like the unmined mineral ore they began as. At worst, bringing them back into circulation may precipitate disaster. Someone unearthing a golden goblet from the dragon's hoard provokes the creature to take devastating revenge on the Geatish kingdom. Looting burial mounds never goes unpunished. The poem closes without disclosing the fate of the treasure in Beowulf's burial mound, and the poet lurches into the present tense to reassure us that the gold is still there. But Beowulf's dying wish was to feast his eyes on it, not to dispense it, and the gloomy future facing the Geats would seem to preclude any lavish displays of wealth anytime soon. Perhaps the best we can hope for is that the treasure remains hidden, even if it lies there *unnyt* (useless). It is worth recalling that Heorot itself, together with all its valuable resources, lay *unnyt* when Grendel's attacks destroyed the cultural heart of the Danish kingdom – the *Beowulf*-poet's only other use of the word.

The actual construction of the dragon's lair seems to have happened long before the poem's time frame, even before the half-mythical pre-history of the Danish royal house. It is a stone burial chamber distinctly reminiscent of a megalithic long barrow – a fitting shape for a sinuous dragon. Its entrance is twice called a *stanboga* (stone-bow), presumably to designate a stone archway. It has a secret entrance – *eldum uncuð* (unknown to people in those days) – and the archway is strengthened by pillars – perhaps the upright megaliths supporting the capstone of a prehistoric tomb. It is roofed with stone, and it is, essentially, an underground space. Dizzyingly, the poet transports us to the time when this ancient monument – this *enta geweorc* (work of giants), as so many megalithic monuments used to be understood – was a new build: it was created for the deposition of treasure by the last survivor of a doomed people, who is given a celebrated elegy spoken in memory of his vanished tribe and their now pointless and useless treasure. The parallels with Beowulf's situation are painfully clear. But this treasure is reclaimed by a vagrant dragon, who, as dragons do in Scandinavian tradition, curls up on the gold as if it were a featherbed, and guards the treasure for three hundred years.

Beowulf's burial mound is constructed in the time of the storyworld during the poet's primary narrative. His people first construct a funeral pyre, and his body is cremated; this is all on his own instructions, just as Scyld Scefing decreed his own funeral rites. Once Beowulf's body is burnt, the Geats begin to build the commemorative mound, but this is not a secret, underground chamber, a dank hole for concealing treasure. It is a tall, broad and imposing structure, which, in an imprecise but forcibly evocative way, recalls Scyld Scefing's passage out of the world across the sea, for it is designed to be visible to seafarers across the wide expanse of the ocean. Beowulf's ashes are placed inside the mound, and with them, the treasures he won from the dragon's hoard. There is a solemn and dignified ceremony as warriors ride around the barrow and praise Beowulf's achievements as they lament his loss. And yet, in spite of all this grandeur and solemnity, the deposition of the treasure raises those disquieting issues I mentioned earlier. We might even catch distant echoes of the parable of the talents in the New Testament, which were neither divested nor invested (to use a contemporary and capitalist term) but interred, and left inert. It is hard indeed to see the burial of the dragon's hoard in Beowulf's tomb as a positive thing in any cultural frame of reference.

Treasure, then, is seen at its best in *Beowulf* when it is being put to use, enjoyed as reward, or proudly gifted, or simply for its aesthetic delights. In some ways, it can be seen as another manifestation of human control over the natural world, the transformation of mineral ore into highly wrought and regarded objects. However, as we shall see, its material durability gives it the possibility of a history, and its material actuality can be shown to be an illusion: in any real world, treasure may be stolen, and weapons may be destroyed in battle, but here in *Beowulf*, swords may melt or, apparently independently of their wielders, fail in a time of need. They may even tell stories.

So far, I have been using the term 'treasure' rather loosely. In *Beowulf*, treasure often comes in large quantities, as hoards, or lavish collections of gifts, and these mostly comprise wargear – weapons and armour – and jewellery. (Pedigree horses are included amongst the marvellous gifts which Hrothgar bestows on Beowulf, but although archaeologists have found evidence of the remains of horses – sometimes disarticulated – associated with richly furnished burial mounds, there is unsurprisingly no mention of horses in connection with funerary treasures in *Beowulf*. It would introduce a note of sensational heathen practice, and possibly, sacrificial rites, at odds with the careful dignity of the Beowulfian funerals, for instance, or the account of Scyld's passing. But one of the inhumations associated with the celebrated Anglo-Saxon ship burial at Sutton Hoo lay next to a horse.)

The treasure which accompanied Scyld Scefing on his final voyage is the first we hear about in the poem. Scyld is himself described as *beaga brytta* (rings' dispenser) and his funerary ship, as befits a reign distinguished by military victory, is loaded *hildewæpnum ond heaðowædum* (with war-weapons and battle-clothes), further specified as sword-blades and mailshirts. As always, it isn't clear whether there is actual specificity here, or just the impression, conveyed through the poetic technique of variation, and serving the poem's alliteration, of a mass of different names for weapons and armour. But the poet is careful to note one significant attribute of these precious things: they come *of feorwegum* (from far-distant parts). We cannot help but be reminded of the rich treasures unearthed at the Sutton Hoo burial, with its impressively cosmopolitan assemblage of artefacts.

There have been many attempts to connect the items from Sutton Hoo with the material objects in *Beowulf*; sometimes partial or damaged artefacts have been reconstructed along lines suggested by the poem, and sometimes, difficult-to-interpret lines of poetry have been construed on the basis of relevant Sutton Hoo finds. And existing similarities can be very striking: the Sutton Hoo helmet, with its aquiline nosepiece and eagle-wing eyebrow guards – which terminate, bizarrely, in boars' heads – offers yet another example of a highly wrought man-made but vividly zoomorphic object. *Beowulf* repeatedly mentions protective images of boars on helmets, and the Benty Grange helmet, found in the nineteenth century, in Derbyshire, and dated to the seventh century, is surmounted by a crest in the shape of a boar. However, the so-called Sutton Hoo standard was reconstructed as such because of an apparently significant double mention of a standard which at the beginning of *Beowulf* was placed in the funeral ship with Scyld Scefing and, at the end, was retrieved from the dragon's hoard by Wiglaf, but it is by no means certain what the original function of the object buried at Sutton Hoo might have been. In the end, the most forcible, if imprecise, connexion between the

Sutton Hoo treasures and those described in *Beowulf* is their richness, and their extraordinarily cosmopolitan origins. One final point is that the treasure in *Beowulf* is insistently golden. Most of the precious objects in viking hoards are silver (plus a large amount of hack silver – bullion used as currency). Gold is relatively rare. Further, jewellery in Old Norse poetry is often described in terms of sparkling ice and frost – clearly silver, and not gold. But *Beowulf* is suffused throughout by the warm glow of gold.

The most prominent item of war-gear – and certainly in terms of its importance in the narrative of *Beowulf* – is undoubtedly the sword. Just like the great assemblages of treasure in the poem, swords can be either passed on, as part of the currency of gift-exchange and reward, or buried in the earth, unused and abandoned to corrosion. But a sword's history as a weapon of violence means that gifts of swords may be – forgive the pun – double-edged. Sometimes, the gift is simply an uncontroversial gesture of thanks for services rendered – as when Beowulf makes a gift of a valuable sword to the Danish coastguard who first challenges, and then welcomes, the hero and his Geatish entourage when they first arrive, and organizes the safe-keeping of their boat (or perhaps rewards the boat-guardian himself). The sword in question is described as being bound with gold, and the poet notes that ownership of such an impressive heirloom will increase its new owner's prestige amongst his fellows. Somewhat similarly, when Beowulf returns in triumph to his homeland, his lord and uncle Hygelac presents him with a sword which once belonged to his father, Beowulf's grandfather, King Hrethel. There is also significant symbolic value in this sword, since Beowulf is the son of Hygelac's sister, and this inheritance from his grandfather serves to pull Beowulf back towards the direct male descent from King Hrethel, although the personal relationship between a man and his sister's son was a special one in itself. However, in a slightly different situation, when the Danish King Hrothgar rewards Beowulf with war-gear belonging to Hrothgar's late brother, Heorogar, a faint sense of unease is engendered: why did Heorogar not pass these heirlooms on to his own son, Heoroweard? What happened to him? The poet tells us nothing, and indeed Heoroweard is only mentioned in the poem itself right here, when we learn that he was not bequeathed the war-gear. The poet adds that Heoroweard was a brave warrior, and that his father was not disloyal to him, as if to dispel that unease, and if we interpret the bestowal of primary war-gear as a gesture of granting succession to the recipient – as many scholars have done – there is perhaps nothing sinister about Heorogar nominating his younger but already established brother Hrothgar as the next ruler of the Danes, instead of his son, who might have been too young or inexperienced. However, if we compare the allusive figure of Heoroweard in *Beowulf* to the corresponding material about the Danish royal house in Old Norse traditions, we find that a Dane called Hjörvarðr (the Old Norse form of Heoroweard) later led an attack on and killed another of Hrothgar's nephews, Hrothulf, who also features in *Beowulf*, although much less prominently than in Old Norse traditions, in which he is presented as the celebrated hero King Hrólfr – 'the greatest of all the kings of the northern lands'. In *Beowulf*, all we learn of Heoroweard is that his father did not pass on to him the sword of the Danish dynasty's male heirs, make of that what we will.

The complex and often allusive background of old feuds and continuing hostilities in *Beowulf* is also figured in the changing ownership of swords. At the very end of the poem, Beowulf's young colleague Wiglaf deals the fearsome dragon its final fatal blow with a sword. This weapon, we are told, had been passed on to Wiglaf from his father, Weohstan. Way back in the deep history of the poem's storyworld, Weohstan had killed a Swedish prince called Eanmund, who together with his brother had been forced into exile when their uncle Onela took over the Swedish throne. Eanmund and his brother found safety in Beowulf's Geatish homeland, which was at that time ruled over by Hygelac's son Heardred, supported by Beowulf. Here, significantly enough, we see a nephew – Beowulf – who did not take advantage of a vulnerable heir to the throne. But Onela invades the land of the Geats, and Weohstan, Wiglaf's father, fighting for Onela, kills Eanmund, Onela's own nephew. The Geatish king Heardred who gave him refuge is also killed. Weohstan presents his lord, Onela, with Eanmund's sword: an *ealdsweord etonisc* (ancient sword of giants), which Onela promptly gifts back to him, as a reward for the killing, even though, as the poet tersely adds, the victim Eanmund was a blood relative of Onela's – his own brother's son. This, then, is the sword with which Wiglaf kills the dragon – a sword which had belonged to a close ally of Beowulf's, but is now wielded by Beowulf's final companion, co-dragon killer, and perhaps

even close relative, for Beowulf formally addresses Wiglaf as the *endelaf |
usses cynnes | Wægmundinga* ('the last remaining one of our kin, of the
Wægmundings'). Following the history of the ancient sword takes us deep into
the tangled threads of alliances and aggressions which make up the poem's
infrastructure.

There is in *Beowulf* one very dramatic – if hypothetical – instance of a
sword's violent history sparking renewed lethal action. When Beowulf returns
to his homeland and describes the outcome of the Danish mission to his lord
Hygelac, he speculates about the fragile future of the Danish royal house.
King Hrothgar has been engaged in a feud with a neighbouring tribe, the
Heathobards, and the Danes have killed their king Froda. Beowulf reports
that there is a plan to reconcile the warring parties by marrying Hrothgar's
daughter Freawaru to Froda's heir, Ingeld – a doomed attempt, according to
Beowulf, who is pessimistic about such strategies, no matter how successful
the match might otherwise seem to be. Beowulf goes on to imagine a scene
in the hall, perhaps at the wedding feast itself, when a Heathobard warrior
may recognize war-gear proudly displayed by the Danes, but previously looted
from the battle in which their Heathobard comrades fell. Such a warrior will
naturally be acutely sensitive to the mischief-making goading of someone who
points out the very sword which belonged to his father before he was cut down
by a Dane. Violence will be inevitable. It is clear that this episode, presented
in the poem as Beowulf's canny speculation, was notorious in the Middle
Ages. A rather similar story about Ingeld is told by the Danish historian Saxo
Grammaticus, and the Anglo-Saxon poem *Widsið* alludes quite explicitly to
a violent encounter between Hrothgar and Ingeld, in which Ingeld attacked
Heorot, but was defeated. And as we have seen, Ingeld's name was picked
out by the Anglo-Saxon scholar Alcuin when he wanted to criticize clerics'
inappropriate interest in heroic themes.

A sword also acts as the provocation to violence during an uneasy truce
in the so-called 'Finn Episode', the story of the Frisians and the Danes, forced
to spend a tense winter together in one hall after an inconclusive battle, and
all too easily roused to vengeance when a sword is placed across the knees of
a Dane in a ceremonial gesture of – what? Loyalty, allegiance or a reminder
of the need for vengeance and therefore a spur to violent action? The cutting

edges of the sword are grimly said to be well known to one of the parties, and the sight of them does its work.

Swords in *Beowulf* are not fully anthropomorphized, but they often have distinct identities and may be given names which reflect their function and appearance: Hrunting is a sword lent to Beowulf by Unferth, a Danish courtier, its name probably deriving from an ancient word for thrusting; Nægling, Beowulf's own sword, probably got its name from nails, or studs, decorating a hilt and reflecting the light as well as strengthening the structure. There are very many poetic synonyms for sword in the poem, and kennings, too; it's not clear, for instance, whether a compound word such as *hildeleoma* (battle-gleam) is a poetic synonym for a sword, or the weapon's actual name. All these allusions to the symbolic power and provocative associations of time-honoured swords make clear their pivotal roles in the poem. I want to conclude this discussion of swords as a central feature of the material world of the poem by exploring Beowulf's relationship with two prominent blades: Unferth's sword Hrunting, and the gigantic (in two senses) weapon Beowulf finds in the underwater lair of Grendel's mother.

When Beowulf arrives at Hrothgar's Danish court in Heorot, he is aggressively challenged in a sort of verbal duel – a flyting – by one of Hrothgar's courtiers, Unferth. Inspired, the poet baldly tells us, by envy, Unferth accuses Beowulf of irresponsible behaviour in his youth, as Beowulf recklessly competed in a dangerous swimming contest and then lost. Beowulf responds to Unferth's challenge by giving his own version of the swimming contest, but then moves the aggression to a more serious level, pointing out that nobody knows any stories about Unferth's brave deeds, and landing what one might expect to be a knock-out verbal blow: that if Unferth were any good at all as a hero, Grendel would not have been able to torment the Danes for so long, and Hrothgar would not have needed a young warrior from across the sea to come and help them out. But then Beowulf goes a step further still and accuses Unferth of murdering his brothers. Of course this is a shocking charge, which, apart from a glancing reference a little later in the poem – that Unferth was not exactly merciful to his own kin in battle – is not substantiated anywhere else. Beowulf underlines the seriousness of such a crime – if it were needed – by describing a brother as one's *heafodmæg* (chief, or closest, kinsman). But an accusation of fratricide also goes right to the heart of the poem, for as we shall see, the monsters Grendel and his mother are identified as the descendants of Cain, the first fratricide. This would seem to put Unferth squarely on the side of the forces Beowulf is opposing. However, Beowulf concludes his speech with a bold vow to take the fight to Grendel, and bring a new dawn to the Danes, and there is general rejoicing in the hall. Unferth seems to be forgotten, and there are apparently no repercussions from Beowulf's scandalous accusations.

And when Beowulf is arming himself for an encounter with Grendel's mother, we learn that Unferth has lent him the sword Hrunting. Possibly the poet did not want to create an awkward scene in which Beowulf and Unferth, their mutual animosity either plausibly festering or implausibly forgotten, would have to meet again for the sword to be passed on. One might further worry that Unferth's gift was given in bad faith, and was this the sword with which Unferth committed the fratricide? However, the poet goes out of his way to praise the sword, and it is certainly a striking weapon. It is first described as *an foran ealdgestreona* (the foremost of ancient treasures); it has an iron blade decorated with 'venom twigs' – perhaps the effect created by a blade made from twisted strips of metal, and then flattened to produce wavy lines. Its blade has been *ahyrded in heaþoswat* (hardened in battle-sweat – that is, blood). This expression combines two ideas: that a sword with previous 'experience' of battle may be extra strong – literally 'hardened in battle' – and recalling the forging of the blade, when in its near molten state the smith would plunge it into cooling water to harden the blade by quenching it.

The sword's past history – fratricide now apparently disregarded – is also praised. The poet asserts that it has never before failed in battle. Here, we may notice a slight shift in agency – one might expect a warrior to fail in battle, rather than his inanimate sword. But the poet elaborates on the familiar idea of a sentient weapon somehow responding to the courage of its owner, going on to say that the sword has never failed anyone brave enough to use it on a daring mission. This idea is underlined by the attribution of the brave deed to come to the sword itself: *næs þæt forma sið | þæt hit ellenweorc | æfnan scolde* (that was not the first time that it had to carry out a brave deed). And Beowulf himself expresses no reservations about the sword, and indeed declares that he will accomplish the deed with Hrunting or die. But that isn't what happens. In spite of its renowned history, its spectacular appearance and its formidable blade, and in spite of Beowulf's undoubted bravery as its wielder, Hrunting did fail Beowulf in battle. Again, we are treated to the sword's own experience: it had endured many hand-to-hand combats, and had often split open helmets. When Beowulf first aimed it at Grendel's mother's head, it even *agol | grædig guðleoð* (sang out a greedy battle-chant). But then it would not bite. This, the poet stresses, was the very first time that the glorious sword failed. However, Beowulf was not overcome – thanks to an even more extraordinary sword.

When Beowulf is on the point of being overpowered by Grendel's mother, he catches sight of an enormous sword in her underwater lair – another *sigeeadig bil* (victory-blessed sword), another *ealdsweord eotenisc* (ancient sword of giants), like Wiglaf's sword which killed the dragon, and another choice weapon. But this sword is distinguished from all others by its immense size: it is the sword of giants in both senses. Beowulf had resigned himself to fighting with his bare hands, although Grendel's mother has a wicked knife which is nearly the death of him. However, he seizes the mysterious sword and decapitates Grendel's mother. In the light that floods the underwater chamber as Grendel's mother dies, Beowulf catches sight of the corpse of Grendel and decapitates that too. The scene shifts abruptly to the lakeshore, where those anxiously waiting for Beowulf suppose that the ensuing gore which rises to the surface of the lake is a sign of Beowulf's own demise. Meanwhile, back in the lair, an extraordinary event is taking place: having been plunged into the battle-blood of both Grendel and his mother, very far from its edge being hardened, the blade begins to dissolve into *hildeicelum* (battle-icicles). The monstrous pair's toxic blood has melted the metal, returning the iron to its molten state.

Around a dozen kennings in Old Norse poetry denote a sword as some variant of 'the ice of battle'. But in all these instances, the ice element functions to convey the hardness, the strength of a blade, even sometimes shattering, loudly and dramatically, like old, solid ice. Nowhere do we see a blade melting away. The *Beowulf*-poet calls this a wondrous thing and immediately compares it to a natural wonder, when God, with His power over times and seasons, causes ice to melt in spring. It's not clear whether this comparison serves to bring home the miracle of the spring thaw, or the singular unnaturalness of the sword's end, or both.

Beowulf is left holding the decorated sword hilt, and swims back up to the lake's surface with that and Grendel's head, a body part and a weapon part, two oddly structurally similar but physically very different remnants of his fatal blow, and both awe-inspiringly oversized (it takes four of Beowulf's men to transport the head back to Heorot). It is worth noting that Anglo-Saxon treasure assemblages – such as the Staffordshire hoard, for instance – often contain not swords *in toto*, but their golden hilt collars, sometimes in large numbers. Perhaps the author of *Beowulf* saw such assemblages, hilts without blades, which had perhaps been broken, or notched, and had been separated from their gold parts which men then collected as treasure, and was prompted to imagine how the iron might have been melted down. Beowulf presents both hilt and head to King Hrothgar, and attention is focused on the hilt, not only as an inherently valuable treasure, but also as a sort of time-traveller, an object from giant realms distant in both space and time. The hilt, like the sword itself, is described as *enta ærgeweorc* (the ancient work of giants), but had an even closer link to the giants, because it is engraved with what is obliquely described as 'the origin of the far-off strife when the flood, the gushing ocean, killed off the race of giants'. It is not clear whether this is a pictorial engraving, or an inscription, although we are told that the hilt is also inscribed with the name of the magnificent sword's first owner, in perfect runic lettering, the alphabet of the earliest Germanic tribes. A visual representation of the Great Flood might be a tall order, even for the *wundorsmiþ* (miraculous craftsman) involved with the making of the sword. But the origin of that age-old strife might be understood as the primal fratricide, Cain's killing of his brother Abel, which led to the generation of antediluvian giants who used to inhabit the world, according to the biblical book of *Genesis*, and the feud between them and God. Grendel and his mother are descended from them, according to our poem, so that the sword is indeed a family heirloom.

Beowulf is a poem which was probably meant for oral recitation, and scholars used to believe that it was even composed orally. It is certainly a poem of stories, speeches, sermons and songs. The possible text on the sword hilt – and certainly, the runic inscription – are the only references to the written word in the whole poem. Hrothgar makes no comment on the text, so we cannot know if he understood its message. But in any case, this scrap of precious metal is hugely significant in the overall design of the poem. Our knowledge of the material world of *Beowulf* is very limited: we know something about warriors' armour, but nothing of costume; we are told of feasting, but there are no details of food or tablewear. We have very little sense of what individuals looked like, and colours are mostly limited to the shadows of night, the glow of burnished gold and the icy glare of frost. But swords are described in lavish detail and, as we have seen, take on some of the qualities a post-medieval audience would feel appropriate only to thinking, feeling entities. So now it's time to explore the world of more conventional sentient beings: the human characters in poem's storyworld.

(ii) The human characters

The human characters in *Beowulf* are presented not as solitary, self-sufficient individuals, but as elements of complex social networks, in close actual or symbolic relationships with other figures. Their identities are either created according to how closely they approach a societal ideal – as kings, queens or heroes, for instance – or by being brought into vivid relief against wicked or inadequate examples of their kind. Superlatives abound: Beowulf is the greatest of heroes; Hrothgar – at least to begin with – the most glorious of kings; Hrothgar's queen Wealhtheow the most gracious of consorts. And individual characters do not so much develop, psychologically, as suffer setbacks or triumphs, and often these reversals of fortune are dramatic. As we shall see, every moment of victory is thus tinged with anxiety about the possibility of reversal – at least, for the poem's audience – and there is always the hope for change when fortunes decline. A non-specific deity is recognized and fulsomely appreciated as the source of good fortune or victory, but – crucially – the powers that be act only for those who help themselves. And finally, resignation to one's fate when times are bad may suggest passivity, but bearing up bravely – keeping calm and carrying on – is applauded as one of the great strengths of the human spirit.

Characterization like this sounds as if it will produce hollow and static human figures, but the characters of *Beowulf* come thrillingly and movingly alive in their interactions with each other. Human relationships are convincingly and naturalistically drawn in the poem, and it is for this reason that I will deal not with either Beowulf the hero, or Hrothgar King of the Danes, but with the relationship between them.

Beowulf and Hrothgar

The first mention of Beowulf in the poem designates him according to his societal position: he is a retainer of King Hygelac, and himself a Geat, like his uncle the king. We move straight to big anonymous superlatives: he was the most powerful in strength of any man living, and noble and mighty. When he sets off to help Hrothgar in his time of need, we see him through the eyes of his fellow countrymen, who do not dissuade him, even though they are attached to him, but applaud his ambition, and he surrounds himself with a handpicked retinue of superlatively brave warriors. There is no particularizing detail here, just a seamless picture of martial excellence. Beowulf and his men land on the shore of Hrothgar's kingdom, and again he is reflected in the coastguard's impression of him – he is the most impressive figure the coastguard has seen in the world and his overall appearance is beyond compare. But such a formidable warrior of course presents a threat as much as a spectacle, and the poet of *Beowulf* may possibly be representing this cautious coastguard – and the audience of the poem – as recalling the fate of a coastguard recorded in an entry in the *Anglo-Saxon Chronicle* for the year 787 CE (perhaps more accurately in 789). Three ships of Scandinavian seamen arrived at Portland in Dorset, and the local reeve (named by a later historian as Beaduheard of Dorchester) came and tried to lead them to his king, thinking that they were merchants. They killed him. According to the Chronicle, 'those were the first ships of Danish men which came to the land of the English' (the *Anglo-Saxon Chronicle* entries are never very clear on the difference between Norwegians and Danes; since these ships were from Hörðaland, the men were actually from Norway). This was before the notorious Viking raid on Lindisfarne only a few years later, so the coastguard's mistaken trust (or, as a medieval historian recounting the episode a couple of hundred years later tells it, his over-confident challenge to them) might be understandable. In *Beowulf*, the coastguard is properly prudent, but as his warm praise for the visitors' appearance seems to imply, his intuition is that they mean well. And although he picks out Beowulf as the most impressive member of the team, he addresses them collectively until Beowulf himself responds on their behalf.

Beowulf's reply as to the purpose of their journey to the Danish kingdom is beautifully pitched and elaborately, formally, courteous. Echoing the poet, Beowulf identifies himself – and his troop – as Geats, retainers of King Hygelac, and then speaks of his own particular identity: that he is the son of a celebrated warrior, Ecgtheow. Next, he very delicately explains the reason for their visit, and with quiet flattery begs the coastguard for his good advice: he and his men have come in peace to offer Hrothgar some help in overcoming the unprecedentedly terrible depredations the Danes have been suffering, if, Beowulf tactfully adds, the stories he has heard are true. Thus Beowulf plays down his own possible intervention – this is no brash young hero barging in to 'save' Heorot – and, at the same time, plays up the horror of what – as Beowulf does not say – Hrothgar has failed to manage himself: the sheer awfulness of Grendel's monstrous attacks. And throughout this whole introduction, Beowulf reveals his sympathetic fellow-feeling for old Hrothgar's trials: he recalls his own elderly father; he raises the possibility of a reversal of Hrothgar's misery, a possibility which he evocatively describes as a cooling of Hrothgar's overwhelming cares; and he sums up what Hrothgar has endured as an *earfoðþrag* (a distressing time) and a *þreanyd* (hard affliction) – the first compound word found nowhere else but here, and the second used only in poetry. As we shall see, a touching quasi-father and son relationship between Beowulf and Hrothgar soon establishes itself.

It is only when Beowulf and his men are guided by the coastguard to Heorot, and questioned by one of Hrothgar's officials, that Beowulf identifies himself: *Beowulf is min nama* – 'Beowulf is my name', an echo of the answer to a typical Anglo-Saxon riddle in which a mysterious object describes itself in the first person and teasingly challenges its audience with the question 'What am I?' Having received this information, Wulfgar, Hrothgar's functionary, passes on the information to the king, who is introduced as *eald ond unhar* (aged, and very grey) – like Beowulf's late father, one supposes. And Hrothgar at once recognizes the name.

Of course, Hrothgar was not always an old, defeated leader. His great-grandfather was the Danish king with whom the poem opens: Scyld Scefing. We learn that he was one of four siblings, three brothers and a sister who was married to a Swedish king. It seems that Hrothgar's two brothers died early, leaving Hrothgar with the kingdom of the Danes, and his late brothers' nephews to bring up – an ominous combination of a kingdom together with more than one possibly rightful heir to it. But Hrothgar's reign was a magnificent one: he is described as having been a great leader, with a large following of loyal retainers. It was at the apogee of his royal and military success that this worthy descendant of Scyld Scefing took the decision to build the greatest ever mead-hall, Heorot. It may have been over-ambitious, but Hrothgar's triumphs are not without a sound ethical basis: he has unrivalled power to dispense favours and riches, but the poet is careful to note that he doesn't trade with human lives, or tamper with people's rightful claims to common land. (It's tempting to identify a slightly anxious topical reference from the Anglo-Saxon poet here.) And yet, at the moment when the poet celebrates the completion of Heorot, we are told of its demise, how it suffered surges of hostile fire – as if the flames themselves were enemy forces – the result of lethal violence arising between those who had sworn oaths to each other: a father-in-law and a son-in-law, Hrothgar and Ingeld, his daughter's husband.

The burning of Heorot is in the distant future of the poem's storyworld, and beyond these dark hints, that distant future is never related. Hrothgar's immediate trial is the conflict with Grendel, and his inability to counter Grendel causes him not anger, or frustration, but acute emotional distress: he grieves for the loss of retainers killed by the monster, and his retainers – their number and loyalty one of the glories of his reign – desert Heorot, and their king. And for the Christian poet, a horror perhaps worse than death is that the Danes lose faith in their leader's ability to protect them, and turn to the worship of idols, and make deals with the devil. Although of course the Danes in the poem are represented as living in pre-Christian times, the poet never directly confronts or describes their paganism, but ironically, here labels their hopelessness and despair as *hæþenra hyht* (the hope of heathens). This demoralized kingdom and its helpless, grieving king form the context into which Beowulf so tactfully and delicately makes his entrance.

When Hrothgar hears who his visitor is, his wisdom and experience – the positive sides of old age – suddenly materialize. He remembers Beowulf's father Ecgtheow who married a Geatish princess, King Hrethel's daughter, and sees at once that Beowulf's arrival marks a hopeful turn of events, partly because of Beowulf's reputation, and partly because, as he relates a little later, he helped Ecgtheow in his time of need and gave him sanctuary in the kingdom of the Danes. So now, he rightly supposes, Beowulf has come loyally to repay the favour. And as if to bolster Hrothgar's reviving spirits, Beowulf begins on a high note, boasting of his previous exploits, his triumphant encounters with giants and sea-monsters, his vengeful and murderous attacks on the enemies of the Geats, and the certainty that he will prove a match for Grendel. With ostentatious modesty, he begs to be allowed to help, and self-deprecatingly points out to Hrothgar that should he fail in his attempt to exterminate the monster, at least Hrothgar will not have the burden of providing him with a funeral, for the monstrous beast will save him the trouble by eating his corpse. Beowulf's grim humour following his nicely judged introductory speech works wonders with Hrothgar, who proudly recalls how well he behaved over the Ecgtheow business, and how the arrival of his son, Beowulf, may be a turning point in the fortunes of the Danes.

But before the Danes and their Geatish guests can settle down to a night's feasting and entertainment, there is one remaining hurdle to overcome – Unferth's aggressive verbal assault on Beowulf's reputation, which I discussed earlier in connexion with the gifting of swords. Rebutting Unferth's accusations of recklessness and folly gives Beowulf the opportunity to return to boastful mode, as he proudly asserts his superiority in the swimming contest, and further claims previous victories over a host of sea-monsters. It is interesting that, as we saw with regard to the sword, there does not seem to be any lasting animosity between Unferth and Beowulf; no-one rebukes Unferth, and there is no sense that he harbours any resentment about Beowulf's response. The Danes simply cheer Beowulf's bravado and the celebrations commence. In fact, there is no sense of any personal relationship between the two men, hostile or otherwise, in direct contrast to the interactions between Hrothgar and Beowulf. It is as if Unferth is simply providing Beowulf with a formal, structured prompt, a conventional if theatrical opening with which to voice his own success. Boasting has not been an admired activity for centuries, and it is a mode of behaviour in *Beowulf,* and in heroic literature more generally, which present-day audiences find hardest to swallow. But Beowulf's boasting certainly lifts the Danes' spirits, and this might be said to be its function, rather than, as it would be in a post-medieval, or non-heroic text, being a mark of Beowulf's disposition.

At this point, it may be worth trying to distinguish between a boast and a vow, as they are used in *Beowulf.* Boasting tends to focus on past exploits, and assessments of present superiority, as when Beowulf boasts of winning the swimming contest, or killing sea-monsters, or slaughtering the enemies of the Geats. The vow is focused on future action, as when Beowulf declares that he will kill Grendel or die in the attempt; it is an admirable assertion of bravery and determination, and may seem less rebarbative to modern audiences. But there are very many instances which fall somewhere between the two, where determination and self-confidence shade into self-praise or arrogance and, at worst, from there to empty bluster. In the context of the celebrating Danes, we can trace Beowulf's course in relation to these two extremes. Hrothgar's queen, Wealhtheow, apparently performing a formal, even ritual task, greets the massed Danes and Geats in Heorot, and offers them – in strict order of precedence, beginning with Hrothgar – a draught from a communal goblet of what is probably imagined to contain mead. This stages another opportunity for Beowulf to speak up for himself: addressing the queen, he describes how, setting off for Heorot, he was determined to give the Danes what they needed, or *on wæl crunge* (die amongst the slaughtered). Now, in Heorot, he renews this vow: that he will accomplish his mission or end his days in the great hall. The poet describes this as a *gilpcwide* ('boastful declaration', with the first element, *gilp*, the origin of another unattractive vocal act, 'yelp'), although Beowulf's vow is more admirable than immodest, and actually not boastful in its recognition that he may not be successful. It certainly pleases Wealhtheow and the rest of the Danes; it is shown to restore the Danes to their former glory, such that *eft swa ær* (as often before) they begin their revels in Heorot.

Two issues remain to be addressed. Firstly, we should pause over the role of Wealhtheow in this scene. Her action in handing round the shared drink seems entirely unremarkable, but it taps into a widespread heroic convention that male warriors address their 'boasts' to women. In Old Norse literary tradition, elaborate martial praise poems – skaldic verses – are presented as being, and were perhaps originally designed to be, recited in formal situations in the courts of kings and earls in Norway. These verses often contain elaborate apostrophes to women, who are addressed in high-flown kennings based on the names of Norse goddesses. In fact, in what are often new prose narrative contexts, such stanzas are rarely presented as being actually recited to women – the whole point is simply that it was somehow held to be fitting, or traditional, for a male warrior to boast to a female audience. And this highly gendered interaction is mirrored in the offer of the communal cup, in Old Norse heroic poetry the gesture of a valkyrie greeting a dead warrior in Valhalla. The amuletic image of a valkyrie extending a goblet is a familiar one to Scandinavian archaeologists, and would presumably have been equally familiar to contemporary audiences. This is not of course to say that Wealhtheow is being identified as a valkyrie, although scholars have pointed out the similarities. Nevertheless, here we have an Anglo-Saxon poet depicting a Scandinavian queen, and apparently drawing on iconic representations, in material and literary forms, of the valkyrie.

The figure of the valkyrie is not consistently presented in Old Norse. The name is based on two elements, the word for those slaughtered in battle, *val* (cognate with the Old English word *wæl* which, interestingly enough, we came across as part of Beowulf's vow to die amongst the slaughtered, like a warrior in battle, rather than the prey of a monster) and a form of the verb 'to choose'. The obvious inference to be drawn from this etymology is that the role of the valkyries was as battlefield demons, choosing from amongst the dead warriors who should be taken to eternal life (and feasting) in Valhalla, the hall Odin provides for this purpose. But Old Norse texts differ in whether the valkyries have the free will to choose for themselves who to convey to Valhalla, or whether they simply carry out Odin's wishes in this regard. Some texts depict the valkyries as little more than glorified waitresses in Valhalla, setting the tables and offering round the drink. But if they are presented as making their own choice of men, we must ask on what basis they make their choice, and why; there is on occasion a suggestion that valkyries who make their own choice of dead male warriors have a post-mortem sexual aim in mind. For all these reasons, then, there clings to depictions of valkyries the sense of supernatural, unnatural and possibly malevolent power.

But Wealhtheow is both more and less than a human rendering of a supernatural battle-demon. Her role at Heorot is at the same time both powerful and vulnerable: she must act as a mediator between Hrothgar and the Geatish hero Beowulf, as their relationship deepens from – on Hrothgar's part – gratitude and admiration to quasi-paternal intimacy. Because impressive as Beowulf might seem, an ideal saviour for the beleaguered Danes, Hrothgar and Wealhtheow have their own young sons, not to mention the residue of nephews, all contenders for the Danish throne. Hrothgar begins by formally entrusting the defence of Heorot to Beowulf, something which he has never previously granted to anyone, so that Beowulf becomes, almost, his surrogate. Beowulf resoundingly proves his bravery and strength by killing Grendel, and Hrothgar returns to Heorot from his safer sleeping quarters elsewhere to find the Danes rejoicing at the sight of Grendel's ripped-off arm, evidence that Beowulf has finally rid them of the monster. The poet tells us that Beowulf is already being celebrated in praise poetry, but is careful to note that none of this was thought to reflect badly on Hrothgar. Respect for him – both in the storyworld and from the poet – is painstakingly maintained.

Hrothgar's reaction to Beowulf's victory over Grendel is also becoming and dignified: he first thanks an almighty deity for the reversal in his fortune and emphasizes again the emotional aspect – the misery which Grendel inflicted on the Danes as they saw their hall ravaged and companions killed. But his characteristic warmth leads him what may be an unwarranted step further in his gratitude to the young hero. With the evident intimacy and simplicity of personal pronouns and Beowulf's given name, he seems to make some sort of offer to adopt Beowulf as his heir:

Nu ic, Beowulf, þec | secg betsta | me for sunu wylle | freogan on ferhþe
(Now I, O Beowulf, you | (O best of men) | as a son to me will | [I] love in my heart).

This is clearly not a formal handover of power or succession. Its affection and tenderness are very plain. Beowulf's response rather skirts the political implications of this avowal, and the poet's focus shifts to the rich gifts which Hrothgar bestows on Beowulf as a reward. But we must not forget Wealhtheow, watching and listening to all this, as the poet has taken care to point out. And it is right here, too, that we have our first mention of another silent witness, Hrothgar's nephew Hrothulf, standing at his side, the son of Hrothgar's dead brother, of whom the poet has told us nothing, and never will, although he slyly notes that relations between Hrothgar and Hrothulf are *as yet* friendly ones.

I don't think that it's over-reading here to sense an impression of Hrothgar as an irreproachable old king beset by an unequalled horror, and graciously rewarding the hero who has rescued him, shifting suddenly to a vision of a foolish, fond old man, vulnerable and even pathetic.

The Danes are entertained – if that's an appropriate word – by a tragic story of a feud between Danes and Frisians, in which a woman, Hildeburh, is caught between the warring factions and suffers heartbreak. I will discuss this story when we come to look at what have sometimes been called the 'digressions' in the poem, although, as I shall maintain, it is not difficult to make out their intense and precise relevance to the primary narrative. Here, though, we turn to Wealhtheow, who has watched her elderly husband declare his love for Beowulf, in front of his nephew Hrothulf, and, we are now told, her and Hrothgar's own young sons, Hrethric and Hrothmund. She sits, perhaps strategically, perhaps symbolically, between the king and his nephew, and the poet again notes that their relations were *as yet* cordial. The sinister presence of Unferth, the fratricide, is also pointedly mentioned.

Wealhtheow's speech as she hands Hrothgar a celebratory cup needs to be quoted in full, and I am using Seamus Heaney's translation, which conveys formality without pomp, and the quiet force of what she is saying:

> Enjoy this drink, my most generous lord;
> raise up your goblet, entertain the Geats
> duly and gently, discourse with them,
> be open-hearted, happy and fond.

Relish their company, but recollect as well
all of the boons that have been bestowed on you.
The bright court of Heorot has been cleansed
and now the word is that you want to adopt
this warrior as a son. So, while you may,
bask in your fortune, and then bequeath
kingdom and nation to your kith and kin,
before your decease. I am certain of Hrothulf.
He is noble and will use the young ones well.
He will not let you down. Should you die before him,
he will treat our children truly and fairly.
He will honour, I am sure, our two sons,
repay them in kind when he recollects
all the good things we gave him once,
the favour and respect he found in his childhood.

If this speech were not part of a poem, but the script of a play, or the screenplay of a film, two different directors could play Wealhtheow's demeanour very differently. We could have a proud, assured Wealhtheow, taking the floor with poise, and intervening to correct her doddering, sentimental husband Hrothgar. With an authoritative display of diplomacy she advises him to give due credit and reward to the Geats, but not to go so far as to make Beowulf his heir, and she boldly defends her sons from the threat of dispossession. She pointedly, if obliquely, reminds Hrothulf of his duty to do right by his uncle and his young cousins, given that, as she claims, Hrothgar brought him up and treated him generously, and she asserts her confidence that he will repay their trust.

But on the other hand, we might be shown a much less buoyant – but more insightful – Wealhtheow, who is anxiously trying to divert her autocratic husband from a calamitous misstep. In fact, her anxiety might be all the more emphatically shown given that Hrothgar has just made public his misguided impulse to make Beowulf his heir, in front of three young men of the next generation who might well feel more entitled to the bequest. Wealhtheow's emphasis on how much she trusts in Hrothulf could easily be played as a desperate attempt to convince herself, and a classic example of a lady protesting too much. That she even has to remind everyone how well Hrothgar treated Hrothulf when he was young might be seen as nervous and unconvinced.

We never do learn from the poem whether Wealhtheow was right to be confident, or right to be in dread of Hrothulf. As we have seen, there are a number of darkly equivocal hints about the future of the relationship between Hrothgar and Hrothulf. But also, as I have noted, Hrothulf corresponds in Old Norse sources about the Danish dynasty to the great and glorious king Hrólfr kraki. Although the sources vary a great deal, one of them recounts how Hrólfr was attacked and killed by Hjörvarðr, the Norse equivalent of Beowulf's Heoroweard, another of Hrothgar's nephews. What we know about the Danish royal house from sources outside *Beowulf* may be confused, partial and contradictory, but one thing remains constant: there was always violence and betrayal either going on, or about to happen.

I pointed out above that there were two issues to be addressed before moving on to Beowulf's encounter with Grendel. The second is part and parcel of the poet's favourite structuring technique in the poem. We learn that once Beowulf has made his masculine boast to the valkyrie-esque Wealhtheow, the Danes finally embark on their evening celebrations. But we have already heard a description of how the Danes used to feast, to celebrate their glory and to accept Hrothgar's lavish treasure-giving. That was just before Grendel's first attack. And now they are doing it again.

The poet seems to excuse their heedlessness. As they and their Geatish guest sink into an exhausted, drink-fuelled torpor, the poet tells us rather disingenuously – and perhaps as an audience, we too should take the words as a warning – that they could not know what was going to happen (*wyrd ne cuþon*) or that a terrible destiny (*geosceaft grimme*) awaited them. But any audience of *Beowulf* must know better. And those inside Heorot did not have long to wait: Grendel's mother makes a vengeful and lethal counter-attack on Heorot the night after their celebrations.

I will discuss in more detail Beowulf's encounters with these two monsters in the next section. For the moment, we need to know only that Beowulf was successful in overcoming them both, demonstrating his physical strength and his bravery, and acknowledging in both episodes that he was helped by a greater power, a controlling deity compatible with, but not explicitly identified with, the Christian God. At this point, I am still following the course of the relationship between Hrothgar and Beowulf, a relationship of course largely determined by Beowulf's interactions with Hrothgar's monstrous foes. As we may have come to expect, Hrothgar's response to Grendel's mother's murderous attack on Heorot is highly emotional. His advanced age is stressed at the outset: he is *frod cyning* | *har hilderinc* (an aged king, a grey-haired warrior). Grendel's mother's victim on this occasion was *þone deorestan* (the dearest one) to Hrothgar, and he is grief-stricken by the loss. He greets Beowulf's polite enquiry about his night's rest after the joyous celebrations with a sharp retort which might be loosely translated as 'How can you even utter the word joy?' For Hrothgar, *sorh is geniwod* (sorrow has been renewed), and he voices a powerful lament for his dead retainer, stressing their close relationship: Æschere, the monster's victim, was Hrothgar's *runwita* (confidant), and *rædbora* (advisor). Beowulf responds directly to Hrothgar's emotional reaction, telling him not to grieve, and echoing a familiar heroic principle that taking action is better than mourning – though in this instance, the sentiment is not merely an heroic commonplace, but is directly applicable to Hrothgar. And this is where the boastful vow comes into its own. Beowulf declares that the best a man can do is to value glory, even if it means his death, and that the monster will never escape him. He urges Hrothgar to bear up, and his words take immediate effect: *Ahleop ða se gomela* (the old man leapt to his feet).

Beowulf is as good as his word and sets off at once to pursue Grendel's mother to her lair. But before he goes, he speaks gently to Hrothgar, asking him to take care of his, Beowulf's, retainers, and to make certain that his valuable treasures already won at Heorot are conveyed to his own lord, Hygelac, back in Geatland, so that Hygelac will know what a gracious and generous host Hrothgar has been. This, says Beowulf, would be for Hrothgar to act *on fæder stæle* (in the role of a father) to him.

Although it is a completely different kind of encounter, the bare bones of Beowulf's successful attack on Grendel's mother follow the same general outlines as his overcoming of Grendel himself – he shows bravery, physical strength, resourcefulness and gives due credit to help from his god. Beowulf's triumphant return to Heorot is also just as one would expect. Beowulf has brought with him Grendel's head and proudly displays it to Hrothgar's court, a shocking sight. But as we have seen, he also presents Hrothgar with the hilt of the magically melted sword. And in a tiny but telling detail, he assures old Hrothgar that the result of his exploit is that the king will now be able to sleep soundly at night, *sorgleas* (free of sorrow), and with his retainers around him – perhaps, one might think, Beowulf's wishful thinking of a fittingly peaceful end to a turbulent reign.

Hrothgar responds to Beowulf with a speech which scholars of Beowulf have conventionally called 'Hrothgar's sermon'. It reflects the wisdom of an old man with a long memory and an extended perspective on the vicissitudes of life. Oddly, Hrothgar begins his formal address to Beowulf and the court (and, perhaps, us as audience) when he has scrutinized the inscription on the hilt of the giants' sword, which, as we saw above, may have depicted or recounted God's war on Lucifer, Cain or the giants. Hrothgar's sermon begins with praise, however: praise for Beowulf, and indeed, for himself, as a leader who can recognize true worth. He seems to have tapped back into the glory days of the Danes, and this is reflected in his vocabulary, which pointedly echoes the terminology of the reigns of Scyld Scefing and his son Beow: *blæd* (that word which seems to mean both glory and the fertile prosperity of the earth) is restored; he has ruled *under wolcnum* (under [the] heavens), as Scyld Scefing prospered *under wolcnum*, and Beowulf will be a comfort (*frofor*) – like Scyld's son – to the people he may one day rule. But then Hrothgar shifts to an explicit contrast, like offering a photographic negative. He begins to speak about another early king of the Danes, Heremod, whose notorious behaviour was the antithesis of good kingship. He urges Beowulf to learn from this (counter) example, and then turns to more general advice: that complacency must not turn to arrogance. There is a dramatic metaphor of the guardian of the soul, who should be its moral gatekeeper, sleeping at his post – an uncomfortable reminder of the careless sleep of the Danes in Heorot? – and a mention of a complacent ruler being shot *of flanbogan* (by [an arrow from] a bow), which seems to be an allusion to a family tragedy in the Geatish royal house, which I shall discuss in another section, when one brother shot another by accident (a fratricide, again, but significantly unlike Cain and Abel). Hrothgar rehearses the paradox of treasure – that by hoarding it, you lose it, so that it's best to give it away. Finally, he speaks of the inevitability of death, in whatever form it takes each person. It is impossible not to see Hrothgar's musings on the end of life as having a very particular, poignant application to his own situation. Hrothgar relates all these issues to his own life history and confesses that the attacks from Grendel were all the more devastating because he had come to believe that he had vanquished all his enemies. Warring tribes he had overcome, but then the monsters arrived.

Beowulf announces his intention to leave Heorot and to return to his homeland. The final picture of his carefully detailed and very moving relationship with Hrothgar is the moment of their parting: Hrothgar embraces and kisses Beowulf, and lets tears fall. In his heart, he believes – rightly, as it proves – that he will never see Beowulf again. And the audience of *Beowulf* will never see Hrothgar again. The troubles facing the Danish royal dynasty are not referred to directly ever again, and Beowulf never returns to Heorot. Hrothgar's precarious status as King of the Danes is all in the unexpressed future of the poem. The poet has balanced dignity with vulnerability, and authority with helplessness, in his unforgettable portrait of Hrothgar, but there is, in effect, no future for him, and the poem continues with the hero, Beowulf.

Beowulf has interactions in the continuing narrative present of the poem with two other major characters, his uncle and lord, Hygelac, back in Geatland, and Wiglaf, who comes to his aid right at the end of his career, when he had to face the dragon. Neither of these relationships is as intimately or subtly drawn as his bond with Hrothgar; they are like fainter echoes of this opening relationship. Beowulf is Hygelac's nephew, and we know from the dark hints in the Danish part of the poem that nephews are a site of potential challenge and rebellion. But in keeping with the poet's technique of positive and negative comparisons, Beowulf is the most positive version of a nephew any ruler could hope for: respectful, loyal and no threat to the direct paternal line of sons. Similarly, Wiglaf is like a son to Beowulf: unswervingly loyal – even to the extent of putting protecting Beowulf ahead of obeying his instructions not to help him. But behind these insistent patterns of male intergenerational relationships, we can see the outlines of an unspoken, unformed but familiar story pattern. The male hero who performs a brave deed in a foreign land and impresses the king – doesn't he usually win the

hand of a princess? And at the end of his life, in his dying moments, wouldn't
we expect him to pass on his wisdom and possibly treasure to his son and
heir? But Hrothgar's daughter Freawaru is promised to the Heathobard leader
Ingeld, and Wiglaf is not Beowulf's son, although he takes the place of a son
to Beowulf. In fact, it's quite hard to work out any blood relationship between
Beowulf and Wiglaf, for the poet tells us that Wiglaf was a Wægmunding,
from a people we have not so far heard of. Although as we have seen, Beowulf
somewhat belatedly, just before he dies, calls the Wægmundings 'our kin', we
have also only just learnt about Wiglaf's father, who killed one of Beowulf's
allies. And in the absence of any blood relative son and heir, there is not even
any hint or mention of something like adoption, even framed as speculatively
as Hrothgar's unacted-upon plans for Beowulf. To understand what is going
on here, we must look at the historical versus the fictional status of the
characters in the poem.

If the poet had elaborated on and fulfilled Hrothgar's idea of making
Beowulf his adopted son – in addition to, or as an alternative to, making him
an actual son-in-law – then he, the poet, would have been involved in a major
re-write of Danish history. The history of the Danes, in Scandinavian sources,
was notorious. Many details differ from how this history is presented in
Beowulf, but there is no sign anywhere of a Geatish incomer called Beowulf. In
any case, as we have seen, there was a tradition about Ingeld, so there's simply
no place for a new son-in-law called Beowulf. Similarly, the bleak ending of
the poem, with Beowulf's Geats facing inevitable annihilation at the hands of
the Swedes, would be altogether different if there were to be a son who might
carry on the Geatish dynasty. Finally, as many have noted, Beowulf's name
fails to alliterate, in the traditional manner, with that of any of the other royal
Geats. The obvious conclusion is that Beowulf is a completely fictional insert
into historical tradition.

Beowulf and Hygelac

Beowulf's lord, Hygelac, is one of the few characters in the poem who, by
contrast with Beowulf, does have a place in the historical record. Of course it's
relatively easy to slip a fictional retainer (and a nephew, and moreover a sister's

son, somewhat sideways to the direct male line of descent) into established history. It is worth noting too, at this point, that we need not be concerned about making a clear distinction between what would stand up as 'actual' history, by modern standards, and known traditions about the past, which may drift into legend, and may or may not be 'true'. A useful analogy is a film version of a Shakespeare tragedy: generally, we are not (unless we are literary historians) too concerned about the actuality of Shakespeare's history, but we would be disconcerted, and perhaps even outraged, to be suddenly faced with a fourth daughter of King Lear's, or a brother of Hamlet's, which would certainly cause a major disturbance to Shakespeare's fictional world, which we are familiar with, and think we know. It's the same with *Beowulf*: there are good grounds for supposing Beowulf himself to be a new fictional character, but his appearance and actions against the background of Scandinavian events in the distant past do not radically upset established traditions, as they are evidenced in Scandinavian sources. The poet anyway has a good deal of leeway: we don't know how much exact knowledge an original audience might have had about those traditions, or indeed, whether they might not have been already patchy and inconsistent, which is more than likely. But at the two extremes, Hygelac is certainly part of the historical record, while Beowulf is almost certainly not. The status of the other (human) characters in the poem is somewhere, indeterminately, in between, but many of them – especially the Danes – would have had at least what we might call a fictional history, and the poet of *Beowulf* is in the end limited in how far those traditions can be altered or manipulated. And finally, the reports of Hygelac's death in historical sources can definitively and uniquely date the events of the poem – that is, the distant Geatish setting of its action. Hygelac, King of the Geats – his name improbably mangled in Latin chronicles as Chochilaicus – was apparently killed, just as the *Beowulf*-poet relates it, on a raid in the continental territory of the Frankish people, in the first half of the sixth century CE.

From the poem itself we know very little about Hygelac. After the closely observed and touching bond between Beowulf and Hrothgar, there is somehow nowhere to go with the relationship between Beowulf and Hygelac, and the poet presents nothing particular or personal, just the perfect, ideal dynamic between a lord and his retainer. This dynamic, as we see it played out not only in *Beowulf*, but also elsewhere in Germanic heroic poetry, was based on mutual obligations of loyalty and reward. The bare bones of the arrangement were that retainers like Beowulf pledge their loyalty, fight on behalf of their lord and can expect to be rewarded with gifts of treasure, and defended in their turn, if it becomes necessary. In *Beowulf*, we see that if a retainer wins treasure himself, perhaps on a lone expedition, such as Beowulf's encounter with Grendel's mother, he must hand it over to his lord, who may then reward the retainer's bravery by handing some back. Loyalty may also entail vengeance: if the lord himself or his family members or allies come to harm, it is a retainer's duty to redress the balance of power by avenging them, if possible, to the death. These principles are necessarily tied up with courage and martial brilliance. Warriors must never show fear or back out of a fight; they must always fulfil any proud boast about vanquishing their opponents, and the very greatest warriors will choose glory before death and, indeed, disdain any threat of death, and certainly never leave alive a battlefield on which their lord lies dead. These are the fundamental ethics of the imagined warrior elite represented in *Beowulf*, and they may even reflect some ancient reality, for they match very closely the martial ideals of the Germanic tribes as depicted in early classical literature.

About to face the dragon, at the very end of his life, Beowulf sums up to perfection this heroic code (and again I quote from Seamus Heaney's translation):

> The treasures that Hygelac lavished on me
> I paid for when I fought, as fortune allowed me,
> with my glittering sword. He gave me land
> and the security land brings, so he had no call
> to go looking for some lesser champion,
> some mercenary from among the Gifthas
> or the Spear-Danes or the men of Sweden.
> I marched ahead of him, always there
> at the front of the line, and I shall fight like that
> for as long as I live …

After this retrospective boast, Beowulf recounts the final obligation he discharged as Hygelac's retainer: he avenged Hygelac by killing – with his bare hands; this was personal – the Frankish warrior responsible for Hygelac's death. And there is one last little kick of the heroic code, as Beowulf exults in the fact that this Frank was not able to present his own lord, the king of the Frisians, with treasure he'd won on the battlefield – that treasure, of course, being Hygelac's war-gear.

So when Beowulf returns to Geatland from Heorot, loaded with the treasures Hrothgar had bestowed on him, events proceed in predictable ways. Beowulf begins with a detailed account of his experiences in Heorot – which is, interestingly, not exactly a reprise of what has already been related, but told from his perspective, as an outside observer. As we have seen, he tells Hygelac about Hrothgar's plan to marry off his daughter Freawaru to Ingeld – a plan which was not made known to us, as audience, at the time, and a plan about which Beowulf says he has the gravest misgivings. Beowulf is proud to tell Hygelac how very generously he was rewarded by Hrothgar and duly hands over the battle standard with a boar image on top, the lofty helmet, the chainmail and a magnificent sword – disturbingly, perhaps, the very assemblage which Hrothgar's brother had not, for some unspecified reason, passed on to his own son. He adds four beautiful horses to the collection. Then he gives Hygelac's queen Hygd a wonderful neck-ring which Wealhtheow had given him and adds three more horses. This largesse may seem simply over the top – a poet trying to convey as lavish an impression a possible, without regard to reality – but there is an edge of precision to it. We were told rather earlier in the poem's narrative that Hrothgar gifted eight horses to Beowulf. And here he is, giving away seven of them, and presumably keeping one for himself.

Hygelac, in his turn, rewards Beowulf in turn for these rewards, as we have seen offering him what may be a symbolic gift of his grandfather Hrethel's sword, pulling him back in towards to main paternal line of descent. But mention of Hygelac's queen Hygd is a reminder that we should now move on from the inevitably male and masculine retainer-lord relationship, and look at the women.

Hygd and Modthrytho

As with the Beowulf-Hygelac relationship, the *Beowulf*-poet falls back on
the representation of the ideal – in this case, the ideal of queenship – when
he introduces Hygd. The Geatish hall is no Heorot, but it is very grand, and
Hygd, though young and inexperienced, is full of wisdom and knows the
fundamentals of the heroic code: that she must be generous with gifts and
free with the treasure giving. The poet then resorts to his characteristic, if
idiosyncratic, mode of characterization: as when Hrothgar, in his sermon,
outlined the virtues of the wise ruler, and contrasted them with the behaviour of
wicked king Heremod, so Hygd is flattered by a comparison with a queen who
did not display ideal virtues: quite the opposite, for Modthrytho committed
firen ondrysne (monstrous outrages). She is the threatening embodiment of
a male nightmare of a powerful woman: no man is allowed even to look at
her on pain of savage tortures and capital punishment. This is the ultimate
repudiation of what feminist critics have called 'the male gaze'. But of course,
the *Beowulf*-poet is no upholder of a 'girls rule' ethos. Modthrytho's repudiation
is itself repudiated: once married to a masculine man – in this case, a king
called Offa – her resistance is overcome and she becomes, like Hygd, an ideal
queen. The numerous variations on the so-called 'maiden king' theme – very
many of them in Old Norse romances – demonstrate how popular the basic
story was in the Middle Ages, and readers will perhaps recognize the outline
of Shakespeare's *The Taming of the Shrew*, with its casual misogyny which still
shocks modern readers.

So who was Modthrytho? Is she a figure from history or an invented
anti-type? The answer is – as so many answers are – both yes and no. The
name certainly doesn't figure elsewhere in any sources, whether historical
or fictional. But it's not even clear that Modthrytho is her name. The final
element – *-thryth(o)* – is fairly common in Anglo-Saxon women's names,
and in fact, in an early medieval Latin life of a real eighth-century king,
Offa of Mercia, his wicked and treacherous wife is called Drida – clearly
a version of the Old English element *-thryth*. But both *mod* and *thryth* are
also common nouns in Old English, both meaning something like 'pride',
so the compound *mod-thrytho* may just mean 'arrogance' and, in this

context, might describe an otherwise unnamed queen of this disposition who commits the offences. Or there's a compromise: the *mod* element may qualify a short proper name, Thryth(o), so she would be called the equivalent of Thrytho the Proud. Some scholars have even proposed that a word which most have taken to be an adjective – *freme* (perhaps, arrogant or imperious, but rather uncertain in its meaning) – used to describe her, might be her name, re-written as Fremu.

However, Offa of Mercia's wife was actually (verifiably actually: her name is on coins and charters) called Cynethryth, and the *Latin Life of King Offa of Mercia* explains (or rather, concocts) the story behind this: once married to Offa she is known as Quendrida – 'Queen Drida', that is, Cynethryth. But to complicate matters still further, the name Cynethryth occurs even earlier in Old English, and it is attached to yet another wicked woman. And although I hesitate to say this, there was another King Offa, too, who lived, if he was not purely legendary, centuries before Offa of Mercia. His wife – strangely enough, like Offa of Mercia's wife – was banished over the sea, but unlike Offa of Mercia's wife, she patiently endured her torments, so that she belongs to a familiar folktale which Chaucer reworks in his *Clerk's Tale*, in which a long-suffering woman endures horrible torments – especially being put out to sea alone in a boat, although as in the *Clerk's Tale* there may be vicious psycho-sexual twists such as forcing her to prepare a marriage bed for her husband and daughter. But in the end she is reunited with her husband. Offa of Mercia's Queen Drida had been banished for some unspecified crime and is washed up on the shores of Offa's kingdom, where the king is foolishly taken in by her, and marries her. Unfortunately for this Offa, marriage did not work miracles on Queen Drida's temperament, so the story is a little bit different from what we see in *Beowulf*. And the poor woman associated with the other, ancient Offa is not wicked at all. Nonetheless, the wicked queen – whatever her name was – in *Beowulf* is also casually, almost as an aside, said to have been sent across the sea at her father's behest. Some feminist critics have seen behind all these stories either a dark implication of incest, in which the female victim, and not the male perpetrator, is banished, or a version of the 'maiden king' romance I mentioned earlier, in which the woman refuses to marry against her will, and is repudiated or violently threatened by her father.

So to get back to *Beowulf*: how much, if any, of all this background might the poet have known, and drawn on, or elaborated? I will explore in the second section of this book the poet's possible frames of reference, from biblical themes to Old Norse myth, from legendary history to oral folk tales. And in a related section, I want to look at how the narrator manages the time scheme of the narrative: what relationship certain stories have with the primary narrative, the present moment of the main narrative, and how the narrator juxtaposes past and present. But for the moment, whilst recognizing the extraordinary complexity of the traditions which may lie behind the story of Offa's amended queen – however we may now view the inherent misogyny of a proud woman being 'tamed' by a dominant male – I'm thinking about how the human characters are presented. We have seen the relationship between Hrothgar and Beowulf, and the utterly convincing portrait of Hrothgar's old age, and how it inflects his words and deeds. But the characterization of Hygelac and Hygd is very different. We see them always from the outside, as resplendent, imposing but oddly static figures, monuments to the ideals of monarchy, leadership and loyalty. And it seems to me that the *Beowulf*-poet is setting up this almost kaleidoscopic picture of the royal couple, but especially Hygd, who is defined and represented as much by a distorted mirror image, a reflection, of what she is not – Offa's wicked queen – as by who she is and what she does.

Beowulf and Wiglaf

When we come to Wiglaf, and his relationship with Beowulf, it seems at first as if we are dealing with another shard in the endlessly reflective kaleidoscope of good and bad versions of key players. For Wiglaf is the ideal retainer, loyal to Beowulf, and totally committed to the reciprocal processes of loyalty and reward. And yet, there's a lot more than this. As we shall see, and have seen, on the one hand, Wiglaf's family history is distinctly edgy, and on the other, his adherence to the principles of the heroic code is dramatically extended to a physical humanity as he tenderly cares for the dying Beowulf.

In what we may now recognize as true Beowulfian style, immediately following the lavish and mutually self-congratulatory gift exchanges between

Beowulf and the Geatish royal couple, we hear first of Hygelac's death in battle, and then about how the ever-dangerous Swedes took advantage of the weakness of the Geats and attacked; Hygelac's son and heir Heardred was killed, and Beowulf took over the throne. But his fifty-year reign is passed over in only a few words, for the next big thing is the advent of the fire-breathing dragon. Now it's Beowulf who is the old king, his glory days behind him, threatened by a marauding monster. And like Hrothgar, his hall too is burned to the ground – this time, by the dragon. Surprisingly, perhaps, when Beowulf hears the news about the dragon, and the destruction of his hall, he at once supposes that this is some sort of divine punishment. He is beset by *þeostrum geþoncum | swa him geþywe ne wæs* (shadowy thoughts | as for him was not customary). But although he soon begins constructive preparations to combat the dragon, the poet warns us right from the beginning that this will be the end for Beowulf. Beowulf brought about a complete change in fortune for Hrothgar, but a sudden change has now come to him, this time a change for the worse.

The poet offers us a quick retrospective of Beowulf's lifetime achievements – including naturally, his debut killing of Grendel. But the Swedes are always lurking on the edge of this history. Beowulf, the positive anti-type of the treacherous nephew, had refused to take on the Geatish throne ahead of his own nephew, Hygelac's son Heardred, who had then – perhaps unwisely – given sanctuary to the rebellious nephews of the Swedish king Onela. Now we learn more about how Beowulf came to the Geatish throne: Heardred was killed because of the refuge he gave to those two nephews. One of the two, Eanmund, is also killed, but Onela seems to have been content to leave Eanmund's surviving brother Eadgils with Beowulf ruling the Geats. This too may have been an unwise decision, because Eadgils, helped by Beowulf, eventually returns to Sweden to take vengeance for the death of his brother by killing Onela. We are not told what had happened to Ohtere, Onela's brother, or why Onela's two nephews rebelled against him and took refuge with Heardred. But it is simplest to suppose that Onela had seized the throne from his brother Ohtere and in doing so dispossessed his nephews. We certainly hear no more of Ohtere. But the Swedes remain a serious threat, as the messenger warns.

The tit-for-tat violence between the Swedes and the Geats can be traced back even further than this lethal split in the Swedish dynasty and the killing of

the Geatish king Heardred. As Beowulf, now an old man, prepares to fight the
dragon, he casts his mind right back to an even earlier set of Swedish wars, when
the Swedish brothers Onela and Ohtere – still young men fighting together
at this stage – were a constant threat to the Geats. In this phase of hostilities,
Hygelac's brother Hæthcyn was killed, and then it was Hygelac's turn to take
revenge; the father of Onela and Ohtere, old Ongentheow, is killed by one of
Hygelac's warriors, and there is then an uneasy peace, as Hygelac rules the Geats
and is supported by Beowulf. But once Hygelac dies in battle abroad in Frisia,
the Swedes swoop in again. Returning to the present time of the poem's main
narrative, a messenger reporting Beowulf's death to the remaining Geatish
troops fills in more of the background. According to his report – which is
subtly different from Beowulf's recall and distinctly sympathetic to the Swedish
cause – it was the Geats who started the hostilities which ended in the death
of Hæthcyn. Worse still, the belligerent Geats had seized old Ongentheow's
wife, the mother of Onela and Ohtere. The messenger relates a gripping story of
overturned expectations: Ongentheow rescues his elderly wife and surrounds
the defeated Geats, cruelly gloating over what he is triumphantly saving until
the next morning: their torture and execution. But Hygelac comes to their
rescue, and this is how and where old Ongentheow met his end.

In Scandinavian tradition, the Danes figure very prominently, although not
all the details of family relationships, alliances and celebrated feats match what
we have in Beowulf. The names, though, chime. The Swedes and Geats are less
clearly represented in Scandinavian sources, however. There are kings whose
names seem cognate with the names in *Beowulf*: Ohtere, the father of the
nephews who rebelled against their uncle Onela, is clearly Óttarr in Old Norse
narratives, but as we have seen, he does not play a very large part in *Beowulf*.
Onela may well correspond to King Áli, who is however a Norwegian king in
Old Norse. Óttarr has a son, Aðils (Eadgils), which seals his identity, but there
is no trace of anyone corresponding to Eanmund. Other correspondences
are patchy and faint; the name Ongentheow seems to relate to the celebrated
Old Norse hero Angantýr, but this correspondence doesn't cast any light on
Beowulfian events.

We learn all this from recall and anticipation: in the poet's summary of
how Beowulf moved from young hero to old king; in Beowulf's recollections

of his childhood, and the early years of his reign; in the grim warnings of the messenger. None of these events are related in the present moment of the poem, either because they are minimally skipped over, or because they are the matter, as I say, of memory or threat. Recollections and prophecies are articulated in the present moment of the poem: the narrator recaps, Beowulf reminisces and the messenger predicts – though with bleak authority, rather than speculation. And this is where the Swedes primarily belong: on the edges – both spatial and temporal, as well as rhetorical – of the main action. But the Swedish menace has insinuated itself into the evolving present moment of the poem. It may have escaped our notice that near the beginning of Beowulf, we are told that Hrothgar's sister was married to Onela, a significant link between the Danish and Swedish royal houses. Suddenly, the old Swedish king Ongentheow's rescue of his queen from the aggressive Geats presents new possibilities. Why did they seize her? Was abducting her just an act of war, or did Ongentheow's wife originally belong to the Geatish people, so that they were forcibly repatriating her? And most pressingly, we need to confront the strange ambiguity of Wiglaf's status *vis à vis* the Swedes, for as we have seen, the sword with which he enables Beowulf to defeat the dragon was given to his father by Onela.

Although Beowulf is given plenty of narrative time to recollect the past, the pull of the poem's present brings him back to the logistics of the dragon fight, although he evidently sees it through the lens of that past: he wants to fight the dragon without weapons – as he grappled hand-to-hand with Grendel – but pragmatically recognizes that this is not possible. However, he is resolved to meet the dragon alone – man versus monster – and instructs his retainers to stand back. This, then, is where Wiglaf, with his complicatedly divided loyalties, comes in. Beowulf explicitly acknowledges that both of them belong to the Wægmunding family, which is apparently divided between Swedish and Geatish ties. But it remains the case that Beowulf's most loyal retainer is the son of one of the Swedish king's champions. Seeing Beowulf in dire straits against the formidable dragon, his retainers, already watching from a safe distance, make a run for it – all except one: Wiglaf. Wiglaf cannot stop himself diving into the fight with the dragon in order to help his lord, even though Beowulf has announced his intention of tackling the dragon alone. At first, though far from reluctant to join the fight, Wiglaf seems to be doing so out of duty rather than personal affection for Beowulf, recalling what he owes Beowulf in the reciprocal relationship of lord and retainer. And he urges on his companions in similar terms, reminding them of the gifts Beowulf had given them, and how they had promised loyalty in return. His final appeal is to the last public duty of the retainers: not to return home unscathed after a defeat, especially not leaving their lord on the battlefield. But his speech is addressed to thin air; the other retainers have gone.

As they fight the dragon together, there is a touchingly symbolic moment when they both share the same shield – Wiglaf's has been burnt up by the dragon's fiery breath. Wiglaf's intervention allows Beowulf to kill the dragon – his sword fails, and a disabling blow from Wiglaf lets Beowulf close enough to the creature to kill it with a short knife. But Beowulf has been fatally injured, and this is where Wiglaf demonstrates extraordinary tenderness towards his lord: he carefully unlooses Beowulf's helmet, and swabs his wounds with water. This is a long way from the reciprocal – even mercantile – framing of the retainer-lord contract, and far too from the indomitable boasting and shouted speechifying of the heroic code. In fact, its nearest analogy – especially if we take into account Wiglaf's Scylfing history – is the biblical parable of the Good Samaritan: the Samaritan who bathes the wounds of the Jew who has been left for dead by the side of the road, and has typified for so many simple humanity from an unexpected source.

Beowulf's dying wish – which many modern readers have found it hard to empathize with – is to feast his eyes on the treasure which the dragon has been guarding, and he sends Wiglaf to fetch it. It is significant that Beowulf takes this opportunity to lament the absence of a son to whom he could bequeath this treasure, but he makes no gesture towards gifting it to Wiglaf. This is in keeping with the powerful sense of an ending here: there is to be no continuation of Beowulf's line, and in the poem – if, perhaps, not in history – the Geats are finished. The treasure too, though magnificent in volume and execution, is a sad remnant of an extinct dynasty: it is *eald ond omig* (old and rusty); the beautiful goblets have no-one to keep them polished, and their decorations – perhaps encrusted jewels, or golden bands – have come off. We are reminded of the speech, recorded earlier in the poem, of the so-called 'lone survivor', the last anonymous voice of a once flourishing society, who in time past consigned that same treasure hoard to the ground where, eventually, the dragon came upon it. That speaker lamented the demise of his people and addresses the earth itself, enjoining it to take back into itself the gold it once contained as a mineral ore. He regrets the absence of someone to take care of the treasure, and the very same word is used – *feormynd* (a polisher, or nurturer, interestingly related to the verb 'to farm') – when the treasure sees the light of day again, as Beowulf's reward for killing the dragon. The treasure has been without human curation ever since it was deposited, and it will now remain so. Beowulf has no descendants to pass it on to, and it is deposited in his burial mound, along with his ashes. As the poet bleakly sums it up, the gold will be *eldum swa unnyt | swa hit æror wæs* (to men of old, just as useless | as it once was). So has all this been pointless, all this glory and heroics and posturing and fighting? Before the ritual mourning of Beowulf's funeral – building of the mound, the cremation, the women's keening and the interment of the ashes and treasure – there is one final, timeless moment of compassion: Wiglaf makes a last, hopeless attempt to revive Beowulf by splashing his face with water.

The temporal and spatial extremities of *Beowulf* are filled with a complex tangle of the past, present and future of Swedish-Geatish feuding. But the narrative present brings to the fore Wiglaf's simple act of kindness. So, to conclude this section about the human characters in *Beowulf*, we can say that viewed from a distance, in terms of either in historical time or geographical space, people form a formidable and tangled mass of threat, tragedy and violence. But seen close up, in the present moment of the poem, their essential humanity dominates the scene.

(iii) The monsters

Beowulf takes on, and defeats, three monsters in the course of the poem: Grendel, Grendel's mother and the dragon. These three encounters are all quite different, and yet the first two are not only paired in the most obvious way – that Grendel and his mother are in some sense the same species as each other, and that the encounters take place in quick succession, indeed the second as a direct result of the first, at the beginning of the poem – but also in the way in which the poet intertwines the two, the narrative shifting almost imperceptibly between them. It has even become a commonplace in *Beowulf* scholarship to refer to mother and son with a collective but technically singular compound noun: the Grendelkin. I won't use that term myself, although I am very engaged by the way the poet presents them as an indivisible unit, whilst somehow maintaining a clear distinction between the two fights. In line, then, with discussing Beowulf as a human character in conjunction with others, in what follows I will treat Grendel and his mother together.

Grendel and his mother

As even the heading of this section makes clear, there is a fundamental inequity built into this mother-son relationship: Grendel's mother has no name, and so is defined solely in relationship to her son. She is, so to speak, an attribute of Grendel's. This is of course not to say that she is less than Grendel in some respect, that she is less terrifying or less of a challenge to Beowulf. The opposite is arguably the case. It is rather that, having seen off Grendel, Beowulf has stirred an even greater threat into action, and this dynamic may remind us of the escalations of human violence: that retribution in human societies – contemporary as well as medieval – tends not to be proportionate. This is the first indication that the poet may be implicitly inviting the audience to make connexions between the fictional, even fantastic, monster fights in *Beowulf,* and the shadowy quasi-historical world of human feuding. In an essay very celebrated by *Beowulf* scholars, J. R. R. Tolkien made a powerful case for the emotional and psychological gravity of the monsters. Until then, many of the poem's readers, guided by the scholarship, had tended to value more highly the quasi-historical 'edges' of the poem, all those tantalizingly partial and shadowy but very evocative references to the distant Scandinavian dynasties of Danes, Swedes and Geats. Following Tolkien's intervention, the monsters seemed to reclaim their place at the centre of the poem, and only recently has the balance begun to shift once again. Rather than embrace either of these pendulum swings, I will be trying to highlight the parity of the human and monstrous threats to security. After all, the storyworld of *Beowulf* contains them both.

Perhaps the most obvious link between the human and the monstrous is also evident in the relationship between these two monsters, for the second monster is insistently, repeatedly, a mother. It goes without saying that the dragon has no mother. In fact, mothers are thin on the ground in *Beowulf*. But where they do appear, they are tragic figures: Wealhtheow, courageously (or anxiously) trying to defend the succession of her own sons with Hrothgar; Hildeburh, mourning her son and brother after the fight at Finnsburh; Hygd, the Geatish queen, wisely and diplomatically hoping to safeguard the kingdom by inviting Beowulf to stand by her young son Heardred when his father Hygelac is killed in battle (Beowulf does his best, but Heardred makes bad choices, and is ultimately killed). These women, one may imagine, passively suffer a fate typical both of female figures in heroic tradition more widely and, perhaps, of aristocratic women in actual history. Grendel's mother shares with these female figures a profound and powerful bond with her son – possibly the only bond in *Beowulf* which is totally inalienable. But she is not at all passive, and at once takes vengeance for the death of Grendel. And there is also a very faint echo in the poem of what would have been for Anglo-Saxon Christians the dominant mother-son relationship, the Blessed Virgin's grief for Christ. Although, as I have said, there are no explicit New Testament allusions in *Beowulf*, just once, when Hrothgar is praising Beowulf for his victory over Grendel, he makes a slightly strange reference to *efne swa hwylc mægþa | swa þone magan cende* (whoever was the woman who gave birth to such a son), declaring that the *Ealdmetod* (God of old) must have been gracious to her – perhaps recalling the grace bestowed by God on Mary. It's strange, because Hrothgar himself has identified Beowulf's mother as a daughter of old King Hrethel. Interestingly, we are also told that no father to Grendel has been identified. In *Beowulf*, the relationship between Grendel and his mother is exclusive and all-consuming: no society, no family, no father, just mother and son.

There is also a significant echo of the mother-son duo in some Old Norse tales of the supernatural in which heroes are beset by trolls. Most people nowadays can picture clearly – and perhaps even quite graphically – what a troll looks like, but much of that visual identity has been built up through centuries of storytelling, and the earliest sources are actually both vague and inconsistent in how trolls are depicted. But they are unfailingly humanoid to some degree – even though the degree to which they depart from normal human form, and their distance from human society, not to mention their size, is variable. But there is a set of Old Norse folk tales which *Beowulf*-scholars have dubbed 'the two-troll tale' in which a male-female duo together terrorize human society. The most celebrated of these 'two-troll' stories occurs in the Old Norse saga of Grettir the Strong (*Grettis saga*), in which the hero, Grettir, himself a somewhat trollish figure, combats first a female troll, and then a male one. *Grettis saga*, a later medieval so-called family saga, cannot have been the source for *Beowulf*, but it may be that both saga and poem drew on the same traditional tale, whilst making very different literature out of it: the prose saga presents something close to actual life in early Iceland (with some trollish additions), while *Beowulf* depicts an imagined landscape from the distant past with monsters as well as humans in it.

We first hear of Grendel after the poet has described the building of the great hall, Heorot. At the highest point of Hrothgar's reign, the poet tells us two things: that ultimately, the hall will be burned to the ground, and that immediately, Heorot, in its celebratory magnificence, has provoked the resentment of a formidable enemy, a *feond on helle* (hellish fiend), a *grimma gæst* (fierce ghost/guest/intruder). He is named from the outset as Grendel, and he is at once, and repeatedly, and consistently, associated with creatures inimical to a divine creator who is in *Beowulf* represented as the guardian of mankind – never explicitly identified as God the father of Judaeo-Christian tradition, but entirely in keeping with him. The Danes are being entertained in Heorot with a story of creation, which is described in terms strongly suggestive of the Old Testament creation story, our world a bright plain surrounded by water, adorned with vegetation for the delectation of mankind, lit by sun and moon, and populated by *cynna gehwylcum | þara ðe cwice hwyrfað* (all things that move and have life). This is what so provokes Grendel. But the poet has a specific lineage for Grendel (and, of course, his mother, who has not yet been introduced). Grendel is a wanderer in borderlands, one of a race of monsters condemned to a bleak exile at the edges of the known world by the Creator who took vengeance on Cain for the murder of his brother Abel. Grendel, then, is a descendant of Cain and shares in the punishment – lonely and long-lasting banishment – which God decreed for Cain. The poet piously points out that God did not take any pleasure in this enduring feud, but neither, of course, did those who were anathematized. According to the poet, all manner of monstrosities – *untydras* (evil offspring) – were engendered as a result of this feud: *eotenas ond ylfe ond orcneas | swylce gigantas | þa wið Gode wunnon.* These terms are difficult to translate: the manuscript is not in perfect condition here, and some words occur nowhere else. But one might hazard 'giants and elves and trolls and such goliaths who contended against God' – in other words, all the humanoid horrors one could think of from Germanic and biblical tradition. Whatever they are, exactly, Grendel is one of them, and he hates the Danes in their quasi-Christian revelry.

So what do Grendel and his mother look like? One of the great skills of the *Beowulf*-poet is to leave the depiction of Grendel indistinct – on the familiar principle that what is imagined is more terrifying than what is described. The very first word denoting Grendel is *ellen-gæst* – a compound word which occurs nowhere else, and so may have been put together by the poet specially for this context. The first element means 'bold', or 'powerful', and the second, related to the modern English word 'ghost', means spirit, or demon, although there may also be a play on a very similar word *gist* which is related to the modern word 'guest', but with the Old English meaning – oddly (or fittingly?) enough – of 'stranger' or 'intruder'. So we have a powerful, supernatural intruder, a terrifying threat. But abruptly, the sympathy shifts: this creature has suffered for a long time, and wretchedly. The Old English word used here for 'wretchedly' – *earfoðlice* – is used throughout the poem of the human characters to denote a physical difficulty, such as, ironically, how hard it was for Beowulf to defeat Grendel's mother, or how Beowulf's retainers find it hard to carry Grendel's huge head back to Heorot as a trophy. It can be mental as well as physical hurt: Wiglaf suffers *earfoðlice* when he watches Beowulf dying. But in a more sinister sense, it is also used to describe how impatiently the dragon waits for night to come, when it can take its lethal fiery vengeance on humankind for the theft of the cup which one of them has stolen from its hoard. The dragon's pent-up fury, its anger and malevolence against its human enemies as it restlessly circles around its barrow are surely what we should understand Grendel feeling here. And the dragon's rising impatience is intensified by the need it feels to wait for nightfall, because like Grendel, it is a nocturnal creature.

And this is the very next thing we are told about Grendel in his wretchedness – that he spent his time in darkness. This darkness is both literal, in that Grendel, like the dragon, is active at night and also spiritual: firstly, because of the obvious metaphorical associations of darkness and light, but also because the word for darkness – *þystru* – used here in the plural is found elsewhere in Old English literature to denote the shades of Hell. In *Beowulf*, as we have seen, the song of creation which so delights the Danes in Heorot is characterized by light, with its descriptions of a shining sun and moon, and a shimmering earth. Indeed, in the kingdom of the Danes, Heorot itself is a beacon of brightness in the darkness, although a thoughtful audience may be reminded of a less happy beacon, given the poet's hints of Heorot ultimately in flames.

The darkness Grendel inhabits, together with the fact that his home on the very edges of the known human world, means that no-one gets a clear view of him or his mother. And their murderous attacks on Heorot are characterized by shock and speed: Grendel no sooner seizes thirty of Hrothgar's retainers, sleeping in Heorot, than he is off, back to wherever he sprang from. (It is perhaps best to understand the figure 'thirty' as simply denoting a large number and therefore a heavy burden; Beowulf himself is said to recover thirty coats of mail from dead Geatish warriors after Hygelac's disastrous raid on the Franks.) Even when Grendel encounters Beowulf, waiting for him in Heorot, his first impulse is to flee rather than fight, literally tearing himself out of Beowulf's grasp with such urgent force that he leaves his arm behind. Grendel's mother makes a similar lightning attack on Heorot, snatching up the nearest retainer who is, as it turns out, one of Hrothgar's closest companions, and making a swift escape. The reader's immediate impression of the sudden and unexpected assault is of the confusion of the retainers in Heorot, who do not even have time to put on their helmets or reach for their mailcoats. Just as there is no time in the storyworld for the retainers, struggling to awake from what might be understood as a drunken stupor, to get a good look at their attacker, so there is no pause for description in the narrative.

But as Hrothgar tells Beowulf, Danes have had distant glimpses of mother and son – not, it seems, from Heorot, but from remoter areas in the kingdom.

The poet is careful to emphasize that there was no clear, close-up view – only *þæs þe hie gewislicost | gewitan meahton* (as far as they could most clearly make out) – but the two were humanoid, that is, took the shape of a man and a woman, except that they were larger than any normal human. This chimes with the difficulty Beowulf's retainers had with carrying Grendel's head back to Heorot. Their humanoid shape also chimes with the account of Beowulf's fight with Grendel's mother. Their wrestling match is vividly dominated by descriptions of Grendel's mother's fingers: grabbing, gripping, crushing, trying to poke lethal holes in his mail coat. Paradoxically, this prevailing sense of physical, humanoid fingers clutching is even extended to the natural world, as we are told that in the monsters' weird underwater lair, the water itself could not get a *færgrip* (a lethal grip) on their mysterious living area.

Grendel's mother is a formidable and frightening opponent, and the poet's rather awkward remark – that the terror she aroused when she made her attack on Heorot was less by as much as the terror of a woman in battle is less than that of a male warrior – is belied by the fight she puts up against Beowulf. It is of course just possible that the poet is indulging in one of those mind-boggling comparative understatements – such as the remark that Scyld left this world not less well provided for than when he arrived destitute, that is, much better provided for, with all the funeral treasures. Here, the poet may be saying that the terror inspired by the unnatural sight of a woman in battle is exceptionally great, and that therefore the terror Grendel's mother inspired was not less, but was, on the contrary, even greater. Understanding such rhetorical devices probably takes practice.

Grendel's attack on Heorot is particularly dramatic because it involves smashing his way into the Danes' stronghold, Heorot, breaking down the door with his bare hands. An added horror is that his aim is not merely violence against the sleeping warriors: he is ravenously cannibalistic, and having seized his victim, he *slat unwearnum | bat banlocan | blod edrum dranc | synsnædum swealh* (tore [him] apart greedily | bit through muscles | drank blood from veins | swallowed great mouthfuls). He even – like a cartoon monster – swallows down the hands and feet. And again like a cartoon monster, he is easily afraid, desperate to escape the moment he senses resistance: Beowulf's powerful grip on him. The violent stand-off between the two – Beowulf struggling to hold on, Grendel struggling to escape – comes close to wrecking Heorot. The poet lingers on the racket their noisy brawling makes, the wooden building resounding and the mead benches wrenched up, but the whole hall somehow holding together because of its ironwork bracing. It seems that only flame – concludes the narrator, ominously – would be enough to destroy Heorot.

And then arises a much stranger sound: Grendel's wail of rage and pain when he realizes he has met his match in Beowulf. The terrible keening noise that Grendel makes is denoted by the word *wop* – related to the modern English word 'weep'. The poet has used this word once before – for the loud lamenting made by the Danes when they discover the results of Grendel's first assault on Heorot. And it is used only once more in the poem, when the Geats weep out loud around Beowulf's funeral pyre. So here again we have an implicit connexion between man and monster: Grendel's eerie lament is no sub-human animal howl, but an utterance indicating a feeling comparable with human grief and anger. In fact, the poet pushes this anthropomorphism yet further, describing Grendel as singing a defeat-song, chanting a terror-tune. Of course, Heorot is no stranger to melody and song; it was after all the Danes' musical revelry celebrating God's creation which provoked Grendel's antagonism in the first place. Grendel's lament is a weird parody of a human performance.

Grendel's mother's attack on Heorot is no mere repetition of Grendel's own. But it is insistently figured as a completely reactive, almost automatic, response, prompted by Grendel's death. To kill Grendel is inevitably to call down the wrath of the monster's mother, and the first word the poet uses of her is *wrecend* (avenger), closely followed by her most usual signifier, *modor* (mother). But her attack on the Danes in their hall is explicitly linked to Grendel's: one of the Danes pays for her attack with his life – just as happened so very often, the poem tells us, when Grendel was doing the attacking. As we shall see, this mingling and intertwining of the duo's actions is a striking aspect of the way the poet depicts them. Many scholars have also noted that masculine pronouns are sometimes used in connexion with Grendel's mother. This has been put down to a sort of sexist absent-mindedness – that it must have been hard to keep Grendel's mother's femininity in mind when describing her fierce thirst for vengeance and ferocious assault on

Heorot, or that her grammatical identity as a monster tended to overshadow her gender. But these masculine pronouns may be another aspect of the poet's conception of Grendel and Grendel's mother as emanations of the same essential monstrous body. Certainly – as mother and son 'naturally' would – they share the same origin as *geosceaftgastas* (demons sent by fate) who were generated after the first fratricide, when Cain killed Abel. Grendel, we are told, was one of these, and his identity is subtly merged with that of Cain, for what is apparently Cain's God-decreed exile is described in terms indistinguishable from Grendel's exclusion from Heorot: 'he' was to occupy the wilderness and *mandream fleon* (flee human joy) – was that Grendel or Cain? The narrative voice continues with a reprise of Grendel's encounter with Beowulf – how they struggled and how Grendel, fatally wounded, dragged himself back to the underwater lair he and his mother occupied. Only then does the poem turn to Grendel's mother's attack, and it is over in no time: she seizes her victim and does not even pause to devour him, hauling him back to her lair. She is said to have set off on a vengeance mission, and once it has been successfully completed, Hrothgar laments the death of the retainer she has carried off and at once attributes her attack to vengeance, a savage reprisal for Beowulf's killing of Grendel – which is again recalled. When Beowulf returns to his homeland, and tells his lord and uncle Hygelac all about his adventures at the Danish court, these priorities are faithfully maintained: Beowulf summarizes his success with an account of killing Grendel, and when he describes both encounters in more detail, Grendel's mother's motivation – vengeance – is what he focuses on. It is significant that Beowulf, having killed Grendel's mother, returns to Heorot with a single trophy: Grendel's head. There is no doubt that without Grendel's death, there would be no vengeance, and no Grendel's mother. But vengeance is not the sole prerogative of monsters. It is, on the contrary, the motivating force of much human violence, and it is not necessarily deplored in heroic society. Beowulf's response to Hrothgar's despair and grief at the loss of his retainer is a proud, positive statement about vengeance: *Selre bið æghwælm | þæt he his freond wrece | þonne he fela murne* (It's better for every man | that he should avenge his kinsman [or friend] | than [that] he should greatly lament). The monsters are only human after all.

The dragon

Just as Grendel's mother attacks Heorot immediately after Grendel – in fact, the very next night, following the Danish and Geatish gift-giving celebrations of Beowulf's victory – so the dragon emerges from a three-hundred-year hibernation only a few lines after Hygelac, King of the Geats, is shown rewarding Beowulf for his success in killing Grendel and his mother. The dragon is a dormant creature which erupts like a volcano. What is repeatedly called in the poem *edwenden* (a reversal, or change in fortune) comes hard on human revelries. But although in the poem itself the dragon's deadly awakening follows straight on from the Geats' celebrations, in the poem's storyworld a rather long time has flashed by in a tiny handful of half-lines: the death of Hygelac, Beowulf's rise to the throne and a remarkable fifty-year reign. Although we do learn, in retrospect, about how it was Beowulf came to rule the Geats after Hygelac's death, we are told nothing of his unusually long period of kingship. It seems that the poet was not interested in constructing the events of this reign – and of course, if the figure Beowulf is indeed a total fabrication, an invention of the *Beowulf*-poet's, then there would be no tradition to draw on or allude to or elaborate. However, to move so very swiftly on to the emergence of the dragon is a clear indication that Beowulf's encounters with deadly monsters are indeed the focal points of the poem – or, perhaps, that the poem's primary concern is the way good fortune is immediately followed by – or even somehow provokes – bad fortune: *edwenden.*

If the dragon is structurally similar to Grendel and his mother in the way it makes its appearance just as a period of celebration dies down, it is nevertheless a very different kind of creature. It challenges us to reconsider what it is we call 'monstrous'. Is a monstrous creature something of preternatural size, recognizable in form, but larger than normal? Is it perhaps a chilling distortion of an almost recognizable being, like the humanoid form of Grendel and his mother? Or simply a fantastical beast? The *Beowulf*-dragon belongs in this latter category, but dragons are far from uncommon in literary traditions from all times and places, even though they may vary in shape and size, so they are both fantastical and familiar to most readers, although individual conceptions will differ, and sometimes dramatically. I myself always imagine dragons as a shifting blend of pterodactyl and crocodile, breathing fire. There are dragons in biblical tradition, and also in Old Norse myth, and I shall talk about those creatures in the next section when we look at the poet's frame of reference. For the moment, I want to examine the form and function of the *Beowulf*-dragon.

The most obvious difference between the dragon and the other two monsters is evident in the very first mention of it: ... *an ongan | deorcum nihtum | draca ricsian* (a single one began | on dark nights | – a dragon – to hold sway). The dragon is a lone creature, and apparently always has been. There is no question of lineage or legacy, of companions or accomplices: it is a one-off. But in its nocturnal habits, and its quasi-human authority (*ricsian*, to rule), it does share some qualities with Grendel and his mother, who were said to take control of Heorot to such an extent that the Danes could no longer occupy it. Clearly, for an Anglo-Saxon audience, as indeed for ourselves, night-time is a site of potential terror, when who knows what may emerge. And while any beasts of the night may be threatening, those which aspire to impose their rule on human society are especially so. The steady consistency of the relationship between Grendel and his mother and human society is carefully judged: humans celebrate, noisily and joyously, the monsters – we are told, or imagine – simmer with resentment, darkness falls, humans sleep and the monsters emerge. The dragon's diurnal rhythms are much the same, although it is provoked not by human celebrations but by the theft of part of the hoard it is guarding (which I will discuss shortly) – arguably, a more justifiable response. The narrator describes the dragon's habit to perfection in the phrase used of it: *eald uhtsceaða* (ancient dawn-ravager). In the darkness before dawn, the dragon reveals its terrifying power – it is *byrnende* (blazing) and *fyre befangen* (enveloped in fire). It is, above all, a *lyftfloga* (air-flyer), shimmering and flashing against the dark sky. And when dawn breaks, and the dragon has returned to its barrow, the devastation it has caused is plain to see.

Dragons habitually guard gold hoards in European traditions. In one Old Norse story, a princess is gifted a miniature dragon in the medieval equivalent of a matchbox, sitting on a single gold coin (and like the reptile pets of modern urban myth, it grows exponentially and uncontrollably). The most celebrated dragon in Old Norse tradition, Fafnir, began life as a giant's son, and is said to have gradually turned into a dragon as he jealously and obsessively gloated over the treasure hoard he obtained when he and his brother murdered their father for ownership of it. The dragon Fafnir is thus imagined as the very embodiment of greed for gold and miserliness. No wonder, then, that the *Beowulf*-dragon is infuriated by the theft of a gold cup from its precious stash. And the dragon is associated with a gold hoard almost as soon as it is introduced. Its own origins are completely mysterious (unlike Grendel's biblically derived inception) but it achieves full dragon-hood when it comes across a *stanbeorh steapne* (steep-sided stone barrow) filled with ancient treasures. In an unexpected shift from the past tense of storytelling – 'this is what the dragon did' – to a chilling present tense – 'this is what dragons do' – we are told that it is in the nature of dragons to seek out abandoned hoards – here called *hæðen gold* (heathen gold). Perhaps the heathenness of the treasure is a nod towards its immense age. Or perhaps we should recall how treasure is prized in *Beowulf* only when it is in flux, moving fluently, almost as if molten, from giver to receiver, and on again, oiling the wheels of social interaction and bonding. Treasure hoarded and buried is bad news, and so it proves here.

The dragon's incendiary powers are very far from merely decorative or sensational. Its fiery breath is more flame-throwing than fairy-lighting, and it burns houses, whole villages, and ultimately, with a faint but unmistakable echo of the fate of Heorot, Beowulf's own hall is reduced to ashes. Preparing to take on the dragon, Beowulf takes the actuality of the dragon's fire with perfect seriousness, commissioning in advance an iron shield, and protecting himself with metal armour. But the outcome of their encounter is not in doubt: both he and the dragon, we are told, are about to experience an end to their transitory lives. In the fight, the dragon proves to be a formidable opponent, fuelled not only by its fire but also by its ferocious anger and malevolence. Beowulf's sword will not cut through its natural amour-plating of scales, and Beowulf himself has ordered his retainers to stand back – in fact, at the height of this dramatic encounter, they have actually run away. Only Wiglaf remains to offer crucial help – ironically, as we have seen, armed with war-gear gifted to his father by Beowulf's enemies, Wiglaf thrusts his sword into the dragon's soft underparts. This enables Beowulf to get closer to the dying dragon and, in an echo of his fight with Grendel's mother, use a short dagger to finish it off.

The death of a hero is a hard thing for an author to manage. The hero's opponent must be suitably formidable, but then the hero can hardly, anti-climactically, be simply overcome by it, thereby losing his pre-eminence. The mutual death of both antagonists, as in *Beowulf*, is the ideal conclusion. Beowulf's dying minutes are the occasion for pathos and admiration. But the dragon is unceremoniously pushed off a cliff, and into the sea – consigned to the waves in a strangely elegiac echo of Scyld Scefing's funeral at the very beginning of the poem. And the dragon itself is granted a surprisingly touching elegy, more touching, perhaps, than merely just enough to establish its worth as a fitting foe for Beowulf. The creature which, when alive, was defined by its aerial acrobatics, its blazing beauty, is now stretched out and stiff, and there is a certain unmistakable regret in the report of its lifelessness: of course it will never be able to terrorize the Geats again, but moreover, *Nalles æfter lyfte | lacende hwearf | middelnihtum | maðmæhta wlonc | answyn ywde | ac he eorðum gefeoll* (Never again through the air | [would it] playfully circle | in the dead of night | revelling in [its] wealth | display [its] figure | but it fell to earth). The dangerous and glittering dragon is very nearly a metaphor for the heroic age itself.

All monsters, whether inherited as traditional, customized to fit a new literary context, or freely invented, will inevitably reflect, or symbolize, or embody the anxieties of the society which produces them, and as we have seen, this is highly likely to be the case with the *Beowulf*-monsters. But we don't have to put ourselves in the shoes of the Anglo-Saxons to feel the power of Grendel, his mother and the dragon. In the hands of an author with sufficient literary expertise, we can see whatever we fear or deplore in any monster. They are not outlandish, alien freaks, but are disturbingly relatable to the pressures which beset any unstable, or threatened, society.

2

Poet, Narrator and Scop

Having examined the world in which *Beowulf* is set, and its human and non-human inhabitants, I now turn to explore the way in which that image is presented, or conveyed, to us, as listeners or readers. It may seem too obvious to be worth mention that the primary figure responsible for delivering *Beowulf* to us is the poet – the author of the poem. But although *Beowulf* is an anonymous poem, so that we will probably never know the name of the poet, or in fact any other details about him – and it's vanishingly unlikely, as I shall shortly discuss, that the poet would have been female – the poem itself can provide all sorts of evidence about this actual figure who produced it. However, some reservations need to be aired. For instance, it's clearly simplest to assume a single author, even though I already raised the possibility that the poem as we have it is the combined result of any number of oral versions across any number of years or even centuries. I suppose it's even conceivable that *Beowulf* was composed by a little consortium of like-minded poets, working collectively. But bearing these reservations in mind, the least clumsy formulation is to use a simple singular, as has been my practice thus far: the *Beowulf*-poet.

We should also be able to infer quite a lot about this nameless figure from the poem itself: from its storyline, tone, ethical viewpoint, mastery of learned information and so on. There's a brief reservation to be made here, though, too: while it might seem straightforward enough to assume that the *Beowulf*-poet was interested in, say, monsters, or Danes or any other aspects of the substance of the poem, again I suppose it's just possible that some imagined commissioner of the poem presented the poet(s) with a list of desiderata: 'Please can we have a poem about Danes/with monsters?', so that the substance of the poem is not necessarily the poet's free choice. Nevertheless, aside from such groundless (but not impossible) speculation, there are certain things we can safely infer about the poet from the poem itself. I shall be exploring what might be called the poet's frame of reference: the intellectual background necessary to produce *Beowulf*, with its biblical references and its repeated allusions to Old Norse myth. I will also offer some guarded speculation about the poet's own ethical standpoint or situation.

It is necessary too to distinguish poet from narrative voice. Although both present the poem to its readers and listeners, the key distinction is that the poet – nameless as he may be – was once a living human person, an actuality in the real world. The narrative voice, by contrast, is a construction, constructed by the poet through the poem itself. The narrative voice is what we hear, either actually, or in our heads, delivering the poem, but is not necessarily identical with its actual human creator. The distinction between author and first-person narrative voice is generally unproblematic in novels: we don't assume that Charles Dickens is straightforwardly writing his own autobiography, or recording his own feelings and situation, in, for instance, *David Copperfield* or *Great Expectations*. It's perfectly easy to accept the first-person narrator of a novel as a fictional construct, an authorial invention like the other characters. But the assumption that the first-person speaker in a poem is the actual poet is very common and in fact rather hard to avoid – largely, perhaps, because poets do very often speak in the first person in their poems, and apparently personally, like, for instance, Wordsworth, describing his lonely wanderings amongst daffodils. Nevertheless, it's always a possibility that the actual poet may be creating a *persona* – an invented first-person voice – such that the thoughts and feelings and indeed whole situation belong to that figure. Third-person narratives like *Beowulf* are even trickier. While the narrator of a poem may well seem indistinguishable from the actual poet, this is not necessarily the case: the actual poet may have created a separate narrative voice specifically to tell the story. In *Beowulf*, for instance, the narrative voice seems – at least to begin with – to adopt the stance of an oral court poet, the *scop*, when in fact the actual poet may well be a cloistered cleric. So I want to uphold a distinction between the anonymous mind which could conceive a poem like *Beowulf*, on the one hand, and the voice which tells the story, which produces the poetic richness of the diction and the poem's metre and metaphor, together with the complex juggling of past, present and future in the way and the order in which events are related, and even sometimes comments on its own storytelling, on the other.

Finally, we have the *scop* (conventionally pronounced 'shope'), a completely fictional figure jointly constructed by both poet and narrative voice. In *Beowulf,* the *scop*, or court poet, a figure in the storyworld, recites stories inset in the primary narrative of the poem itself. Explicitly or implicitly, the *scop* is introduced into the narrative as the speaker – if not necessarily the author – of what scholars used to call 'digressions' in the poem, stories indistinguishable in form and style from the main body of the poem, but telling of characters and events outside of it. These recitations are of course not irrelevant to the main body of the narrative, but neither are they as straightforwardly barbed as, for example, the play within a play about the killing of a king in Shakespeare's *Hamlet.* They are received simply appreciatively by their audiences in the poem, who are not shown arguing over their import, or pondering their significance. These activities belong instead to the audience outside the poem – us – and engage us with the themes and implications of the poem's events and characters.

I begin, then, with a consideration of what kind of a person might have been able to produce a poem like *Beowulf.*

(i) A Christian poet

There are two fundamental assumptions about the identity of the *Beowulf*-poet which have not been credibly challenged: that he was male, and that he was a Christian. These two identities – based on gender and religion – are in fact bound together. Christianity is essentially a religion of the book, associated with literacy and learning. And in the Middle Ages, clerics – monastic scholars especially – were overwhelmingly male. Thus a male Christian identity for the *Beowulf*-poet is a commonsense assumption based on what we know of the history of the period. There is also what has been called the masculine 'economy' of the poem: that it is a text mostly about men, and about male virtues. Of course, you don't have to be a male author to write about men – just as you don't have to be a warrior to write about the heroic society or an aristocrat to write about royalty. In fact, at least with regard to these two last analogies, the opposite might be held to be the case. And it is true that in Anglo-Saxon times, some female monastics – nuns – were both learned, and sometimes powerful, women. Hild, Abbess of Whitby in the seventh century, is a prime example. She founded and ran what is called a double monastery – monks as well as nuns, sharing the same church, and the same rule, but living in separate communities next door to one another – and hosted there the Synod of Whitby, a hugely prestigious and influential conference which was of the utmost importance in aligning the English church with Roman, rather than Irish, that is, Christian Celtic, practices (although Hild herself argued on the losing side). The most celebrated re-alignment concerned how to calculate the date of Easter, and the method adopted by Northumbrian rulers paved the way for the one still used today. Hild's Old English name, incidentally, means 'battle', and she was the grandniece of King Edwin of Northumbria. She was clearly not only an immensely capable administrator, but also a politician at the highest level in Northumbria, and a considerable scholar, or at least, fosterer of learning: five of her monks became bishops.

Curiously enough, the most famous story associated with Hild is the account of the cowherd poet Caedmon, who hid out one night in a cowbyre at Hild's Whitby Abbey because he couldn't come up with a sung party-piece at a feast. There, he was visited by an angel who commanded him to 'sing Creation', whereupon Caedmon miraculously began to transform the substance of the Old Testament into Old English verse – essentially, in the same language, metre and poetic style as *Beowulf* itself. According to the Northumbrian scholar Bede, who wrote about her around half a century after her death, it was Hild herself who recognized Caedmon's remarkable talent as a gift from God, doing all she could to encourage it, and Bede describes his poetic genius as being like that of a 'clean beast chewing the cud'. What an extraordinary story to account for the beginnings of English poetry. Bede praises Hild's rule over Whitby Abbey, singling out for special mention the egalitarian lines along which the monasteries were run and her care for everyone associated with the foundation. So here we have a cowherd (at a feast), someone whose job is to look after the clean beasts – the ruminants – ruminating on the matter of the Old Testament, and producing poetry. And an abbess who sees that this is not a mere party-trick, but a precious gift from God, which she recognizes as being her duty – even as the leader of a large and prestigious foundation – personally to foster.

Hild's stature may not be representative of Anglo-Saxon women, but it is at least not unique amongst them. Nevertheless, the fact (or legend) remains that the poet is Caedmon, a man, and the scholar who recorded the story is the Venerable Bede, a male cleric. Given that we know so very little about the *Beowulf*-poet, beyond what we can infer from the poem itself, it would be quite a stretch to make a case for a female poet. And although in the early days of *Beowulf* scholarship it used to be thought (although it was really wishful thinking) that the poem was a pre-Christian composition with later Christian interpolations (almost like vandals spray-painting graffiti on a revered ancient monument), the sheer scale of Christian and biblical allusion in the poem now makes the presumption of the poet's Christian context a very secure one. It's also worth noting, along commonsensical lines, that even though Anglo-Saxon England was for a long time divided into separate kingdoms, whose individual rulers converted and recidivized at different dates, nonetheless Christianity was run by the Church authorities as a sort of state religion, an institution with its own rules and even courts, with fines and punishments, and a passion for orthodoxy, in which heresy was diagnosed at best as error, and at worst, as a sort of insanity, and paganism denounced from the pulpit. It is of course likely that ordinary people (whoever this might mean) in Christian Anglo-Saxon England were superstitious and perhaps remained attached to certain pagan beliefs, or even practices, but it is beyond question that anyone with the resources and standing – intellectual or material – to produce a poem of this magnitude and scope would have been part of a Christian institutional elite.

In reviewing the Christian elements in *Beowulf,* I will look at: references to the Old Testament and the New Testament (including, crucially, those books which are now regarded as apocryphal); to the liturgy (the words of the Mass); to Anglo-Saxon sermons; and to the Church fathers, in their patristic writings. More speculatively, I will also consider ethical qualities which, as framed in the poem, seem either to chime with Christianity, or to undermine it: such issues as vengeance, loyalty, pride or generosity. I will also look at any representation of religious practices in the poem. In spite of a great deal of Old Norse mythological material having come down to us from medieval Icelandic authors, these literary texts afford remarkably little insight into actual religious practices. They may reflect the outline structures of pagan religious beliefs, but they have been transformed into literature – which is why contemporary New Age neo-pagan religions supposedly based on them are essentially fictions, resting on little or no evidence of doctrine or ritual. Nevertheless, there are a very few instances of the *Beowulf*-poet decrying Danish practices which are arguably un-Christian, and therefore betraying a Christian standpoint.

Throughout, I will be concerned to open up and maintain a distinction between what the narrator of *Beowulf* tells us, and what the characters within the storyworld are shown as saying and believing. This turns out to be a crucial distinction, because of course it lays bare an obvious and gaping gulf between the poet-narrator (I think it makes sense to conflate the two voices in this particular discussion) together with his original audience (and us, to some degree), on the one hand, and the storyworld he is portraying, on the other. The poet and his narrative voice are Christian, and the world of Hrothgar, Heorot and Beowulf is not. But this chasm is not something that the poet of *Beowulf* exploits: quite the opposite, in fact, because the poem is not by any means a triumphalist expression of the benightedness of pagans and the superiority of Christians. Rather, it's a complicatedly positive representation of the good things about a pagan, heroic past. The poet scrupulously avoids the anachronism of presenting the pagans as Christians, but there is no suggestion that he has any sympathy with paganism itself. This is a narrow line to tread, and I will begin by considering the language used in the poem to refer to a higher power directing human events.

Just as the Christian Anglo-Saxon narrator not only tells his story in Old English, but also represents the speech of his characters in that form, making no attempt to characterize their speech as in any way foreign, so he uses a personal idiom dotted with Christian turns of phrase, whether in third-person narration or as the direct speech of his characters. For instance, throughout

the poem Danes and Geats are casually described as thanking God for large
and small mercies – a safe sea-journey from Geatland; the arrival of the hero
Beowulf to Heorot; Beowulf's boldly stated determination to seek out and kill
Grendel's mother. Of course, the same word, 'god', in Old English as in modern
English, can be used both specifically, of the Christian god, or generically, to
denote any divine being. This distinction between the two meanings would be
even less obvious to an original audience, whether hearing the word, or seeing
it written in the manuscript, in which proper nouns – names – are customarily
not capitalized.

'God' is not the only word used by the narrator or his characters to designate
a divine, and mostly supreme, being. In *Beowulf* there are a host of synonyms
on display: *frea* (Lord); *ælmihtig* (Almighty); *metod* (Creator); *waldend* (Ruler);
dryhten (Prince, Lord); *kyning* (King) and more. I've capitalized the modern
English forms so that it's evident just how much the capital letter – not used
in the manuscript – seems to predispose us to see the Christian sense of these
words. Some also have a non-religious meaning, and are familiar epithets for
God in modern English: king, lord, ruler. And sometimes they are used in
conjunction with other words, such that the two-word phrase gives an even
more familiar 'Christian' impression: *wuldres kyning* (King of Glory); *ece
Drihten* (Eternal Lord); *waldend fira* (Ruler of Men). Others, however, find
parallels in pre-Christian literature, or in Old Norse literature which refers to
pre-Christian deities, and have not continued in Christian usage, possibly for
that very reason: *frea* (evidently the same word as the name of the Old Norse
god Freyr); or *metod* (probably the Old English version of the Old Norse term
Mjötuðr – the measurer, one who measures out human lives).

Whether serving dual purpose as common nouns for authority figures
in heroic society, or echoing unfamiliar pre-Christian terminology for the
divine, the *Beowulf*-narrator's words for God were early on established in
Christian contexts. I recounted the story of Caedmon, the Whitby cowherd
who transformed Holy Writ into Anglo-Saxon verse. The Venerable Bede,
telling this story in his *History of the English Church*, quotes Caedmon's first
few lines of poetry in Latin (the language of the text itself) and explains,
'This is the sense but not the order of the words which he [Caedmon] sang
as he slept. For it is not possible to translate verse, however well composed,

literally from one language to another without some loss of beauty and dignity.' But in many of the manuscripts of Bede's work, lines of Anglo-Saxon verse corresponding to Bede's Latin paraphrase have been added, squeezed into the margin of the manuscript or in the little cramped space at the bottom of the page. It seems simplest to suppose that this poetry pre-dated Bede's prose, perhaps having been known more widely as an oral poem, and was included (although it is just possible, but not in my view very likely, that someone translated the Latin and it was added later). But the significant point is that whether the poem (or at least, these lines of it) originated at the time when Bede sets his miracle story – that is, during Hild's time as Abbess of Whitby – or whether it was translated from Bede's Latin, it is still almost certainly the oldest surviving fragment of Anglo-Saxon verse, because the oldest manuscript containing it has been dated to around the time of Bede's death, in 735 CE. And the text is packed full of the sort of epithets for God – in this unequivocally Christian context – that we find in *Beowulf*. They include both the familiar ones which are still used today, and others which seem to us – and perhaps also to an original audience – to evoke ancient pre-Christian deities.

The earliest – and maybe the most authentic – version of Caedmon's Hymn is written in the Northumbrian dialect, which Bede himself and his fellow clerics, and Caedmon, would have spoken. But I quote it here in the form of Old English we find in the *Beowulf*-manuscript, so that the similarities in the diction are clearer:

Nu sculon herigean **heofonrices weard**	Now let us praise [the] heavenly kingdom's guardian
meotodes meaht ond his modgeþonc	the creator's might and his mind-thought,
weorc **wuldorfæder** swa he wundra gehwæs	[the] work of the glory-father in that he, each wonder
ece drihten or onstealde	– eternal lord – first established.
He ærest sceop eorðan bearnum	He first of all shaped, for earth's children,
heofon to hrofe, **halig scyppend**	[with] heaven as a roof, – holy shaper –
þa middangeard **moncynnes weard**	that middle-earth – mankind's guardian –
ece drihten æfter teode	- eternal lord – [and] afterwards adorned
firum foldan **frea ælmihtig**	for men, the earth: lord almighty.

I've added some punctuation, to give a sense of the possible relationship between all the half lines, and emphasized the Old English terms for God. It is a miraculous survival and also a lovely piece of poetry, with its steady, poised alliteration and carefully balanced half-lines. There is, as in the best Old English poetry, a meditative quality, created by the implicit invitation to ponder the relationship of half lines linked by alliteration but not syntactical sense: *heofon to hrofe* next to *halig scyppend*, or the final resounding clash between *firum foldan* and *frea ælmihtig*. There is a different formula to denote God in almost every line, and still current and familiar terms (Guardian of the Heavenly Kingdom; Eternal Lord) share space with *Frea* and *Metod* – just as they do in *Beowulf*. Caedmon's Hymn is the clearest possible evidence that the *Beowulf*-poet's use of these terms is not an attempt to give pre-Christian or Scandinavian colouring to the text. But I should mention here a slight counter-example. Before his encounter with Grendel, we are told that Beowulf will in fact prevail over the monster, and will be granted *wigsped gewiofu* (victories' weavings) – thanks to the intervention of the lord. This clearly denotes a Christian deity. But the phrase used for Beowulf's successes in war is full of heathen and mythic connotations, for it recalls the familiar Old Norse trope of the fate of warriors in battle being a web woven by valkyries. So the narrator, having dealt out this small whiff of Scandinavian paganism, launches emphatically into the present tense with a resounding acclamation of how almighty god showed his power here, as he does now and forever. That little nugget of Norse lore is tightly wrapped around with unequivocal references to an all-powerful and eternal god.

If the words the poet uses for god are securely Christian in their connotations, we must return to an initial difficulty: that the Christian poet of *Beowulf* repeatedly – and, some might say, carelessly – includes them in the speech of his pre-Christian characters. In fact, a very careful look at the poet's usage here reveals some interesting nuances. For a start, terms for a Christian divinity which involve New Testament references – Saviour, Christ, Redeemer and so on – are never used in the poem, by anyone, although they are perfectly common in Old English religious poems. There are no references at all to the Blessed Virgin, the apostles, the Crucifixion or Resurrection. The Christian

Trinity – Father, Son and Holy Ghost – is completely absent. Although one of the words the poet uses for God is *fæder* (father), there is no reason to connect this with Christianity, since in Old Norse texts the god Odin is referred to as *Alföðr* (father of all) – and since we are mentioning Old Norse gods, Thor is also called *hinn almáttig Áss* (the almighty god). But in spite of both Christianity and Old Norse paganism being in some sense pantheistic, *Beowulf* conveys to us an invariably and determinedly monotheistic poet and world.

The distribution of references to a god in *Beowulf* is also very interesting. Although the poet acknowledges a divine presence and represents his characters – at least sometimes – as doing so, there are significant stretches in the poem in which there are no such references. Perhaps the most striking is the celebrated story of the fight at Finnsburh, not least because this is an episode in the poem which bears a close (but not exact) resemblance to a substantial fragment of Old English heroic verse usually known as *The Fight at Finnsburh*. I shall be looking at what have been called the 'digressions' in *Beowulf*, of which the Finnsburh episode is one, in the next section of this book, but the important issue here is that the substance of this story is seemingly a bit of old Danish history, and it is presented in the poem as the recitation of Hrothgar's *scop*, or court poet: a poem within a poem. So the immediate narrator of the story is not, ostensibly, the narrator of *Beowulf*, and there is no direct speech from the characters in it. It is, as it were, doubly insulated from the ethos of the narrator on the one hand, and the world of Heorot on the other. The poet is not speaking in his own – Christian, though monotheistic – voice, and, again ostensibly, is not creating the characters. The upshot of all this is that the poet avoids the anachronism of presenting his characters as Christians, but, at the same time, avoids alienating his audience by shining a light on their historical paganism (even presuming that he would know what that was like, or was concerned with historical authenticity: medieval authors were not often interested in period detail). He therefore moderates the expression of his own Christianity, by reducing it to an uncontroversial monotheism, and rather similarly moderates the historical paganism of his characters, by having them refer to one god with a non-specific but familiar enough set of qualities: power, authority, eternal existence and so on. Poet and characters meet in the middle, and this makes room for the sympathetic and broad-minded take on their society which the poet (almost always) maintains. A quick count shows that of all the characters in the poem, it is Hrothgar who makes the greatest number of references to God. Here we see how well-disposed the poet is to his own creation, an old man beset by terrible monsters. But he leaves unmoderated the externalized story of the Finnsburh tragedy.

All this shows that we must be very careful about supposing Christian references in *Beowulf* to be inadvertent lapses by a poet so steeped in Christian literature that he didn't always notice that he was echoing its characteristic terminology. A very striking example of what seems at first sight to be a careless oversight is the narrator's use of the phrase *non dæges* ('nones' – the ninth hour of the day, the mid-afternoon fixed time of monastic prayer, named because it was about nine hours after dawn). It is at this ninth hour that Beowulf's retainers, anxiously waiting on the shore of the lake, see blood rising to the surface and give up hope that they will ever see Beowulf again; they remain there, but the Danes waiting with them give up altogether and go home. It seems strange that the poet should have included a specific time of day for this loss of hope. After all, practical details of time and place are otherwise notably absent: Beowulf's expedition to Grendel's mother's underwater lair is said to take a part of a day to swim down to. Although it's not quite clear from the Old English here just how much of the day it took, obviously this is not in any sense a realistic detail. Even the cave at the bottom of the lake is more an imagined space than a plausibly realized one. So why would the *Beowulf*-poet have introduced this anachronistic detail of medieval life into an otherwise fantastical episode?

But as all Christians know well, it was at the ninth hour of the day of Christ's crucifixion that, according to three of the four New Testament gospels, Jesus himself seemed to give up hope and shouted out 'My God, My God, why hast thou forsaken me?' For this reason, medieval theologians associated nones with the lowest point of human hopefulness, a time of vulnerability for humans, which the devil might take advantage of. The *Beowulf*-poet's use of the term is thus full of significance and must have been purposefully used. There is a similar, though less clear-cut, example when the narrator of the poem recounts how the original human owners of the dragon's treasure hoard had laid a curse *oð domes dæg* (until doomsday) on anyone stealing the treasure. It might be argued that the Christian poet was simply using 'doomsday' as a term for the end of time. But from the poet's perspective, the pagan view of the world is time-limited, and very much not eternal. Their pre-Christian curse could not endure until the end of time, because for a Christian the Day of Judgement will intervene. Furthermore, the poet himself shows that God is above and beyond the extent of pre-Christian time. As if in answer to those who would worry about whether the curse would catch Beowulf, and consign him to a pagan version of hell, *hergum geheaðerod | hellbendum fæst* (confined in heathen temples | held fast in hellish fetters) the poet carefully constructs an escape clause: the curse would apply to any man *unless* God chose to exempt him. It is very suggestive that God is here emphatically called *God sylfa | sigora Soðcyning* (God himself | victories' true king) as if to make clear that we are talking about the all-powerful god of Christianity, and not just a pagan divinity.

To see how closely the characters in the poem can be aligned with a Christian viewpoint, and to what extent the poet himself reveals his own Christian sympathies, we need to be aware of whether God is presented as actually intervening in the events of the poem, and whether this is reflected in the attitudes of both characters and poet. Again, as with the casual references to God, what we see is a careful and diplomatic coming together of the poet and those who inhabit his created world. It is several times pointed out by the poem's narrator that God has always ruled over the world of humans, as He still does – this of course extends God's presence right back into the heroic age of the poem, even if the characters are not Christians. But Hrothgar himself readily acknowledges that a god has the power to put a stop to the depredations of Grendel, if he wished to – thus raising the old Christian conundrum about the place of evil in a god-created universe. Beowulf too, equally readily and regularly, concedes that his successes against the monsters are down to God's help, a view which the poet-narrator invariably underscores. This acknowledgement of the prevailing power of a supreme deity aligns very well with a Christian viewpoint, whatever the Danes and the Geats are presumed to have believed. It also grants Beowulf an attractively modest quality, in spite of all his bravery and boasting. But when he returns to Geatland and recounts his adventures to his lord, Hygelac, there is no mention of God's intervening support at all. The quasi-Christian bubble extends only so far from Hrothgar's Heorot and the virtual location of the poet.

The biblical allusions in the poem are also very meticulously distributed: only the poet-narrator makes any direct reference to biblical tradition. These references are dominated by the identification of Grendel and his mother as descendants of Cain. According to the biblical book of *Genesis*, Cain, the son of Adam and Eve, killed his younger brother Abel, apparently because Cain jealously believed that God showed Abel more favour than him. After denying the murder to God, Cain was cursed and sent into exile 'in the land of Nod, on the east of Eden'. He was destined to wander in this wilderness forever, because 'the Lord set a mark upon Cain, lest anyone finding him should kill him' and thereby put him out of his misery. A little later on in *Genesis*, we are told that 'there were giants in the earth in those days', and almost immediately following that 'God saw that the wickedness of man was great in the earth'. This prompts Him to create the Flood, 'and every living substance was destroyed which was on the face of the ground, both man, and cattle, and the creeping things, and the fowl of the heaven; and they were destroyed from the earth'. Only Noah and those with him on the Ark were saved.

Early commentators on the Bible linked these references and created a coherent narrative out of them: that the evil giants who so provoked God's anger were the progeny of Cain. Alcuin, the eighth-century Anglo-Saxon scholar I mentioned earlier, complaining about monks listening to heroic stories instead of readings from the Bible, sets out a really quite sensational rationale to make sense of these puzzling statements. The biblical book of *Genesis* mysteriously refers to interbreeding between 'the sons of God' and 'the daughters of men' immediately before introducing the giants. Alcuin identifies the daughters of men as the descendants of Cain, and the sons of God as the descendants of Adam's son Seth – the sons of God because they have 'an ancestral religious blessing'. He continues: 'The sons of Seth were overcome by concupiscence and joined in marriage with the daughters of Cain; and through such a union were procreated men of immense size, arrogant men of mixed natures, whom Scripture calls giants'. Other commentators added all kinds of monstrous creatures to Cain's progeny. This is clearly the learned exegetical tradition which the *Beowulf*-poet was following, and it is stated explicitly when

Grendel is first introduced in the poem: *þanon untydras | ealle onwocon* (from him [Cain] evil offspring all arose). This statement is followed, as we have seen, by a daunting list of humanoid monsters, which I discussed earlier.

So the *Beowulf*-poet's learning encompassed the teachings of the early scholars who 'glossed', or interpreted, the Bible. This is not surprising: most Anglo-Saxon clerics would have known the Bible through the lens of those scholars such as Alcuin, and Bede, who tried to make sense of it, and explain its contradictions and *non sequiturs,* rather than at first-hand. These interpretations of *Genesis* encouraged the development of a long-lasting and engaging tradition about the origins of monsters. But one difficulty remains un-glossed-over. How did this monstrous race survive the Flood, if, as is unequivocally stated in *Genesis*, all living things were wiped out, unless they were with Noah in the Ark? This knotty problem still engages biblical fundamentalists in heated debate. The *Beowulf*-poet does not address it directly. But it may be the case that he was familiar with another exegetical ploy to explain the giants' survival. It is emphasized in *Genesis* that all living things 'on the face of the earth' were destroyed. But it is also made clear that Cain was originally banished from 'the face of the earth'. In *Beowulf,* although at first Grendel's dwelling place is not clearly stated, his mother (and, we may assume, Grendel too) lives at the bottom of a mysterious lake. It seems likely that the *Beowulf*-poet knew a tradition in which monstrous creatures survived the Flood by lurking in underwater lairs.

Repeated allusions to Grendel's descent from Cain dominate the biblical references in *Beowulf.* But there are a number of others, although they are not as clear-cut. For example, similarities have been noted between the poem and the biblical account of David and Goliath: David taking on the giant on behalf of King Saul, decapitating the monster with his own sword and so on. But as is true of so many attempts to link literary works with biblical sources, the archetypal nature of biblical narrative – in this case, an attempt by a brave young warrior to take on a formidable opponent, and to succeed, against all the odds – means that very many narrative elements in many literary traditions may look similar to Bible stories. And the Old Testament is so packed with stories that it's hard *not* to find examples of similarity – not to mention the fact that Beowulf fights twice, against both Grendel and his mother, so that there are double the number of possible similarities even within the poem itself. In fact, a strange law of diminishing returns seems to operate: the more parallels we find, the less significant they seem to be, and the less powerful their evidence for purposeful borrowing by the *Beowulf*-poet. I will therefore not consider what can in any case never be a full list, ranging from the pretty convincing, to the actually very tenuous, or really not very probable at all. However, I do want to mention just one more instance, because it raises so many interesting issues which can help us to understand the scholarly milieu of *Beowulf*. This is the purported relationship between the poem and the apocryphal *Book of Enoch*.

Which biblical books are accepted as scripture – that is, as canonical, established elements in a Bible – varies according to different Judaeo-Christian religious traditions. Some books recognized by Christian tradition are not included in the Hebrew bible; Protestant bibles categorize as apocryphal those books which are acknowledged by Roman Catholic authorities. Anglo-Saxon Christianity accepted more books than are officially recognized today, but the *Book of Enoch* was already regarded as spurious by most Christian churches centuries even before Anglo-Saxon Christianity was established. It has only survived in Ethiopian manuscripts, although fragments of it have been discovered elsewhere, in other languages. One such fragment is a tiny portion of what may once have been the whole text, which has been translated into Latin, in England, in the Anglo-Saxon period, so it seems perfectly possible that the whole book was known – at least by some learned people – in Anglo-Saxon England. Looking at the full text, it is easy to see why it might have interested the poet of *Beowulf*: it's all about giants, their origins and their sinful behaviour (including blood-drinking), and the ensuing Flood.

It is possible to suggest a number of correspondences between the *Book of Enoch* and *Beowulf* – particularly in the poem's presentation of the figures of Grendel and his mother. It should be said that such parallels are open to the charges I levelled earlier against the many apparent connexions between *Beowulf* and the Bible: that some narrative elements, especially those concerning heroes and monsters, are almost inevitably similar. But there is one intriguing point which stands out from these more general similarities. It concerns Grendel's actual name.

Proper names in *Beowulf* have prompted a good deal of scrutiny from scholars and critics. The name Beowulf itself, for instance: is its literal meaning 'bee-wolf', and is it therefore a kenning for 'bear' (as in, a wolf is a predator, and a predator on bees is a [honey]bear)? This suggestion accords very nicely with the hero Beowulf, who fights without weapons, and killed another warrior, Dæghrefn (literally, 'Day-Raven'), with his bare hands – perhaps squeezing him to death in a kind of bear hug? Is the name of the wise Geatish queen Hygd purposefully derived from the Old English word *ge-hygd* (thoughtfulness)? Is the antagonistic Unferth's name a form of the negative Old English compound *un-frið* (un-peace, that is, discord)? Opinions have varied, but it does seem that some names in the poem have a significant meaning. Grendel, however, is different. The first syllable echoes a number of Germanic words which have unpleasant connotations: grind, grim, Grettir [the scowler], grimace or even just 'grrr'. But the ending *-el* is not familiar as an element of a proper name at all in Germanic languages such as English or Old Norse, in which proper names are often a combination of two common nouns or simple word elements (such as Beo-wulf or Dæg-hrefn). The name doesn't sound Anglo-Saxon, and there are no other characters in literature or real people in the historical record with the name. But in the *Book of Enoch*, the vast majority of the names of the ancestors of the giants (here identified as fallen angels, a tradition, to be fair, never alluded to in *Beowulf*) end in the element *-el*.

Of course the *Beowulf*-poet was not completely free to manufacture names for his characters – some of them, after all, relate to figures who exist in other Scandinavian sources, especially Old Norse legends about the Danish royal house, although Hygelac is the only Geatish character who crops up elsewhere. But it is tempting to suppose that the name Grendel was constructed by an expert and learned wordsmith who combined the grating sound and connotations of a familiar Germanic lexical element with a novel foreign element found in an uncanonical biblical text which may have been arcane even then. However, there is a complicating factor: we do have, in the poem, another name ending in *-el* – that of the Beowulf's grandfather, Hrethel, King of the Geats. This plunges us back into the realms of speculation: was there some record – which had not come down to us – which named Hrethel, and that this suggested the form 'Grendel' to the poet? Or did he invent the name 'Grendel' and then use that as the basis for the name of his – apparently – fictional Geatish king? And as we shall see in the next part of this chapter, there is good reason to believe that the *Beowulf*-poet invented the story of Hrethel and his sons' tragic accident as a fake analogue to an Old Norse myth.

We are back amongst the unanswerable questions. Another way to discover the *Beowulf*-poet's intellectual background is to look at the echoes of Christian writing in the poem. This involves a slightly different perspective on the poet's Christianity: it is not so much a measure of his purposeful manipulation of or reference to Christian or biblical material, but rather a measure of how far Christian religious texts influenced the style of his poetry – just as those casual references to God might be seen as reflecting his own personal idiom, rather than being a deliberate strategy. In this way, the many echoes of Christian texts in *Beowulf* can reveal to us a poet steeped in the literary traditions of Christianity. A clear example is the description of the weird lake which Grendel's mother is shown living at the bottom of. I have already noted, in the section of this book about the setting of the storyworld, that the description seems to be an assemblage of forbidding features, rather than a coherent imagining of actual landscape. In fact, there is a very similar description of just such an uninviting locale in a tenth-century collection of sermons in Old English. The collection is known as the Blickling Homilies, named after Blickling Hall, in Norfolk, where the manuscript was once kept. One item in the collection is a translation, from a Latin source, of a vision of hellmouth attributed to St Paul. The correspondences are remarkably close. In both, there are frost-covered groves, grey stone and streams descending though mist, and the words used for these features are nearly identical in the homily and the poem. In both, the waters are inhabited by terrifying water monsters. Scholars have argued about whether the details in *Beowulf* are borrowed from the sermon, or vice versa, but one very interesting difference suggests that the poet, creating a landscape as grim as possible, had in his mind a Christian description of hell and was adapting it. St Paul's vision includes the horrible detail that human souls were hanging from the frosty branches, while in the poem, the branches themselves are hanging down. It seems to me that the *Beowulf*-poet would have found plenty of inspiration in St Paul's vision for his depiction of a haunted mere in pre-Christian Scandinavia, but he couldn't possibly have included souls hanging from branches, and therefore adapted his source, and not the other way round.

There are other stylistic echoes of sermon literature in *Beowulf*. Hrothgar's lecture urging Beowulf not to give way to pride and complacency has long been dubbed 'Hrothgar's Sermon' because of its distinctively homiletic mode, and at times it seems to draw on biblical wisdom, as a Christian sermon would, and Anglo-Saxon sermons actually did. A clear instance is Hrothgar's warning to Beowulf that if the soul's guardian sleeps, an archer – the Devil himself – will take the opportunity to shoot fatal arrows, which is based on a biblical source, and was re-worked by an Anglo-Saxon homilist. It is interesting, too, that this mention of sleeping guards and lethal arrows, as well as echoing biblical examples, also evokes episodes from the storyworld of *Beowulf*: of when the Danes, in what might be uncharitably called a drunken stupor, sank into sleep the night Grendel's mother made her vengeful attack, or of the death of Hrethel's son Herebeald, accidentally killed by his brother's arrow.

The verbal texture of 'Hrothgar's Sermon' is also distinctively homiletic, with its pairs of near-synonymous verbs – for instance, *weaxeð ond wridað* (grows and flourishes) or *forgyteð ond forgymeð* (forgets and overlooks). It's no coincidence, I think, that the first, lengthy description of Grendel's mother's mere, with its clear resemblances to St Paul's vision of Hell, is also spoken by Hrothgar. There is little doubt that whether the original audience of *Beowulf* was a monastic one, or simply composed of lay people, they would have recognized at once these sermon-like features of style and content. And finally, there is certainly no mistaking in what follows the New Testament cadences and sentiments of the Sermon on the Mount from the Gospel of St Matthew:

	Wa bið þæm ðe sceal
þurh sliðne nið	sawle bescufan
in fyres fæþm,	frofre ne wenan,
wihte gewendan.	Wel bið þæm þe mot

æfter deaðdæge   Drihten secean
ond to Fæder fæþmum   freoðo wilnian.

(Woe is he who shall | through terrible wickedness | thrust [the] soul | into
[the] fire's embrace | not to expect comfort | [or] any whit of change. |
Blessed is he who may | after [his] death-day | go to the lord | and in the
father's embrace | crave protection.)

Again, and in spite of the impression this short passage gives of forceful and
unequivocal Christian orthodoxy, there are echoes of the heroic substance of
the poem itself: the hostile embrace (*fæþm*) of fire, which engulfed Heorot,
and Beowulf, on his funeral pyre; and the dead at Finnsburh; or the protective
embrace of a human father such as Beow experienced at the poem's opening –
a son who was the embodiment of the comfort (*frofor*) which God sent to
Scyld Scefing and the Danes. The narrative about pre-Christian Scandinavians
is suffused with Christian rhetoric – or, to see it another way, the Christian
sentiments in the poem are underlaid by a subtext recalling the pre-Christian
action and characters in the poem.

The passage echoing the Sermon on the Mount is spoken not by Hrothgar
in sermonizing mode, but, perhaps more unexpectedly, in the narrative voice.
It follows immediately from an unusually overtly Christian – or at least, anti-
pagan – passage, in which the despairing Danes, made weary, shamed and
terrorized by Grendel's attacks, resort to what the narrator plainly intends to
represent pagan practices: they made vows to honour idols (*wigweorþung*)
at heathen temples (*æt hærgtrafum*) and prayed to the 'destroyer of souls'
(*gastbona*) – the Devil – for respite. It is evident that the narrator is openly
decrying the Danes as heathen, the only point in the poem at which this
happens. Most devastatingly, the narrator concludes that not knowing God,
these abhorrent practices were the only recourse they had: the empty and
delusive *hæþenra hyht* (hope of heathens).

There have been various attempts by *Beowulf* scholars to mitigate the
bleakness of this condemnation, which stands out markedly from the carefully
balanced line the narrator usually follows. Some have argued that only a small,
renegade group of Danes are being censured here. Others compare the poet's
representation of the pre-Christian Danes to Old Testament people, who are

on occasion said to worship idols in bad times. What is especially unusual about the passage is that it purports to describe actual practices – something which, as I have said, we know very little about (and the poet may not have known much about them either). Anglo-Saxon clerics were usually extremely careful not to describe heathen practices, even in order to condemn them, presumably so as not to give anyone any ideas. This may explain why the narrator responds so robustly to the mention of idol-worshipping with his fierce miniature homily about damnation and salvation, the fires of Hell as opposed to God's embrace. In the overall scope of the poem, the shocking activities of the idol-worshipping Danes may be seen as having been provoked by Grendel, the creature from hell whose implicit mission is to drag the Danes down with him. To extend this further, we can identify Beowulf, then, as saving them from more than just being eaten alive by a monster.

Apart from a fleeting and ambiguous reference to the Geats consulting omens before Beowulf sets out on his journey to Heorot – presumably they were favourable; the narrator makes no comment – the only other developed representation of pre-Christian practices is the description of cremations on a funeral pyre: Beowulf's own funeral, and the burning of Hildeburh's kin after the Finnsburh fight. Cremation was very much not a Christian funeral rite in the Middle Ages; burying the body – inhumation – was the only practice consonant with resurrection, with respect for the integrity of the body, and to avoid any association with the fires of Hell, or, indeed, paganism itself. But Anglo-Saxons almost certainly knew that cremation was a pre-Christian custom. And the thirteenth-century Icelandic writer Snorri Sturluson, in his history of the kings of Norway, divides early Norwegian history into two great phases, the *brunaǫld* and *haugsǫld* (the Age of Burning and the Age of Burial Mounds) – cremation for him was not so much a possibly dangerous precursor, superseded by his own Christian era, but something belonging to the very distant past, a fact of prehistory.

Beowulf's funeral is a stately and impressive affair: the funeral pyre is built up high and hung with war-gear. There is roaring fire and billowing smoke as the blaze takes hold, and the sound of general lamenting. The body burns. A Geatish woman – a sort of ritual mourner, it seems – sings terrible predictions about the bleak future of awaiting the Geats. Once the fire has died down,

Beowulf's men begin to construct a magnificent memorial mound which can be seen from far out to sea, and his ashes are interred in it, along with the dragon's treasure hoard. Dirges are chanted as warriors on horseback ride around the mound. There is no hint whatever of any Christian disapproval, or even uneasiness or reservation. The spectacle of cremation, with all its vivid details, is allowed full expression. The final, exquisitely poised comment on the process is that *Heofon rece swealg* (Heaven swallowed the smoke).

The poet is remarkably broad-minded about possible immediate afterlives for his characters. Scyld Scefing, as we have seen, drifts off across the sea, a traveller to an unknown bourn from which he will not return. Beowulf's corpse-smoke ascends to heaven. Hell is a constant threat, but even the poor idol-worshipping Danes are not explicitly damned to hell, though they certainly risk it. We may assume that Grendel and his mother are destined for Hell after their deaths, but the poet does not insist on it. The rest of us – soul-bearers, the children of men, earth dwellers – must face death as inevitable, and go to a place already prepared for us, where the body will be held fast. This is the grave, our deathbed, where the body will *swefeþ æfter symle* (sleep after [the] feasting). See how even here, as the Christian author addresses his Christian audience, life is figured in heroic terms, as a banquet. Heorot, in remote and exotic sixth-century Scandinavia, with its kings, retainers and warriors, can nevertheless serve as a microcosm of human life on earth.

The vision of the hall as a microcosm of human life is not unique to *Beowulf*. Its most celebrated expression is found in Bede's eighth-century *History of the English Church*, as we see King Edwin of Northumbria consulting his advisors about the wisdom of converting to Christianity. His chief priest, Coifi, supports conversion, on the bitterly resentful grounds that in spite of being such a pious pagan, the king has favoured other men more, so paganism hasn't done much for him. But another councillor advances a deeply moving justification for going with the new Christianity:

> This is how the present life of man on earth, O King, appears to me in comparison with that time which is unknown to us. You are sitting feasting with your ealdormen and thegns in winter time; the fire is burning on the hearth in the middle of the hall and all inside is warm, while outside

the wintry storms of rain and snow are raging; and a sparrow flies swiftly through the hall. It enters in at one door and quickly flies out through the other. For a few moments it is inside, the storm and wintry tempest cannot touch it, but after the briefest moment of calm, it flits from your sight, out of the wintry storm and into it again. So this life of man appears but for a moment; what follows or indeed what went before, we know not at all.

This is an extraordinarily poignant and sympathetic depiction of the lives of pagans: a brief, bright interlude in a fire-warmed banqueting hall, but no notion – just a dark, chilly dread – of what might have come before or what might come after. It is diametrically opposed to the Christian view, according to which life is a weary passage through this valley of tears but – at least at best – there may be a heavenly home at the end of it all. We must remember, of course, that Bede the arch-Christian is representing how he thinks a pagan might envisage life, but then the sympathy with which the flight of this little bird is described is all the more remarkable. So, to return to the poet of *Beowulf*: his vision of a Christian burial is developed into an image of death as a sleep after a period of bright banqueting. This idea recurs in the poem in an elegiac context, when Beowulf, facing certain death fighting the dragon, recalls the story of a tragedy which befell the Geatish royal house. One of Hygelac's brothers accidentally kills the other (I will discuss this in detail shortly, when we come to look at the Old Norse element in *Beowulf*). The father of the two brothers is compared, in his inability to take vengeance for the killing, to a father whose son has been executed – another kind of unavengeable death. The bereaved father is imagined as viewing the desolation after the son's death, the banqueting hall now empty of all its heroic retainers: *ridend swefað | hæleð in hoðman* (horsemen sleep | warriors in [their] graves).

This seems to be a good moment to discuss the interface between Christian and pre-Christian ideas in *Beowulf*: the question of values, virtues and attitudes to life. The trouble is that virtuous values tend to be universal. It has become common for politicians, in a show of patriotism, to claim for the nation they govern certain values – let's say, justice, fairness, tolerance and diligence – as if other nations valued injustice, unfairness, intolerance and laziness. So it is that even if we – or the *Beowulf*-poet – knew what distinctive values pagans endorsed, it is hard to imagine that they would differ very markedly from Christian ethics. Before going any further with this, it may be worth clarifying some terms. Religious and secular are opposites, and the term 'Christian' refers to religion, as does 'pagan'. 'Pre-Christian' as a term is in some ways preferable to 'pagan', because 'pagan' suggests a unity and homogeneity amongst pre-Christian Germanic religions which almost certainly did not exist, and also has a note of censure in it. Distinctively religious ethics – for example, Christian ethics such as we find in the New Testament, as recommended and divinely sanctioned ways of living in the world – are not so relevant in *Beowulf*, since there is so very little reference to the New Testament. And Old Testament ethics – for example, 'an eye for an eye' – can sound as alien to Christians as pagan ethics might be imagined to be.

Heroic society, as depicted in early medieval literature like *Beowulf*, was based on the idea of a warrior elite, with its kings, heroes and retainers, and might be thought to have its own secular, that is, worldly, rather than religious, ethics. But again, the values of the warband have wider applicability than just to heroic society: loyalty, bravery, steadfastness and integrity are universal values as applicable to followers of the Christian religion as to anyone else. Perhaps vengeance is a site of difference, embraced by warriors such as Beowulf, and even the monsters he takes on. But again, strictures against vengeance belong to New Testament teachings, as in the biblical statement widely quoted in the Middle Ages, 'Vengeance is mine, saith the Lord, and I will repay.' Even violence itself, eschewed by Christian clerics, was enthusiastically adopted by Christian kings, ever more so as the theology of the so-called 'just war' began to develop.

Finally, whether pride is a virtue, or better recognized as a vice, one of the seven deadly sins, is still debated by Christian theologians. In addition, it can be hard to make out the exact connotations of Old English words for emotions such as pride: the word *mod*, for example, the origin of the neutral modern English word 'mood', seems to have been used for a range of emotions: pride, spirit, courage, arrogance, temper and more. All in all, then, the ethical world of *Beowulf* is immensely accommodating, embracing religious and secular virtues, Christian values and heroic ethics, and even – for all we know – the kinds of behaviour pagans would have approved of. Hrothgar's wise words, and accounts of Beowulf's bravery sit happily alongside the poet's own Christian milieu, and belligerent Unferth, the savage monsters and treacherous contenders for ancient thrones are deplored by everyone.

(ii) An Old Norse scholar

It is obvious from this exploration of the Christian elements in the poem that the *Beowulf*-poet was a learned person. The exciting accounts of Beowulf's encounters with three formidable monsters are set in a rich and detailed context of Scandinavian history, and many of the individual details are echoed in a great range of medieval texts, historical, legendary and fictional. Even the monsters, as we have seen, are contextualized in biblical or patristic tradition. This is just what we might reasonably expect from an educated Christian poet creating a poem set in early medieval Scandinavia. Perhaps less predictable is the likelihood that the poet knew enough about Scandinavian mythology – which has largely come down to us in Old Norse-Icelandic texts, and is therefore usually termed Old Norse mythology – to bring oblique and – I shall argue – on occasion subtly doctored allusions to it, and to work creatively with Old Norse-Icelandic analogues to the poem, that is, narrative elements which resemble, but are not exactly the same as, material found in the poem.

As I promised in the Introduction, I will not be re-hashing learned debates about the possible dates for the poem's composition. But when *Beowulf* came into being is much more than just a simple matter of scholarly curiosity. For one thing, it radically affects the way we as readers regard the poem. Is *Beowulf* a remarkable, even miraculous, survival from the very distant past, preserved by chance when similar works were irretrievably lost? Or is it a literary achievement – different only in its length – to be ranked and perhaps dated alongside other great Anglo-Saxon poetic works, expressive elegies like *The Wanderer* or *The Seafarer*, or the weighty transformations of Old Testament narrative such as *Exodus* or *Genesis B*? Or is it a late summation of a whole culture, an elegy both for a heroic past long gone and for an Anglo-Saxon literary tradition nearing its own end?

But even more than these considerations, whether we think the poem was produced at the beginning, the middle or the end of the Anglo-Saxon period also bears on how the undoubtedly Christian – and Anglo-Saxon – poet might have related to, understood and represented the stories and beliefs (and hence perhaps the behaviours) of his sixth-century Scandinavians characters – that is, what, with certain important qualifications, we now call Old Norse myth. An early poet might have had no direct contact with actual Scandinavians or their stories, but, perhaps knowing about the shared ancestry of the North Germanic peoples – such as the continental Germans whom the eighth-century Anglo-Saxon missionary priest Boniface reported as calling themselves 'of one and the same blood and bone' as the Anglo-Saxons – drew on a shared literary inheritance from pre-Christian times. Or perhaps an early – that is, pre-viking – poet had contacts with Scandinavian merchants, and learnt from them some of the stories and characteristics of his poem's setting. In either case, it is important to bear in mind the qualification that Old Norse myth in its late, written, form could well be quite unlike these hypothetical early beliefs and traditions. And it is by no means certain that the pre-Christian cultures of the many and various Germanic tribes were ever the same, or even similar. So we need to be very careful about attributing differences between what we see in *Beowulf* and what has survived in Old Norse-Icelandic mythological texts to the poet's intervention.

A middle period dating for Beowulf must take into account the obvious obstacles to cultural exchange presented by hostile relations between Anglo-Saxons and Scandinavians – from the apparent savagery of the raid on Lindisfarne in 793 and subsequent strikes (of which monasteries were the prime targets) to the depredations of the Great Army of 865, whose success rested on the extensive Scandinavian settlement of much of northern and eastern England which came to be known as the Danelaw, and the renewed attacks of the later tenth century. Proponents of a ninth- or tenth-century date for the poem have reasonably argued that the hostilities were not continuous, and that attacks in Northumbria would not necessarily preclude peaceful and culturally productive relations in, say, Mercia or East Anglia. Or maybe we don't have to decide between hostility and appreciative cultural interaction – the poet of *Beowulf* perhaps learned about Old Norse myth from his new Danelaw neighbours, and nevertheless took it upon himself to undermine and counter it. This would explain why what we see in *Beowulf* is Old Norse myth in a form not only arguably different from its later, written form, but also perhaps purposefully modified rather than uncritically imported.

The latest possible date for the poem presents what is ostensibly a perfect fit of poem and audience: the court of the new Scandinavian rulers of England, Sveinn Forkbeard and his son Knútr (King Canute). And yet, the literary culture of conquering dynasties has more usually accommodated native traditions in new colonial forms; *Beowulf* is after all an Anglo-Saxon poetic representation of Scandinavians, not the other way around. Nevertheless, a late date for the poem accounts very well for the poem's range and perspective, its mighty frame of reference, and the poise and wisdom of the narrator's voice as he seems to look back on and show us an era long past, commenting on its strengths and weaknesses, its lessons for the present and its irrecoverable pastness.

So given the history of Anglo-Saxon relations with raiding, invading and settling Scandinavians, it is hard to fit the poem and its audience into any appropriate niche in Anglo-Saxon England, any time and place in which allusions and analogues to Scandinavian myth would be both known by the poet and appreciated by his audience. And yet, as we shall see, so long as we do not expect uncritically imported mythic material which precisely reproduces what has come down to us in Old Norse written sources, there are a surprisingly large number of echoes of Old Norse myth in several different forms in *Beowulf*. And it seems that the poet did a number of very different things with them. I shall begin with three examples which show how alien Old Norse mythic traditions might have seemed to our Anglo-Saxon Christian poet – move on to show how differently what is clearly the same fundamental story material appears in the two traditions, and conclude with a brief discussion of the interaction and possible harmony – or not – of these two apparently contrasting belief systems.

Sigurðr or Sigmundr?

Allusions to Old Norse myth are especially significant because they are selected by the poet and brought in to the narrative at will – by which I mean that they are not essential to the core events of the poem. They are not, that is to say, indispensable aspects of story material which might have originated in pagan

Scandinavia, and needed to be included to make the storyline of *Beowulf* coherent and comprehensible. Instead, we can see the poet using them to build up a suitably Scandinavian-seeming context for the main action. Beowulf's climactic encounter in the poem is his fight with a malevolent dragon which threatens to destroy his kingdom. Nothing could be more natural, then, than for the poet to compare his Scandinavian hero Beowulf with the great dragon-slayer of Old Norse legend, Sigurðr the Völsung – especially given the likely familiarity of some Anglo-Saxon audiences with this Scandinavian hero, if Viking Age stone sculpture from northern England is anything to go by. However, a close look at this apparently straightforward allusion shows the poet engaging with the story of Sigurðr in quite complex ways.

Hrothgar's court poet, the *scop,* just like our own poet, is *guma gilphlæden | gidda gemyndig* (a man loaded with eloquence | [with a] mind full of stories). He is again like the *Beowulf*-poet, *se þe ealfela | ealdgesegena | worn gemunde* (someone who very many | ancient stories | called to mind). He does not introduce his Sigurðr story in the context of Beowulf's final dragon-fight, or even just after it, but much earlier in the poem, when the Danes are celebrating Beowulf's first big success against the monster Grendel. He begins by praising Beowulf for his very recent success against the monster Grendel, and only then does he reach far back into Scandinavian myth and legend and launch into a recitation about the legendary dragon-slaying hero. Suddenly delving into his ancient story hoard, he *[w]elhwylc gecwæð | þæt he fram Sigemunde | secgan hyrde* (related everything he had heard tell about Sigemund).

But in Old Norse tradition, Sigmundr (to give him the Old Norse form of his name) is actually the father of Sigurðr, and the fight with the dragon is always attributed to the son, not the father. In Old Norse, Sigmundr doesn't fight a dragon. Has the *Beowulf*-poet simply mistaken father and son, or inherited a version of the story which confused the two? This is certainly the commonsensical explanation. But I shall argue that identifying the dragon-slayer with the father, Sigmundr, has enabled our poet to associate him with much darker and less heroic behaviours than the uncomplicated and widely celebrated heroism of his famous son Sigurðr.

At first sight, the poet seems to be demonstrating the essential similarity between Beowulf and Sigemund. Like Beowulf, Sigemund's fame is attributed to his slaying of a dragon which, like the dragon in the poem itself, was guarding a hoard. Sigemund faces the dragon alone, as Beowulf does, and pins the dragon to a wall with a mighty sword thrust which pierces the creature's body. According to *Völsunga saga*, the Old Norse source with the most detailed account of both Sigmundr and Sigurðr, and itself based on Old Norse poems about the Völsungs, Sigmundr had a prized sword which had been given to him by the god Odin – or at least, a strange visitor to the hall of the Völsungs, an old one-eyed man with a hat pulled down low over his face. In a curious parallel to Arthurian tradition, and the sword in the stone, Excalibur, this sword had been impaled by Odin in the trunk of a mighty tree which grew in the centre of the Völsungs' hall, and only Sigmundr could free it. However, in the Old Norse sources, the dragon fight itself is quite different from what is described in *Beowulf*: Sigurðr spies out the dragon's habitual path, digs a pit along the route and crouches in it so that when the dragon slithers overhead, he can stab its soft underbelly and thus kill it. In *Beowulf*, Sigemund's fight with the dragon is like Beowulf's, a fierce face-to-face confrontation, and the dragon is no slow slug-like slitherer but a formidable opponent.

Opening his account, the *scop* remarks that Sigemund's many heroic exploits were not widely or well known; the only person who knew much about them was his nephew Fitela, who was with him, as his companion and support, and, the narrative voice somewhat otiosely adds, was told about them by his uncle (but if he was with his uncle on these exploits, he wouldn't need to be told about them, would he?). Fitela was not by his side on the occasion of the dragon fight, we are told (so why is he being mentioned at all here?). The implication of the *Beowulf*-poet seems to be that though everyone has heard of the dragon-fight, there were other tales to be told about Sigemund and Fitela which required much more arcane knowledge, and further, that these stories might have involved less wholesomely heroic exploits than dragon fights, for they included *fæhðe ond fyrena* (feuds and monstrous/sinful deeds). A modern reader who has read the Norse sources might well concur: according to *Völsunga saga* Fitela – Sinfjötli in Old Norse – was the son of Sigmundr and his sister Signý, and thus both nephew and son; together, Sigmundr and Sinfjötli spent a period in exile as werewolves, killing their enemies with vulpine savagery. And Sigmundr, detecting cowardice in his other nephews, the young children of Signý by her legitimate husband, mercilessly murders them.

The incest, the shapeshifting, the Odinic sword: none of this is referred to in *Beowulf*. And yet it would be hard to claim that it is not implied, or at least slyly hinted at. We are left with a strangely ambivalent model for Beowulf: a celebrated dragon-slayer who, in the poet's conflation of Sigemund and his son Sigurðr, is nevertheless associated with much less admirable deeds.

The story of Sigemund and the dragon leads the *Beowulf*-poet to the case of Heremod, apparently a Danish king who found himself *mid Eotenum* – amongst the Jutes, the giants, or just figuratively, his enemies. What happened to him there is not altogether clear: the poet tells us simply that he was lured away into the control of his enemies, and put to death. It seems, though, that he had been a Bad King: he had put his subjects in fear of their lives, and they were unable to rely on him to help them when times were perilous. While Beowulf, the poet tells us, became *freondum gefægra* (dearer to his friends), sin took hold of Heremod. Later in the poem, Heremod is again brought up as an example not to be imitated, when Hrothgar is counselling Beowulf on the principles of good kingship. Heremod was the cause of slaughter amongst the Danish people, and *breat bolgenmod | beodgeneatas* (swollen with rage, beat to death his table-companions). In spite of the privileges of kingship, which God had given him, he was at heart ungenerous and violent, and paid the price with a long period of misery for both himself and his people. He eventually died a lonely death after a joyless life. Hrothgar concludes that the example of Heremod should be a lesson to Beowulf.

Heremod as a Danish king does not figure anywhere else in Old English literary traditions, although he is mentioned in a semi-historical genealogy of West Saxon kings. However, Hermóðr, to give the Norse form of his name, appears in Norse in three very early (perhaps tenth-century) Old Norse poems, probably as a god, since he is presented in company with the other Æsir, the Old Norse pantheon. There is no hint there of the wicked and doomed figure in *Beowulf*; if anything, he is a benevolent figure who, for example, volunteers to brave the goddess of the underworld, Hel, in what in fact proves to be a failed attempt to bring Baldr back from the dead. This disparity might even cause us to suppose that the similarity of the two names is no more than chance. But what is significant is that in all three Old Norse poems, Hermóðr is presented alongside the legendary hero Sigmundr in Valhalla. So Sigmundr and Hermóðr appear together in Old Norse traditions, and in writing of Sigemund, the first name which springs to the *Beowulf*-poet's mind is Heremod. The obvious conclusion is that the *Beowulf*-poet was drawing on sources like Old Norse myth which paired these two characters. The poet's hero, Beowulf, is contrasted favourably with both Sigemund and Heremod, implicitly, in the first case, and categorically in the second. Sigemund, the pre-eminent Norse dragon-slayer, is associated with murky deeds which the *Beowulf*-poet does not care to elaborate on. And the name of a Norse god or hero is used to denote a Danish heathen king who is morally evil but, tellingly, does not appear in historical traditions about Denmark. The Norse colouring brings darker shades with it. And the point to remember is this: the stories of Sigemund and Heremod are not an integral part of the *Beowulf* story. The poem has no pressing need to bring them in at all. And he certainly doesn't need to mention Fitela.

Brísings or Brosings?

The more incidentally the *Beowulf*-poet introduces an allusion to the supposed background to his story, the more convincing the detail will seem as a natural, even inevitable reference to a body of relevant tradition, and perhaps one shared by poet and audience. This lightness of touch is evident in the poet's brief but vivid allusion to Hama and the necklace of the Brosings. After his success against Grendel, Beowulf is rewarded with praise and with treasure, including the most magnificent neck ring the narrator has ever heard of – apart, that is, from the necklace of the Brosings, which Hama carried off to a bright fortress when he was fleeing the ingenious enmity of King Eormenric. The casual tone of this allusion somehow carries the implication that everyone will know what the poet is referring to, and that there is no need to explain further, or labour the point. Hama does figure in another Old English poem – *Widsið*, itself an allusive collection of obscure names of people and places apparently from Germanic tradition. In *Widsið*, we learn little about Hama except his association with twisted gold; such treasure is mentioned as included in Beowulf's reward, and one wonders if the phrase particularly suggested neckrings, elaborately coiled light-catching torques. Eormenric – an Ostrogothic king who appears relatively often in both Old Norse and Old English sources – is mentioned in *Widsið* too, but not in connection with Hama. In the much later Old Norse *Þiðreks saga*, a figure with a possibly cognate name – Heimir – steals various treasures from King Eormenric, though there is no specific mention of a magnificent torque. This Heimir is said eventually to enter a monastery – which might correspond with how the *Beowulf*-poet concludes his allusion: Hama *geceas ecne ræd* (chose everlasting gain) – or even refer to the *byrhtan byrig* (bright fortress) to which Hama fled.

The centrepiece of Beowulf's reward, the magnificent necklace itself, is named by the poet as the *Brosinga mene* (necklace of the Brosings). There is also an iconic necklace in Old Norse, and it has a tantalizingly similar name: the *Brísinga men*. The two forms are not linguistically related, but it is hard to believe that they do not both denote the same treasure. So the commonsensical explanation of the name difference is that either there were different traditions about the great necklace, and names varied between them, or, simply, that the poet or scribe(s) of *Beowulf* got the name wrong, given that the *Brosinga mene* is just a brief allusion in the poem, while in Old Norse sources the *Brísinga men* is mentioned a number of times, in different texts. But a look at these Old Norse sources reveals that the necklace had a very racy history.

Basing his work on Old Norse mythological poems, the thirteenth-century Icelandic antiquarian and literary historian Snorri Sturluson identifies the goddess Freyja by her ownership of the *Brísinga men*, and cites an early Old Norse poem as evidence for the theft of the necklace from Freyja by the malevolent demi-god Loki: in the ninth-century Norwegian poem *Haustlöng*, Loki is termed 'the thief of the Brísing-circlet'. Only in rather later sources do we learn more of the story, and as always it must be remembered that later versions may be unreliable. And yet it's always possible that they may provide a strong indication of how a memorable mythic motif had captured the imagination of later writers. This is precisely the case with the *Brísinga men*. The Eddic poem *Þrymskviða* begins dramatically: the giants have stolen Thor's hammer, a mythic attribute even more iconic than Freyja's necklace. The only chance of reclaiming the hammer is for the gods to pay the giants for its return by giving them the goddess Freyja herself. Predictably, she is enraged by their plan, so enraged indeed that 'the great necklace of the Brísings fell from her'. But her explicit objection is an interesting one: she complains that she will be thought 'the most sex-crazed of women' if she agrees to be taken to giantland as a bride. The Æsir come together in council to devise another plan, and Heimdallr – the watchman of the gods – has an idea: Thor can dress up as Freyja, and the key element of his disguise will be that he will wear 'the great necklace of the Brísings' – a phrase which through repetition has become a resonant refrain in the poem.

Thor does not exactly play his part to perfection. He eats the whole wedding breakfast single-handedly; he drinks all the mead; and his eyes beneath the bridal veil glitter dangerously. But Loki – dressed up as a bridesmaid – has an answer for all these excesses: Freyja, he explains, has been unable to eat, drink or sleep, so full of desire is she for her giant wedding. Loki plays on what the giants expect – or hope for – and what Freyja herself fears will be believed of her: that she has an unbridled sexual appetite. At the end of the story, Thor gets his hammer back, his masculinity symbolically restored after the cross-dressing pantomime.

A second late Old Norse source, a short story known as *Sörla þáttr*, also associates Freyja, the necklace, and sex bought and sold. This narrative explains that Freyja commissioned the necklace from four dwarves (perhaps the eponymous Brísings) and paid for it by sleeping with each of them in turn. In Norse tradition, then, the *Brísinga men* is a highly charged treasure with powerful sexual associations. The tenth-century Icelandic poem *Húsdrápa* contains a reference, picked up by the immensely learned and knowledgeable Snorri Sturluson, to Heimdallr (whom we have already seen suggesting that Thor wear the *Brísinga men* in an otherwise highly improbable attempt to pass himself off as Freyja) struggling with Loki over an unspecified jewel. In his explanatory prose, Snorri simply states that Heimdallr (whose name recalls that of Hama in Beowulf) 'contended with Loki for the *Brísinga men*'. It is clear that the *Brísinga men* was a hugely significant and resonant object in Old Norse myth, with intensely powerful sexual associations.

Of course we would not expect such associations to play a part in the morally upright world of Hrothgar and Beowulf, and the poet seems to clean up the whole episode with his vague assertion that Hama came to a good end. But if he wanted to compare Beowulf's treasure with the most extraordinary necklace in the whole Germanic world, the *Brísinga men* is the only real comparator, a treasure repeatedly the object of theft and desire. Beowulf's treasure has its own problematic history, however. Beowulf gives the gold torque with which Hrothgar rewarded him to Hygelac's queen Hygd, and it is indeed stolen – but not from her. It was being worn by King Hygelac, the poet tells us, when he fell in battle against the Franks. A Frankish warrior – a lesser hero – made off with it. Would the theft of the neckring from the woman it belonged to be a dangerously close parallel to the *Brínsinga men*? Might the change of the neckring's name have helped to shift the attention from Freyja to Hama? And in the poem, the neckring was looted in battle – an unhappy, but uncontroversially heroic fate for this counterpart to a highly controversial Norse treasure. Further, the theft of the necklace has been aligned with the distinctive structure and themes of *Beowulf*: typically, moments of celebration and triumph, especially treasure-giving, are juxtaposed with eventual doom, making the implicit point that great treasures are never safe. Those who give them away, our Christian poet seems to suggest – like Hama, or indeed Beowulf himself – do better than those – like Hygelac, or the Æsir – who try to hold on to them.

An accidental death

The *Beowulf*-poet returns to the death of Hygelac when Beowulf is facing his final great challenge against the dragon. Beowulf has successfully maintained the Geatish kingdom since his uncle Hygelac's death in battle, first by supporting his son Heardred's precocious rule, and then taking over the kingdom himself when Heardred is attacked and killed by the Swedes. His reign has lasted fifty years – this must have seemed an astonishingly long period to the poem's Anglo-Saxon audience – and, oddly pessimistic about his chances of success, Beowulf the old king reminisces about his happy childhood as a beloved foster son of Hrethel, King of the Geats. But the first incident he recalls is a grim one: one of Hygelac's brothers, Hæthcyn, accidentally killed another brother, Herebeald. For Hrethel, this tragedy involved more than the death of a son. In the normal heroic way of things, revenge would be taken on the killer, but Hrethel cannot avenge one son by killing another, and in any case the accidental nature of the killing complicates the issue. Hrethel, paralysed with grief and unable to see any way forward, simply loses the will to live: *gumdream ofgeaf | Godes leoht geceas* (he gave up human joy [and] chose God's light). Like Hama, he turns away from the world, and this choice is ratified by the Christian poet, for he moves from the darkness of grief and powerlessness into God's light.

Many scholars have remarked on an apparent parallel between Hæthcyn's killing of his brother Herebeald and the Old Norse myth of Baldr's death, caused by an inadvertent shot from his brother Höðr. The correspondence of the names alone (Here*beald* and Baldr, *Hæth*cyn and Höðr) – the similar elements are precise cognates in Old English and Old Norse – cannot be simply coincidental. The name Hæthcyn does not occur anywhere else in Old English and Herebeald is extremely rare. Though the killing in *Beowulf* is presented as a simple, perfectly plausible, accident, while in the Old Norse it is the result of a malevolent (and deliberate) plan by the demi-god Loki to use the otherwise blameless Höðr as the instrument for causing 'the greatest misfortune ever to have befallen the gods', nevertheless, the outlines of the event are identical: one brother accidentally kills another with a missile, and great distress is caused to the family, whether royal or divine. Hrethel, as we have seen, can do nothing. His impotence is compared by the poet to that of a father whose son has been hanged – as the result of a legitimate execution, we may suppose. His grief is the same as Hrethel's – indeed, in detailing that misery, it is sometimes not clear whether the *Beowulf*-poet is speaking of Hrethel or the unnamed bereaved father in the comparison. In the world of the poem, their dilemma, and their lack of possible remedy, is the same.

The death of Baldr is a different matter, however, and not just in terms of the accident as opposed to the murderous plan. After Herebeald's and Hæthcyn's deaths, Hrethel's next son, Hygelac, is in line for the throne. But amongst the Norse Æsir, all dynastic hopes have rested on Baldr. The gods, and Odin in particular, are not only suffering bereavement, and frustrated vengeance, but also facing a crisis of succession. Odin cannot leave one mythic world for another, for he is already Lord of the Dead. But he can act outside the constraints of the actual human world, and he does. According to Snorri Sturluson's thirteenth-century account, Baldr's mother Frigg is the first to act.

When Odin and the other gods, rather like Hrethel, are paralysed by grief, she calls for a volunteer to travel to the goddess Hel's underworld and try to buy back Baldr. As we have seen, Hermóðr responds to the challenge and pleads with Hel to give up Baldr, citing the Æsir's great grief at his death. Hel takes him at his word and offers to return Baldr to the gods if 'all things in the world, alive or dead, weep for him'. Hermóðr's visit to the underworld ends with a charmingly improbable exchange of gifts – some jewellery, including the great ring Draupnir, and a nice linen dress – as if he had been at a family reunion and not on a desperate rescue mission. But on his return, the Æsir send messengers all over the world to weep Baldr out of hell – Snorri likens such ubiquitous tears to the natural phenomenon of the melting of frost on objects brought in out of the cold into warmth, as if the attempted resurrection of Baldr were a spring fertility ritual, bringing the god back to life after the winter. But the great thaw is incomplete: a hard-hearted giantess in a cave refuses to melt: she 'will weep dry tears at Baldr's funeral'. This giantess, Snorri's narrator presumes, is Loki, who has successfully fought to prevent a reversal of his plan to have Baldr killed.

So now it's up to Odin to do something. In Old Norse poetic traditions (which scholars automatically but not necessarily rightly assume preserve more authentic traditions than Snorri's later, Christian re-telling of the death of Baldr), Odin contravenes the law of nature, and begets a son, Váli, who magically reaches maturity in the space of one day, solely to wreak revenge on his half-brother's killer. Snorri – perhaps fastidiously – does not allude to this fantastic genesis, and so to have a fully articulated account we must piece together a series of poetic allusions. In the poem *Völuspá*, which is perhaps to be dated to around the year 1000 CE, immediately after Höðr's fatal shot at Baldr, the poet tells us that a brother to Baldr, son to Odin, was born and 'began fighting at one night old'. In *Baldrs draumar* ('The Dreams of Baldr') the same line is repeated, with the addition of two names: the miraculous baby is Váli, and his mother is Rindr. Both poems include the detail that Váli would not wash his hands or comb his hair before the duty of vengeance was fulfilled. A third poem, *Hyndluljóð*, notes that Váli was born to avenge his brother Baldr, and a tiny fragment of skaldic verse attributed to the tenth-century Icelandic poet Kormákr ties up the last loose end: *Oðinn seið til Rindar* (Odin performed sex magic in order to seduce Rindr). In short, Odin has done everything in his considerable magical powers to avoid the emotional, dynastic and cultural impasse of the inability to take vengeance for a son who has been killed.

To return to *Beowulf*: the poet has presented us with the accidental killing of one brother by another which seems to mirror a similar incident in Old Norse myth. But could it be that the *Beowulf*-poet invented this similarity? Has he in fact fabricated an analogue, creating names for the Geatish brothers – known nowhere else – which echo those of the corresponding mythic figures? Literary analogues are usually defined as narrative elements in separate literary traditions which present obvious similarities. As we shall shortly see, the term analogue is very useful in denoting a similarity which is not necessarily the result of one author borrowing from another – so we don't have to argue that one text is earlier or later than the other, or even, that one author knew the other text. Similarity, however it might have arisen, is all that is needed. But one of the most interesting aspects of analogue comparisons is in fact *not* similarity, but difference within that overall sameness. And here in *Beowulf,* there is a marked difference in the responses of the bereaved fathers: while Hrethel, King of the Geats, surrenders to the hopelessness of his situation, Odin, Father of the Slain, resorts at once to sorcery. It seems, too, that the *Beowulf*-poet deliberately played up Odinic elements in his account of the brothers' tragedy. For instance, it is possible to argue that there is an allusion to Odinic sacrifice if the death of Herebeald and the story of the old man whose son is hanged – already intermingled – are conflated, for victims whose deaths were dedicated to Odin were both pierced and hanged. That the hanged man is described *hrefne to hroðre* (as a treat for the raven) perhaps reinforces the Odin connexion, and the Old English verb *ridan*, which means both to swing on the gallows and to ride, may be argued to evoke the myth of Odin's own self-sacrifice, when he hanged himself on the World Tree, Yggdrasill, whose very name means 'Odin-steed'. But there is even stronger evidence that the poet is going out of his way to evoke, obliquely, Old Norse myth, in his observation that the old man with the hanged son *oðres ne gymeð | to gebidanne* (does not care to wait for another [son]) – in marked and perhaps pointed contrast to Odin's efforts.

The Icelandic warrior-poet Egill Skalla-Grímsson, in the Old Icelandic saga based on his life, is also shown grief-stricken for the loss of his sons;

one has died of sickness, the other has been drowned, and both are therefore unavengeable. Egill's response is like Hrethel's: he takes to his bed, refuses to eat or drink and prepares to die. In a deeply touching scene, his step-daughter Þorgerðr (actually the daughter of Egill's late brother, whose widow Egill has married) first tricks him into drinking some milk, and then persuades him that he should try to capitalize on this small lease of life and compose a funeral poem for Böðvarr, the son who has been drowned. The resulting poem, quoted in full in some manuscripts of the saga, is a magnificent lament, the *Sonatorrek* (this is usually translated as 'A Lament for Sons'). In the course of the poem, Egill first expresses his paralysing sense of loss and complains that he has been unfairly treated by the god Odin. But as the composing of the poem becomes itself the poem's subject, Egill recognizes that his god has not deserted him and that Odin's gift of poetry has been the saving of him.

In his lament, Egill seems to make specific reference to the one impossible route to vengeance: 'This is also said – that no-one can get recompense for a son unless he himself can beget another descendant who will be for others a man born in place of his brother.' And just like the old man in *Beowulf*, who also, as we have seen, does not want, or indeed have, the option of waiting for another son, Egill has one remaining consolation: he can compose a lament – *gyd wrece*, as the *Beowulf*-poet initially puts it. A little later, even more closely resembling Egill, the old man *gewitað þonne on sealman | sorhleoð gæleð* (then takes to his bed, recites a song of grief). It seems, then, that Odin's response was a bizarre, daring – and necessarily divine – exception to the accepted course a bereaved and elderly father might take.

So to sum up these three examples, which all turn on similarity and difference in names as well as story, matter: in all three, the versions of the elements in Old Norse sources are associated with distinctly un-Christian and essentially sinful elements: incest, shapeshifting, sorcery, dubious sexual practices and Odinism. These elements are presented in the poem as belonging to the world of the poet's otherwise worthy pre-Christian Scandinavian characters, but the difficult balance the poet must strike is to show or suggest that Old Norse myth was full of such wickedness, without including explicit, and possibly rather thrilling, references to it in his poem. So into the apparently positive comparison of two great dragon-slaying heroes, Beowulf and Sigurðr, is smuggled the murky deeds of Sigurðr's father, Sigmundr. The sexual deviancy associated with the *Brísinga men* in Old Norse is never mentioned; the great necklace has a slightly different name; the focus of the story is not on Freyja who bought the necklace with sex, but on Hama, who came to a good end; and the treasure itself is part of the poet's conception of valuable objects being better bestowed than hoarded. Finally, it might be argued that the poet has invented an analogue to one of the central elements in Old Norse myth, the killing of Baldr by his brother Höðr, in order to show in an oblique way the alien characteristics of the Norse god Odin, who resorted to sex magic when his dynasty was threatened. To be sure, each individual instance might be explained in a simple, comonsensical way: that traditions differed, that the poet got his names wrong. But cumulatively, an obvious pattern emerges: Old English, good; Old Norse, bad. If we do assume skilful use of mythic sources, we can see a poet who knew so much about Old Norse myth and legend that he could not only allude to it and echo it, but also manipulate it for his own ends.

Three heroes: Beowulf, Thor and Grettir

In the examples above, the *Beowulf*-poet reveals his active and engaged knowledge of Old Norse myth and legend. He consistently shows up the Old Norse as antithetical to Christianity, contrasting it with the beliefs and behaviours of the characters in his poem, who are, ironically enough, themselves Scandinavian pagans. But there is another, completely different way in which we can see the imprint of Old Norse literature in the poem. Although widely separated in time, geographical origin and even literary form, several Old Norse texts are sufficiently, if sometimes only faintly, similar enough to be called analogues to *Beowulf*. As I explained above, the term analogue is particularly useful here, because there is no need to claim any direct borrowing from one text to another. We can bring together as analogues not only an Anglo-Saxon poem – *Beowulf* – and some Old Norse poems perhaps contemporary with it, but also the thirteenth-century mythic stories of Snorri

Sturluson, and a late Icelandic saga – *Grettis saga* – which probably dates from the fourteenth century. There is obviously no question of the *Beowulf*-poet having borrowed material from these two last prose works, and virtually no likelihood of Snorri or the saga author having known *Beowulf*. It isn't even very likely the Anglo-Saxon and Old Norse poets had any direct contact. And yet, similarities are evident, if, as I say, faint. The explanation for the similarities is almost certainly that all the texts were themselves re-telling the same, or similar, shared sources. What links all these analogues is the depiction of a hero: the Geatish warrior Beowulf, the Norse god Thor or the Icelandic (and ultimately historical) sagaman, Grettir the Strong.

Beowulf's career has been compared with the exploits of the Norse god Thor, most obviously in their final, mutually fatal, encounters with a monstrous serpent. Thor is the hero of the Æsir, fighting their battles, defending Ásgarðr and taking on giants (and giantesses), the old enemies of the gods. His giant-killings feature widely in Old Norse poetry and prose; a number of eddic poems are given over to such episodes, and Snorri Sturluson adds to their number in his *Prose Edda*. A fragment of verse from the tenth-century Icelandic poet Þorbjörn dísarskáld enthusiastically lists the names of some of Thor's victims; we do not know how many more there may have been. Of course, protection from monsters, or enemies, is just what heroes offer, and as Lord Raglan pointed out long ago, the biography of the hero is remarkably similar in narratives across many times and places; in fact, its climax is very often a fight against a monster or other powerful figure. It would be surprising if Beowulf the champion of the Geats did not share certain features with the god whose physical courage and might were his primary attributes. Beowulf is a fictional figure set in a semi-historical Scandinavian past; the *Beowulf*-poet was unconstrained by historical actuality in his depiction of the hero, and pitting him against monsters might well have encouraged the poet to draw on mythic models since they too faced fabulous foes. But I hope to show that there is more to it than this. I will begin by setting three of Thor's exploits – his first attempt at hooking the World Serpent, and two of his adventures at the court of the giant Útgarðr-Loki – against arguably similar episodes in Beowulf's career.

Thor and the World Serpent

Thor's dramatic first encounter with the Miðgarðsormr, or World Serpent, was evidently a popular and widespread story in north-western Europe. Most people nowadays who know this story have come across it in the version Snorri Sturluson tells. But there are references to it in much older Old Norse verse. Úlfr Uggason's tenth-century poem *Húsdrápa* is said by the author of *Laxdoela saga,* in which its recitation is described, to have been inspired by the carved panelling in the magnificent Icelandic farmhouse where the aptly named Óláfr *pá* – the peacock – held a wedding feast for his daughter; the poem contains an account of Thor's encounter with the World Serpent. And the earliest known skaldic sequence to have come down to us, the probably ninth-century *Ragnarsdrápa,* also purports to describe a visual representation of the episode – Thor hooking the World Serpent was one of the four scenes supposedly depicted on the four quarters of an elaborate, perhaps ceremonial, shield. Finally, there are extended allusions to the episode in the eddic poem *Hymiskviða* which contains a lengthy and dramatic account of how Thor and the giant Hymir set out together on monstrous fishing expedition; Thor baits his line with an ox-head; Hymir manages to hook two whales at once. But Thor's bait attracts the World Serpent – the 'encircler from below of all lands'.

Snorri's account in his *Prose Edda* plays up the element of comedy inherent in the episode, especially the giant Hymir's cowardly cold feet about the whole trip, but there is real drama in his account of how Thor and the Serpent face each other out: moments when the stability of the whole cosmos may be in the balance – hanging by a thread, one might say, since Thor's fishing line threatens to haul the World Serpent right out of the water until Hymir ends the stand-off by cutting it. This moment plainly caught the imagination of artists and sculptors as well as poets; on the Hørdum stone, in Denmark, for example, we can see Thor's boat raked at an improbably steep angle as the hooked serpent, out of the picture except for one sinister coil beneath the boat, tautens the line. There are representations of the scene on the so-called 'Fishing Stone' at Gosforth, in Cumbria and on stones in Sweden and Gotland. In Old Norse skaldic verse, two poems purport to describe visual depictions of the scene.

At first glance, this thrilling episode with its focus on the stand-off between the mighty Thor and the World Serpent, and its potential for comic treatment – brought out most clearly in Snorri's prose re-telling – seems to have no counterpart in *Beowulf*. The root of the comedy as Snorri presents it is that after the giant Hymir has patronized Thor – whom he imagines to be a young boy – as a feeble rower on account of his age, and one who will not be able to stand the cold conditions of a lengthy trip, we see his growing fear of rowing so far out to sea that they might encounter the World Serpent. We can infer from this that fishing for the World Serpent was no part of Hymir's agenda, and Snorri tells of a secret plan on Thor's part; he 'made up his mind to seek an opportunity for a meeting' and hijacks Hymir's fishing expedition for this purpose. A stanza from the skaldic sequence known as *Ragnarsdrápa*, quoted by Snorri in his *Prose Edda*, also implies that Thor deliberately sought out his foe: 'The son of the Father of Men wished to pit his strength against the twist of the earth, splashed with sea-spray.' But if we shift perspective from the hooking of the monster to the rowing far out to sea, then faint parallels with one of Beowulf's exploits – the swimming contest with Breca – seem possible.

A careful reading of Snorri's account, for example, reveals traces of a competition between Hymir and Thor: god and giant are in the same boat, rowing together, and very fast. Hymir is taken aback by Thor's evident strength. In *Hymiskviða*, there are also implications of a rowing competition: here, as in Snorri's account, the giant Hymir is disconcerted by Thor's energetic rowing, but unlike Snorri, the poet of *Hymiskviða* does not have Hymir cut the line to release the World Serpent, nor does Thor throw the giant overboard. When Thor and Hymir row back to shore 'the giant was not happy', and he prolongs what seems to have been a competitive expedition: 'and still the giant, accustomed to being pig-headed, contended with Thor about strength'. He proposes another contest – might one assume he does this because he has lost the original one – and was it a rowing contest?

We can compare this rather shadowy rowing competition with how the *Beowulf*-poet presents the contest between Beowulf and Breca. On arrival in Heorot, Hrothgar's royal hall, Beowulf is challenged by one of Hrothgar's closest hall-companions, Unferth, who jeers at a rowing contest Beowulf had in youth against a figure called Breca (his name is cognate with the word 'breaker').

As we have seen, Unferth claims that the contest was undertaken rashly, for reasons of pride alone, and that furthermore, Breca won the contest. Beowulf challenges Unferth's verbal attack first by defending himself – he and Breca were both young – *cnihtwesende* (being boys) – then with a proud claim to victory: he prevailed against enraged sea monsters, even when dragged down to the seabed by these savage creatures provoked by the incursion into their element. Thus he outdid Breca in his reputation for heroism. But did Beowulf win the original contest, in the end? It is hard for Beowulf to refute Unferth's primary charge that he lost to Breca, because it is not made clear what the terms of the contest were. Unferth only says that Beowulf and Breca – like Thor and Hymir – ventured into *deop wæter* (deep water). So was it a race, with a finishing point? Or was it a competition to see who could row out furthest to sea? No indication is given. The next day, Unferth alleges, Breca was washed up on the shores of the land of the Heatho-Ræmas, in the south of Norway, and from there made his way back to the Brondings, his own people, wherever that might be. Beowulf, according to his own account, found himself washed up somewhere on the shores of northern Norway. But since we have no idea where he and Breca started from, or where they were headed, the question of which of them 'won' is unanswerable. Were they in the same boat?

Beowulf's contest with Breca has been much discussed by scholars, both in terms of the aggressive challenge from Unferth – identified as an example of Germanic 'flyting' or verbal sparring, a form paralleled in Old Norse texts – and how the episode prefigures Beowulf's later struggle with Grendel's mother – in deep water, beset by water monsters, dragged down to the depths, but ultimately victorious. But the dramatic focus of Thor's expedition with Hymir, that is, the face-to-face encounter with the terrifying World Serpent, has tended to overshadow an underlying, and rather patchily preserved, story: that of the hero, young and rash, rowing far out into the ocean in competition with a companion, risking his life against a water monster and yet managing to return to the shore. Though the details are different, in broad outline this plainly accords with the story of Beowulf and Breca. And we can see how the *Beowulf*-poet has incorporated this narrative element – an episode from Beowulf's early career, before he came to the Danish court – into his main storyline, his narrative present: when the hero arrives, Unferth begins by raking over the past, in a challenge to Beowulf's reputation, and Beowulf sets the record straight. It is, in this sense, a story from outside the timeline of the primary narrative.

The giant's glove

Snorri Sturluson incorporates the story of Thor's encounter with the World Serpent into a larger narrative. He presents the fishing expedition, as we have seen, as having been planned by Thor precisely in order to land the monster – significantly, in revenge for a previous failed encounter. In the first part of his treatise on Old Norse poetry, *Gylfaginning*, Snorri gives a lively, dramatic and entertainingly comic account of Thor's adventures in giantland, specifically at the court of a giant called Útgarða-Loki. Útgarða-Loki presents Thor with a series of apparently friendly and, ostensibly, laughably easy physical challenges, as part of the entertainment at an evening feast. For one of them, Thor is challenged to lift up a rather large cat from the hall floor, but taking hold of the creature under its belly, no matter how far Thor stretches up, the cat's paws remain in contact with the floor as its back arches higher and higher; eventually it raises one paw from the floor, but this is not enough for Thor to succeed in the feat. Thor – the mightiest of the gods – is humiliated in this task, as in all the others. The next morning, however, the giant reveals that none of the tasks were as they seemed, and in particular, that the cat was actually the giant World Serpent itself, so that Thor's achievement in detaching even one of its paws from the earth was a feat both astounding and, to the giant audience, apparently in on the deception, quite terrifying. But Thor is furiously angry, not at all mollified, and it is now that he vows to engineer another meeting with the monster. This is what leads to his dramatic encounter with the World Serpent.

The stretch of narrative in *Gylfaginning* containing these stories from giantland is, unlike most of the rest of Snorri's work, not derived from surviving Old Norse poetry. Its origins remain unknown. But it contains two elements – both humiliating to Thor as presented by Snorri – which find echoes in *Beowulf*. On his way to giantland, Thor and his companions make an epic journey eastwards, across the sea and through a large, dark forest. Searching for a place to spend the night, they come across a large building whose doorway is as wide as the structure itself, and entering, they find a smaller room off to the side, about halfway down, and huddle there, with Thor guarding them. Their night is disturbed by terrifying noises, and Thor remains on watch, his great hammer Mjöllnir at the ready. In the morning, all becomes clear: the noise is a giant, asleep beside them and snoring. And their night shelter is his mitten, their bedroom the thumb of it. The comedy is broad, and Thor is a figure of fun, looking all the sillier for the giant's grave politeness towards him in their exchanges.

Beowulf too has a close encounter with a monstrous glove, but there is no comedy to be had from it. Interestingly, as with the story of Beowulf and Breca, the poet does not include this episode in his main narrative, but again introduces it as part of the reported speech of one of his characters – in this case, Beowulf himself, who, once returned to Geatland, describes to his lord and uncle Hygelac how he fought and killed the monster Grendel. Though it was not mentioned in the earlier direct account of Beowulf's fight with Grendel, Beowulf now reports that Grendel was carrying a great glove made out of dragon skins – perhaps a sinister allusion to Beowulf's eventual fate. Beowulf tells Hygelac that Grendel's intention would have been to put him – and more victims – in this extraordinary rucksack. It may be worth mentioning incidentally that Beowulf describes the glove as *searobendum fæst* (bound together with ingenious fastenings). This is an odd feature for a glove to have, but it does recall the giant's rucksack in Snorri's *Gylfaginning*, which is tied up with 'trick wire' so that Thor's inability to open it is yet one more humiliation at the hands of the giant.

So why didn't the poet include the detail about the glove in his own narrative of Beowulf's fight with Grendel, instead of introducing it, somewhat improbably, only in Beowulf's summary? I would suggest that the poet was trying – successfully, in my view – to avoid a difficulty only too obvious in Snorri's account of Thor's adventures in giantland: the issue of scale and proportion. It is a weakness in Snorri's otherwise very skilful and funny account that it is simply not possible to envisage the sort of interaction between Thor and the giant which he describes – conversation, sharing provisions and so on – if the disparity in size were so great as to allow Thor and his companions to spend the night in the thumb of the giant's mitten. Of course the disparity in size, given Thor's reputation as a fearsome giant-killer, is part of the comedy, and it may be thought over-literal to demand strict and realistic scaling. Nevertheless, Beowulf's fight with Grendel would have been an altogether different encounter if the poet had represented Beowulf as tiny enough to fit – with room to spare for other victims – inside Grendel's glove.

Another detail from Beowulf's fight with Grendel which the poet includes only as part of Beowulf's own account is the name of the Geatish warrior whom Grendel came across first that night, and ate. He was Hondscio, whose name, literally 'hand-shoe', is a kenning for glove (a covering for the hand, as the shoe is a covering for the foot). Was the poet preparing his audience for the introduction of the glove? Or did he have the detail already in his mind as he devised a name for the eaten Geat? Speculation is pointless, but it is a curious coincidence, and a tellingly curious name.

Wrestling with old age

Perhaps the greatest of Thor's humiliations in giantland is his wrestling match with Elli, an old woman whom the giant, ostensibly despairing of Thor's ability to meet even the feeblest of challenges, brings on as a suitable opponent. Thor struggles hard against Elli, and when he stumbles to one knee, the giant steps in and stops the fight; with this encounter he calls a halt to all the challenges. But again, as is explained the next morning, Thor was deceived. The name Elli means 'old age' in Norse, and as the giant points out, no-one can be expected to prevail against her. The giants marvel that Thor was only brought down to one knee by her. Beowulf also fights a woman – Grendel's mother, savage with revenge and a powerful opponent for Beowulf, who is, like Thor, brought to his knees by her. But there is no big friendly giant to stop the fight; instead, Beowulf's mail coat protects him against her potentially fatal knife thrust, and once he reasserts himself, God – *witig Drihten* (wise lord) and *rodera Wealdend* (Ruler of the Heavens) – grants him victory.

Grettir the Strong

The clearest and most extensive Norse analogue to events in *Beowulf* is very well known to scholars: in the fourteenth-century Icelandic *Grettis saga* (The Story of Grettir), the eponymous outlaw-hero takes on the physically intimidating ghost of a mysterious Swedish stranger, a zombie-like creature which has been terrorizing the district. Grettir, himself a visiting outsider, like Beowulf, volunteers to help and fights the creature in a remarkably Beowulfian encounter. On another occasion, he again acts as visiting hero when he fights a female troll in hand-to-hand combat; like Beowulf fighting Grendel's mother, Grettir follows her to her lair, a dry cave deep beneath a waterfall, and like Grendel struggling to get away from Beowulf, she leaves her arm behind. The similarity of the outlines makes it clear that here we have two versions of what must essentially have been the same story, but even more remarkable is a set of minor details – in terms of both narrative motif and even terminology – common to the two accounts. In both, for instance, the hero's companions give up hope when they see his opponent's blood staining the water, mistakenly assuming that their hero has been mortally wounded, and both saga writer and Anglo-Saxon poet use similarly unusual words for the sword carried by the hero. The killing of the monsters is presented in both texts as a cleansing of the locale they were terrorizing, and the hero himself as a saviour of the community. As I have said, the favoured explanation for these clear similarities is that both *Beowulf* and *Grettis saga* derive from the same source – the so-called 'two-troll tradition' – and the widespread existence of this tradition has seemed increasingly likely as more similar Old Norse stories are added to the list.

At this point, it may be worth pulling together some of the parallels considered so far, and pondering what they might signify. We have three hero figures – Beowulf, Thor and Grettir – who fight female humanoid opponents: Grendel's mother, Old Age and a nameless female troll. Clearly there can be little question of any direct relationship between *Beowulf* itself and either Snorri's thirteenth-century story-telling on the one hand, or the *Grettis saga*-author's fourteenth-century text on the other. So the most obvious explanation is that Snorri and the author of *Grettis saga* drew on older sources for the basic story matter, and either themselves adapted the material, or used material which had already been adapted, to fit the story into these different literary contexts.

Now the question of Snorri's sources for this material is a particularly interesting one. For one thing, the account of Thor's adventures in giantland is the only part of Snorri's *Prose Edda* which does not have an identifiable source in Old Norse poetry or prose. The fact that there is no surviving poetic source for these stories prevents us from arguing confidently for their basis in earlier traditions – if it were not, of course, for those tantalizing similarities in *Beowulf*. It seems reasonable to suppose that either early poetic sources have for some reason not survived, or Snorri based his stories on oral folk-tales. But perhaps the humiliations of Thor could never have been part of a myth at all close to any actual belief in his power and divinity. And there is another thing: there is something inherently non-narrative, or unrealizable, about the challenges Thor is faced with in Snorri's narrative. We have already seen that the relative size of the protagonists and the glove raises issues of plausibility. Similarly, the identity of the figures which the giant invites Thor's companions to compete against is impossible to envisage. The entity pitted against Loki in an eating contest – Logi, or wildfire – belongs more to the riddle, or cryptic word game, than to a narrative realization. Wildfire of course devours meat – and the trough it is contained in – faster than any other living creature, but how could one envisage the contest as taking place? Would there be a humanoid shape made out of flame? Thor's other companion runs a race against Hugi – 'thought' – and naturally cannot cover the ground as swiftly; but again, what kind of figure would Hugi have cut? And is the revelation of their real identities not spoiled, both inside and outside the world of the narrative, by the transparency of their names? In Old Norse, 'elli' means old age, so any original audience would guess her identity at once. In many literatures, allegorical abstractions are common literary devices. But this mode is foreign to native Old Norse literature, in which narratives are almost always concretely realized, and rooted in reality. All this, in my view, points to a non-narrative source for some at least of Snorri's storytelling: possibly, the cryptic allusions of a solemn mythic poem. Crucially, it seems more likely that Snorri, the clever and learned Christian author, would transform pre-Christian material into an entertaining burlesque than that the *Beowulf*-poet would shift that comedic mode back into one of high seriousness.

It may be, then, that the three authors drew on similar sources, in which a figure fought humanoid monsters of both sexes. Snorri has inherited, or transformed his sources into, tales in which the hero – identified as Thor – is

successively ridiculed. The tone is completely different in *Beowulf*; here the
hero's deeds are successful and exemplary; his opponents and their attributes
are terrifying; the narrative is epic and serious. The story in yet another version
of the material – *Grettis saga* – is tailored to fit the ethos of the Old Icelandic
family saga. Typically, in family sagas the setting is a plausible recreation of
an actual, historical society peopled with characters who may have had some
basis in history. Though there may be some supernatural elements, such as
hauntings or witchcraft, there are none of the fantastic motifs we associate
with folk tales or myth. However, *Grettis saga* has much in common with the
fornaldarsögur (sagas of olden times), a genre in which the hero's adventures
with his adversaries are much more obviously fictional and even fantastic. It
is not surprising, then, that it is from amongst the *fornaldarsögur* that further
analogues to the *Beowulf* story have been identified. Nevertheless, Grettir
remains a human hero, part of a real and fully realized historical society.
Certainly more work remains to be done on the re-use and transformation
of myth in the family sagas, but there is no doubt that many saga authors
developed mythic patterns to a greater or lesser extent and adapted them to fit
into their naturalistic narratives.

Beowulf, Grettir and Thor share a surprising number of attributes,
even allowing for the common heroic biography mentioned earlier, and
especially if we set to one side Snorri's unserious depiction of Thor in
the giantland section of *Gylfaginning*. As well as the similarly physical
fights with humanoid monsters of both sexes, Beowulf and Grettir have
unpromising childhoods, and all three pit themselves against the sea,
Grettir, for instance, swimming in his youth across a dangerous sound
between Norway and one of its many offshore islands. It is suggested of
Thor and Beowulf that their rowing contest was a rash and youthful deed.
Thor and Grettir both ford a raging river in a heroic exploit concerning
a woman, the god being helped by the giantess and the outlaw-hero
carrying the woman across. Most notably (but perhaps by the same token,
most stereotypically, and therefore less significantly) all three heroes are
protective of their society to the point of being almost salvific figures. It
should be said at once that this aspect of their hero-status is really only very
clear in the early, poetic sources: *Beowulf* itself, and Old Norse verse. As we

have seen, by the thirteenth century, Thor is reduced to a comedic figure, as in Snorri's narrative, and in the even later *Grettis saga*, with its naturalistic picture of Icelandic society in the early years of settlement, there is little scope for truly superhuman heroes. And yet even in the saga, we are told that Grettir's actions in clearing out the trolls have a cleansing effect on the district. In saga literature, farmland believed to be haunted by trolls is liable to be deserted and let go to waste. This was a deep and abiding anxiety amongst Icelanders who had struggled so desperately to settle and make productive a very harsh environment. Grettir's achievements thus resonate far beyond exciting hero versus monster escapades. In *Beowulf,* the significance of the hero's achievements is quite different: Beowulf as a young warrior rescues Hrothgar from the misery of Grendel's depredations, and at the end of his life, as a king, defends his people from the dragon's destructive attacks. Here, personal relationships and the duties of kingship are at the heart of the poem, carefully balanced against each other. And in Old Norse mythological poetry about Thor, we see him defending the gods against the ever-present and ever-threatening Other: the giants.

Intriguingly, none of these conflicts represents an uncomplicated confrontation between good and evil. Grettir is an extremely complicated character, a misunderstood sociopath dogged by bad luck. Beowulf is beset by doubts before the dragon fight, and was perhaps rash and/or arrogant in taking on the dragon alone and over-keen to take possession of the dragon's hoard. The last word of the poem, in what we would expect to be a eulogy for the hero, is *lofgeornost* – its sense in this context has been much debated, but the meaning of the word itself is 'most eager for praise'. Thor – even before his reduction to a comic character – is portrayed in Old Norse mythic sources as hot-headed and violent. Most of these texts were composed or transmitted by Christians about pre-Christian figures, such that we couldn't expect unadulterated hero-worship. But there is a clear echo of Christian salvation – in the figure of Christ himself – in the poetry.

That scholars have seen echoes of Christ in the figures of both Thor and Beowulf is the most fundamental link between the two heroes. There are significant parallels between Thor's hooking of the World Serpent and the Devil as Leviathan, on a fish hook baited by Christ himself. Thor is presented in Old Norse sources as the son of Odin – the father of men – and Jörð (Earth). This parentage resembles Christ's earthly mother and all-powerful Father. Further, in the part of *Hymiskviða* which describes the hooking of the World Serpent, Thor is openly called 'the one who saves mankind'.

Art historians have proposed that the depiction of mythological scenes on Viking age Christian monuments in Britain – for example, the Gosforth Cross, and the 'Fishing Stone' which may have formed part of a frieze decorating the church in Gosforth – may indicate that a strong typological connexion was perceived between Christian and pagan motifs. Typology – rather like the use of analogues in literary tradition – is concerned with similarities between figures and narrative elements often far-removed in time and geographical space. In the Middle Ages, Christian thought focused on the (divinely inspired and in fact prophetic) typological relationship between the Old Testament and the New. For instance, the sacrifice of a beloved first-born son in the story of Abraham and Isaac prefigures, in a typological reading, God the Father's sacrifice of Christ on the cross. Medieval artists very often emphasized these parallels, so that visual depictions of the sacrifice of Isaac sometimes show him carrying the kindling for his own sacrificial pyre on his own shoulder, just as Christ is depicted shouldering his own cross. So it seems possible, and even likely, that an Anglo-Saxon audience, trained to see meaningful similarities between the Old and New Testaments, might be receptive to accommodating some elements of Old Norse myth as 'types' of Christian images. The similarity between Thor and Christ taking on the enemy of mankind with a fish-hook – an implement suggestively equidistant in form to Thor's hammer and Christ's cross – could reinforce the parallel. The celebrated reference in the Old Norse *Landnámabók* – a record of the original settlers in Iceland – to Helgi, nicknamed 'the thin', who believed in Christ and invoked Thor on sea journeys, might be reinterpreted not as a somewhat cynical Viking pragmatism, but as recognition that both heroes were appropriate protectors against the perils of the sea, and against threats both monstrous and spiritual. They were not mutually exclusive, but avatars of the same salvific entity.

The existence of such syncretism raises the possibility of a new kind of attitude from the poet of *Beowulf* towards Old Norse myth: a poet who was not disapproving, or rivalrous, but ready and willing to draw on both traditions in his depiction of a celebrated hero. It may even be worth making a distinction between the acceptability of Thor, the god of farmers and settlers, like the Danish Scandinavians in eastern England, and the much more risky figure of Odin, the necromancer the god of aristocratic Norwegians, whose country is never once mentioned in *Beowulf*, and whose presence in the poem is oblique and sinister.

If we can see traces of a Christ-Thor figure in *Beowulf*, it may be that poet did not himself invent this composite, and, on the evidence of Anglo-Scandinavian sculpture, that it was familiar to his audience as a site where Old Norse myth might be held to meet the Christian beliefs of the Anglo-Saxons. But it is also clear that Thor's final encounter with the World Serpent, in its context of the final battle between the gods and their adversaries as Ragnarök, was not something easily paralleled with Christian eschatology. To conclude, in what follows I will suggest that the echoes of Ragnarök evident both in Beowulf's fight against the dragon, and in the ethos and outline of the whole poem, mark out the epic, heroic and in many ways glorious pagan past depicted by the poet as something wholly foreign to Christian traditions.

The key element of Ragnarök is that in a series of cataclysmic encounters, the gods engage in single combat with their enemies, and neither side survives. Odin fights Fenrir, the great wolf, and the poet of *Völuspá* gives us to understand that this is the death of him, for it is his wife Frigg's second sorrow, her first being the death of Baldr. Fenrir perishes too, when Odin's son Viðarr avenges his father by stabbing the monster. Týr fights the savage hound Garmr, and both are killed. Freyr advances on the fire-giant Surtr and falls; Surtr later sets fire to the whole world, so that the flames lick the heavens themselves. But before this all-consuming conflagration, Thor meets the World Serpent, and although he attacks the creature with characteristic vigour, his strength fails in the face of its deadly poison, and both fall. Here, then, is the clearest parallel between Thor and the hero Beowulf: both die fighting a mighty dragon, and with them ends a whole epoch – in Beowulf's case, the end of the whole race of the Geats. Beowulf has no heirs; there is no successor to the throne, and though his helper Wiglaf survives the dragon fight, there is no indication that the Geats have any future, especially in the face of attacks from their old enemies the Swedes. As we have seen, Beowulf is burnt on his funeral pyre, and heaven swallows up the smoke. The Danes, as we know from analogous Norse sources and could infer anyway from the poet's own dark hints, have been engulfed in another conflagration: the burning of Heorot – once a beacon of civilized heroic life built with such pride and hope – and the notorious internecine violence amongst the generation after Hrothgar.

The pessimism of this conception of the end of the world (though to some extent tempered by rebirth in *Völuspá*, perhaps under the influence of Christian theology) runs quite counter to Christian belief. One might consider the contrast between the triumphant closing passages of Old English biblical poems such as *Judith* and *Andreas* and the grim prognostications of the future at the end of *Beowulf*. Parallels between *Beowulf* and Ragnarök are hard to resist. The poet insists – in spite of Wiglaf's loyalty and bravery, in spite of historical evidence suggesting that the Geatish line did not in fact end here – on a mood of hopeless resignation for the end of his poem, and it seems that for this he turned to Old Norse myth.

(iii) The narrator

Having looked at the various subjects of *Beowulf* – the setting, the human characters, the monsters – and having tried to recreate the mindset and intellectual background of the real author of the poem, however irrecoverable as an historical person he may be now, we can turn to the poem's narrator, the voice we imagine as we read the poem. Listeners to a recitation of *Beowulf* would be disposed to identify this narrator with the reciter – the actual flesh-and-blood person speaking the verse. Readers may not picture a person, or conjure up a particular quality of voice, but nevertheless will be aware at some level of abstraction of a voice delivering the poem. This is what I mean by the narrator. I will attribute to the narrator not the subject matter of the poem – its setting and characters – nor its intellectual framework; I see these as the poet's choices and attributes. I will be looking at the way in which the story is told; not what is told, but how it is told. There are obvious poetic conventions any narrator of a poem adopts: metre, that is, the rhythm of the lines; and diction, that is, use of words, and by extension, metaphor. I will begin this section by describing and illustrating the narrator's choices under these headings. After that, I will look at the way the story is told: how the narrator varies the pace of the narrative and arranges the sequence of its events, sometimes telling the story chronologically, but at other times skipping backwards and forwards in time to create distinctive special effects. Finally, I will explore the narrator's perspective on the events related.

Words and rhythm: Poetic diction and metre

The basic form of the poetry of *Beowulf* is very evident from the opening few lines quoted at the beginning of this book. The original text is usually printed in modern editions as a long, continuous succession of pairs of half-lines, with a clear gap between the two halves. To save going back to that original quotation, here is another set of half-lines, set out in the usual way, this time from the closing lines of the poem:

Ongunnon þa on **b**eorge **b**ælfyra mæst	Then they began on [the] cliff the greatest funeral fire,
wigend **w**eccan; **w**udurec astah	the warriors, to kindle; wood- smoke rose up
sweart ofer **s**wioðole **s**wogende leg	dark above fire, roaring flame
wope be**w**unden – **w**indblond gelæg –	with weeping intermingled – swirling wind dropped –
oð þæt he ða **b**anhus ge**b**rocen hæfde	until it [the flame] the bone-house had destroyed,
hat on **h**reðre.	hot in [the] heart.

As well as the characteristic appearance of the poem on the pages of modern editions (incidentally, the Icelander Grímur Jónsson Thorkelin's early nineteenth-century edition of *Beowulf* set out the poem as a long, spindly column of single half-lines), we can recognize the patterns of alliteration (picked out here in bold). Where there is standard alliteration (one or two alliterating syllables in the first half-line, followed by a second or third in the second half-line), it is possible even for a reader unfamiliar with Old English to piece together the regular two-stress beat of each half-line by leaning on the alliterating syllables (although it helps to be able to recognize and discount unstressed prefixes such as be- or ge-). This two-stress beat is maintained from the poem's very beginning to its very end. But the number of unstressed syllables in each half-line varies, and so too does their placement in relation to the stressed ones. This produces a surprising variety of effects and prevents the metre from becoming hypnotically regular. For instance, in the few lines quoted above, the last half-line – *hat on hreðre* – has four syllables, in the simple alternating pattern stressed-unstressed-stressed-unstressed, while in another half-line – *sweart ofer swioðole* – there are two, not one, unstressed syllables following each of the two stressed ones. It is of course difficult to illustrate this, because you have to know enough Old English to recognize that diphthongs (two vowel sounds together) are counted as one sound, so that this half-line, for the purposes of metrical analysis, should be read (and indeed was perhaps pronounced – who knows?) as having six syllables, something like 'swart over swiðoler'. The interesting thing is that there seems to be no way of knowing whether the extra unstressed syllables make the line last longer, or whether they are simply recited (or imagined to be recited) much more quickly, so that in effect any half-line – no matter how many syllables it has – takes up the same amount of actual time as any other, and the beat of the lines remains steady.

A different effect altogether is produced if the unstressed syllables precede the stressed ones, as in the long line *oð þæt he ða banhus | gebrocen hæfde* (until it the bone-house had destroyed). Here, the bringing together – a virtual collision – of the two key words in the line (*banhus* and *gebrocen*), which even bridges the gap between the two half-lines, with both words stressed and alliterating, makes them dominate the line, the focus being on how the fire destroyed the body (the 'bone-house'), in much the same way as a phrase like 'broken body' would stand out in a poem in modern English. Similarly, from the beginning of the poem, the metre of the half-line which introduces the progenitor of the Danish royal house forces attention and emphasis on his name: *Oft Scyld Scefing* ... One of my own favourite examples of metrical effects is the first description of Grendel's attack on Heorot:

Ne wæs þæt forma sið
þæt he Hroðgares   ham gesohte

(it was not the first time | that he Hrothgar's | home sought out).

The introductory 'it was not the first time' is merely scene setting, necessary background information. Again, the key phrase 'Hrothgar's home' (Heorot) pulls two half-lines together and speeds up the flow of the verse. The pronoun 'he', more usually unstressed, is emphasized here (it is Grendel, after all) and the close succession of alliterating stressed syllables produces an effect of inexorability: there is no escape from Grendel's depredations.

The metrical analysis of Old English poetry, and of *Beowulf* in particular, has filled many books, and there is little consensus. In fact, the technicalities of some published works are often incomprehensible even to other Old English scholars. And yet, somehow, the effects are evident, and the rhythm easy to pick up. And quite unlike the more familiar poetic conventions of syllable counting, end rhyme and an iambic metre – the regular succession of unstressed and stressed syllables (di dah di dah di dah di dah di dah) – the form and metre of *Beowulf* sounds very like the flexible, emphatic delivery of a carefully worked speech ('*I* have a *dream*'; 'We will *fight* them on the *beaches*'), its rhythm echoing formalized speech patterns (with half-lines like sound bites!) still evident in modern English.

One way of demonstrating the difference between syllable-counting iambic metres and what might be called 'natural' stress patterns is to take this first line of one of Shakespeare's sonnets:

Shall I compare thee to a summer's day?

Although this line can be scanned as a perfectly regular iambic pentameter, that is, a ten-syllable line which alternates weak and strong stresses – Shall *I* com*pare* thee *to* a *summer's day* (I've italicized the stressed syllables) – it would utterly destroy the poetry to recite it, either in your head, or aloud, like that. Read 'naturally', as if it were prose, the stresses fall rather differently, on the key words in the line: Shall I com*pare thee* to a *summer's day*. It may even be that the mysterious tension between the two ways of reading it is what gives this line – and, of course, so many others like it (try, for instance, the first line of John Keats's 'Ode to Autumn': Season of mists and mellow fruitfulness) – its almost sub-consciously perceived power.

Although the metre of *Beowulf* is to some degree flexible, and its stress patterns more like those of English speech, it is clear that we are nevertheless dealing with a quite definite metre, a poetic form with a fairly limited number of stress patterns and syllables, as well as the regular demands of alliteration. But the relationships between the half-lines are very fluid, whilst the usual, familiar and linear word order of English prose tends – and almost always strives – to convey one conclusive sense. Nevertheless, with the aid of the very literal, almost word-for-word translation I have provided, we can perhaps appreciate the loose, even impressionistic way in which the untethered half-lines in *Beowulf* interact with one another to produce multiple meanings.

This basic poetic structure continues unchanged from the beginning to the end of the whole poem. There are no stanzas, and no clear subdivisions. Perhaps tantalizingly, there are indications that someone – whether it was the poet, or one of the poem's two scribes, or whoever might have written down a version of the poem which the existing manuscript was possibly copied from – thought that the poem *ought* to be broken down into sections. There are various different indications throughout the poem that some sort of sub-division of the poem was envisaged: the periodic use of capital letters; spaces sometimes left between lines; even sequences of Roman numerals. But the really curious thing is that although some of these marked-out sections (which have conventionally been called 'fitts') do correspond to the substance of the narrative – beginning with an introduction to a formal speech, for instance, or ending with a rounding-off aphorism – it can be quite impossible to see why a new 'section' has been indicated, or an old one ended. Sometimes, for example, what seem to be indications of divisions come in the middle of a speech; and the fitts vary enormously in length, from a few dozen to over a hundred lines. Their rationale remains a mystery, and they certainly don't mark natural breaks in the poem. So essentially, the poem moves from beginning to end in one continuous and unbroken succession of half-lines.

However, at the level of narrative content – what the poem is actually saying – *Beowulf* is a dramatic patchwork of different voices: speeches from the main characters, as recollections of the past, or boasts about the future, all patched together and coordinated by the narrator as the poem moves from voice to voice, and ranges back and forth through time and place. These shifts in perspective also produce marked fluctuations in the pace of the narrative. This will be the subject of the second part of this section. But I want now to

look more closely at how the poem's style and diction contribute to its effect
on the reader or listener. I will start with an analysis of the five and a half-lines
quoted above.

These lines describe the burning of Beowulf's body on his funeral pyre. Such
a graphic and detailed description of an open-air cremation is a remarkable
thing in itself: as we have seen, a medieval Christian poet would have been
very conscious that the religious orthodoxy of his day abhorred the ritual
burning of a dead body, negating as it does any possibility of physical afterlife
or bodily resurrection. I have already noted that the poet allows no trace of
disgust or condemnation to colour the description. Instead, we have a sensuous
evocation of this – to an Anglo-Saxon poet – strange and perhaps distinctively
foreign practice. There's the smell, as well as the sight, of the dark wood-smoke
curling up from the newly lit pyre, and then the dramatic roaring of the flames
as the fire takes hold. The noise of the blaze is mingled with the sound of
ritual keening, which suddenly becomes more audible as the wind fanning
the flames drops, and there's an almost synaesthetic connection between the
swirling wind and smoke, and the voices of those grieving Beowulf's death
aloud. Finally, the fire destroys the body. The last phrase in this quotation, *hat
on hreðre* (hot in the heart), has a sharp double meaning. On one level, it refers
to the physical burning of the heart within the corpse's chest cavity, but on
another, since it was conventional in Old English poetry to figure sorrow as a
burning sensation in the breast, it also conveys the attendant grief at Beowulf's
death. Here we have the crudely physical and the passionately emotional
qualities of Beowulf's cremation brought together in one simple phrase.

I want to take this – the bringing together of contrasting ideas – as my
starting point for illustrating the poet's skill in his use of poetic diction, not
just in certain purple passages, but throughout the whole poem. I will begin
with a detailed discussion of the word *banhus* (bone-house) – one of the few
kennings in *Beowulf.*

Kennings are a key aspect of Germanic poetic diction. I have already
alluded to the way these poetic circumlocutions, defined in the strictest way,
have a metaphorical dimension: *hronrad* (whale-road) is not a road, but the
sea; *beowulf* (bee-wolf) is not a wolf, but a bear; *hondscio* (hand-shoe) is
not a shoe, but a glove. The key to unlocking the riddle is to understand the

base word (road, wolf, shoe) as broadly as possible (route, animal predator, covering for a human extremity) and then redefine it as directed by the other word, the determinant – the route a whale uses; the predator associated with bees (and honey); the covering for a hand. This metaphorical shift will force the reader or listener to see the object or concept which is being denoted from a novel perspective: to a whale, the sea is the usual, mundane way of travelling. But by the same token, the idea is floated (sorry!) that the sea is an alien, and perhaps dangerous, route for humans to travel. Two worlds – the human and the animal – are brought together in the kenning.

In Old Norse poetry, kennings may be very elaborate, consisting of more than two elements. Applying a technique of extension to the Beowulfian kenning 'hand-shoe', we could extend 'shoe of the hand' to 'shoe of the perch of the hawk' – and so on. In some kennings, especially those associated with battle or warriors, it might seem that this principle of infinite regression could have no limit. 'Tree of battle' (warrior, that is, an upright living thing associated with a battle) could be extended to 'tree of the storm of Odin' (a storm being any kind of noisy, dangerous turbulence) or 'tree of the storm of the god of battle' and even, if you will, 'battle' itself as 'clangour of weapons' and so on – except that Snorri Sturluson pronounced that kennings with more than five (five!) elements would be lacking in taste, and Norse poets seem, thankfully, to have shown the way in this. But, as with the example just given, Old Norse kennings often replace an element in a kenning with the name of a god or goddess, and may therefore rely on an audience's knowledge of the god's identity, or of a mythological event, to decode the circumlocution. So, for instance, the circumlocution 'enemy of the giantess' relies on the audience's knowledge that the god Thor was celebrated for fighting giantesses. I would myself differentiate these sorts of circumlocutions from 'proper' kennings, because there is no metaphoricity: the god Thor actually *is* an enemy in relation to giantesses. But the degree of metaphoricity – the linguistic practice of calling something that which it is not – may vary in kennings, and while kennings in *Beowulf* do not go beyond a simple, two-element structure, do not make overt mythological references and are, moreover, used very sparingly, we can still trace this spectrum of metaphoricity. Thus, in the kenning *hronrad*, as I have pointed out, the sea is precisely *not* a road; there is in fact what might be called an elemental paradox – the sea as land – in the kenning. *Hondscio*, though, is slightly different: a shoe is not a glove, but the two nouns belong more closely to the same category (an item of clothing for a human extremity). Literary theorists would call the relationship between them metonymic rather than metaphorical, I think. Finally, we have the kind of circumlocution which is hardly metaphorical at all, such as the compound word *bælfyr* (literally, pyre-fire) in the lines describing Beowulf's cremation. 'Pyre-fire' actually *is* a fire, but the determinant *bæl* (pyre, a funeral pile for burning a corpse) simply specializes, rather than completely changing, the core meaning of the base word *fyr*, to denote the particular kind of fire associated with a cremation pyre.

This at last brings us to the important kenning *banhus* (bone-house). The kenning denotes a body. Although very often the relationship between the two elements of an Old English kenning can be expressed by a single compound – two words joined together to make one, for example, whale-road – we can almost always re-structure the kenning by adding the preposition 'of' – as in 'the road of the whale' (or 'the shoe of the hand'). But this doesn't quite work with *banhus*, because the body is not 'a house of bone', where the word 'of' seems to mean 'made of'. More loosely, to understand the kenning we need to understand 'a house for or associated with bone[s]' or, fully explicated, 'a sort of container which provides a house for bone[s]'. The body is imagined as housing the human skeleton.

All kennings – like all metaphors – invite us to see one thing in terms of another. Sometimes, as with *hronrad*, the connection is immediately evident. But pondering the term *banhus*, a number of figurative connections begin to emerge. Firstly, there is an unstated but evocative connection between the wood of the funeral pyre – presumably a complex but conventionally designed construction – and the bones of a skeleton, with logs as leg bones, and finer branches as ribs. The burning corpse is almost a grisly microcosm of the whole pyre. But mention of ribs directs us to an even more significant connection. The word *hus* (house) in Old English denotes not just a dwelling place, but any kind of building (think of the modern terms 'greenhouse' or 'Opera House'). The iconic burning building in *Beowulf* is of course Heorot, its conflagration always just outside the primary time of the poem's narrative, an immanent symbol of the destruction of the overreaching ambitions of the heroic world, just like events culminating in the death and cremation of Beowulf. The kenning brings together these two very different burnings by designating the burning corpse in terms of a burning building.

Kennings in *Beowulf* are inevitably significant because they are so sparingly used. But the poem is chock full of compound words. Compound words are simply long words formed by sticking together (usually no more than) two elements which are each words in themselves. In *Beowulf,* kennings take the form of compound words, unlike in Old Norse, in which kennings usually have the grammatical equivalent of the preposition 'of' (technically, the genitive case) to express the relationship between the two words – 'battle's tree' (the equivalent of 'tree of battle'), rather than the compound 'battle-tree'. But in most other Old English poems, as in *Beowulf,* there are all kinds of combined pairs of words, not just kennings, and all kinds of relationships between them. Some compound words are nouns, and some adjectives. There are even some adverbs. Thus, Grendel can be called a *mearcstapa* (borderland-wanderer) who came *under misthleoþum* ([from] under mist-slopes), attacked the *Gar-Dene* (Spear-Danes) in Heorot and carried his *wælfyllo* (slaughter-fill) away, causing Hrothgar *hreþerbealo* (heart-misery). Adjectival compounds are common too: it was when the Danes in Heorot were noisily celebrating the creation of the *wlitebeorht wang* (appearance-bright earth) established by a *sigehreþig* (victory-triumphant) god, that Grendel, a *wonsæli wer* (dark-fated person), made his *bealohycgende* (evil-intending) way to Heorot. Finally, there is a whole class of compounds in which the first word is what is known grammatically as an intensive – 'very', 'extremely', 'much'. The word *fela*, for instance, meaning many, or much, is combined with a whole series of very different adjectives to give a range of compounds including 'very wise', 'well-informed', 'extremely sad' or 'exceedingly brave'.

The most obvious effect of these compounds is that they do away with the need for 'little words' – pronouns, prepositions or particles. If *mearcstapa* (borderland-wanderer) were not expressed as a compound, we would need something along the lines of 'wanderer in the borderlands', and the direct combining of 'mist-slopes' would need the first element to be changed into an adjective ('misty') or linked more wordily to the second element ('slopes covered in mist'). The result of all these compounds in the poem is a dense, compact poetic style, heavy on nouns, adjectives and verbs, and also, in a way which mirrors how the half-lines themselves relate to one another, it tends to leave unstated and inexplicit a series of possible shades of meaning, the compound 'mist-slopes' suggesting many more possibilities than the conventional 'misty slopes', and certainly more than the prosaic 'slopes covered in mist'. The heavy use of compound words is one of the features of poetic style which most vividly characterizes Old English poems in general, and *Beowulf* in particular. It works in apparently opposite ways: to reduce the number of words used, but expand the range of meanings by leaving the precise way in which they relate to each other unspecified.

Old English poetic diction – and again, *Beowulf* in particular – is also characterized by large number of poetic synonyms for key objects and concepts – sword, battle, warrior and so on. Obviously this is useful in a poetic tradition which relies heavily on alliteration, and it is in fact hard to know whether alliteration as a poetic technique developed because of this tendency in the language to have a multitude of synonyms, or whether, conversely, the synonyms were coined to serve the needs of alliteration. But compound words are quite different: since the alliteration always falls on the first element of a compound word, it doesn't matter how many compounds the poet creates from that first element: they will all alliterate on the same first syllable, the first stressed syllable of the first element. The profusion of compound words does not, then, make alliterating any easier. But amongst the most productive first elements in *Beowulf* are words for gold, battle, heartache, sudden and fen, each giving rise to half a dozen or so compounds, the vast majority found nowhere else. One might almost recreate the poem from these first elements, and the productivity of these fundamental themes, with the resulting compounds scattered throughout the poem, knits together the poem's narrative.

The degree of repetition in the use of synonyms and compounds is clearly very great. And repetition has never been accounted a positive quality in poetry. In Old English poetry, the repetition evident in a number of poems fuelled a very persuasive and once widely accepted theory usually termed 'oral-formulaic'. This held that poems such as *Beowulf* were hardly original, individual, thoughtful compositions at all, but were orally composed using pre-existing words and phrases – and compound words – or were perhaps even extemporized, that is, made up on the spot for each performance. And it is indeed the case that a number of alliterative half-lines – formulae – recur across a number of Old English poems. For instance, the half-line *wod under wolcnum* ([he] strode [forward] under the heavens) is more or less applicable to any hero arriving anywhere.

But no two contexts are exactly the same, and using the same phrase, or formula, in different contexts has two powerful poetic effects. First of all, repeated formulae may point out shades of difference in meaning, sometimes introducing irony. The phrase *wigend weccan* (warriors [began to] waken) occurs, as we have seen, in the lines I quoted earlier describing Beowulf's funeral pyre, and how warriors kindled the fire. Almost the same phrase – *wigend weccean* – occurs a little earlier in the poem, when a messenger, bringing news of Beowulf's death to the Geats, and launching preparations for the funeral pyre, runs through all the things that will not happen now that Beowulf is dead – and they are all the good things about the heroic life which have been routinely celebrated in the poem. But now there will be no more treasure giving, no more gifts of neck rings, no more harp-playing. The verb *weccean* in this second context still means to waken, but here, the grammar is different: the narrator wonders what will waken the warriors – *wigend weccean* – if the harp falls silent. Warriors are (not) being roused, not warriors doing the kindling, though the verbs used are the same. There is a distinct suggestion that sleeping warriors will end up on a pyre, but the narrator answers his own question with a grim prediction: spears will be snatched up as warfare begins, and the sound of the harp will be replaced by the grotesque sound and scenario of a non-human messenger, the raven, a carrion bird, calling to the eagle, another corpse-feeder, to alert it to the imminent slaughter of warriors, which will provide food the two of them can share with the wolf.

These three 'beasts of battle' – the raven, the eagle and the wolf – themselves occur as a sort of extended formula in Old English and Old Norse poetry, always as macabre portents of warriors' deaths. And a number of other connections are sparked by the mention of warriors being woken: warriors sleeping in the hall, being woken by the incursion of Grendel; warriors who will shortly be sleeping the euphemistic sleep of the dead, never to be woken. There may even be an echo of the very specialized, but here very relevant, sense of the verb 'to wake' meaning to keep vigil, over a dead body. How will these warriors be waked? Thus the repetition of the formula in the scene of Beowulf's funeral pyre both recalls the violent deaths which have preceded his own, and portends the doomed future of the Beowulf's people, the Geats. This, then, is the second effect of formulaic repetition: the repetitions in the poem create a dense web of associations. As we have seen, warriors wakening a funeral fire and burning a body also conjure up the catastrophic burning of Heorot.

It is worth pausing here for a moment to ponder the evocative and yet precisely judged compound adjective the poet has probably coined to describe the spears which the waking warriors will have to snatch up: they are *morgenceald* (morning-cold). It is a striking feature of Beowulfian poetic style that like *morgenceald,* many compound words – and indeed, every one of the noun compounds I detailed above – are found nowhere else in Old English literature. The technical term for them is *hapax legomena,* and *Beowulf* is full of them. There are two issues here that need addressing. One is the obvious fact that we do not have a full record of all Old English words in circulation in the early medieval period, but only those which happen to occur in the surviving texts. Just because a word isn't found in the surviving texts doesn't mean that it didn't exist. Added to this, it is also the case that in Old English literature, certain words are only found in poetic texts, apparently constituting a distinctively 'poetic' vocabulary, and it seems likely that only a fraction of the poetry composed in early medieval England has come down to us. Nevertheless, the sheer quantity of *hapax legomena* in *Beowulf* is remarkable, and very many of them are compound words. So, for instance, the word *gold* (gold) is a perfectly common word in Old English prose as well as verse, but in *Beowulf* there are at least seven compound words, found nowhere else in Old English literature, in which *gold* is the first element ('gold-guardian', 'gold-curse', 'gold-adorned' and so on). It looks as though the *Beowulf*-poet was wonderfully freely inventive with his compound words.

The second major issue is a fundamental problem with the interpretation of compound *hapax legomena,* words which appear nowhere else. How can we know what they mean? And some hapaxes, whether compounds or not, are very hard to get any sense out of. But rather than giving up hope, and just accepting tiny blank holes in the poem, investigating their uncertain but possible meanings can suggest a whole poetic and cultural world which the poet – and probably the audience – of *Beowulf* were alert to.

Essentially, there are two ways of determining the meaning of an otherwise unknown word: considering its immediate context, and/or looking at cognate, or related, words, in other texts or languages. Using these methods, I want to examine two notoriously difficult hapaxes in *Beowulf*: *ealuscerwen* and *facenstafas*.

The context of the word *ealuscerwen* is the violent and destructive encounter between Beowulf and Grendel, an encounter which smashes up mead-benches and shakes the great hall of Heorot to its core. The poet tells us that *ealuscerwen* came upon all the Danes when this encounter took place. So it seems an obvious inference that the word means something like 'terror' or 'distress'. But if we look at the two elements of the compound, it's very hard to see which of them, if either, conveys any or all of this meaning. The first element, *ealu*, is the common Old English word for 'ale', and it's found as the first element in other unproblematic Beowulfian compounds such as 'ale-benches', 'ale-drinking' or 'ale-cups'. The second element is a little trickier, since there is no recorded verb '*scerwan' (the asterisk denotes a word which doesn't actually exist, but has been hypothesized). But there is a verb *bescerwan* which means 'to deprive of', so given that the prefix *be*- usually indicates something being taken away, it seems reasonable to suppose that *ealuscerwen* means 'provision of ale' – which would be totally fitting in the series of other *ealu*- compounds in the poem, and totally fitting in the usual context of ale-drinking in Heorot. But there is no hint of terror or distress – quite the opposite, in fact. The loose overall sense would be 'When Grendel and Beowulf fought so furiously, the Danes were certainly given ale-provision' – on the face of it, a nonsense, and completely contrary to the drift of the context.

It has been pointed out that the element *ealu* could be related to the name of a Norse rune, *alu*. Letters of the runic alphabet had names, and the runic letter corresponding to 'A' was called *alu*, which may mean something like luck or fate. So the Danes would have been given a share of luck – that is, really bad luck – when Grendel fought with Beowulf. But at this point, we need to turn to a very similar compound in another Old English poem, *Andreas*, an exciting verse narrative about St Andrew the Apostle. God has visited destruction on Andrew's enemies with a catastrophic flood, and here, as in *Beowulf,* the victims experience terror and distress – specifically, *meadoscerwen* (mead-provision) is visited on them. As with *ealuscerwen* in *Beowulf,* this is the only occurrence of the compound in Old English. There may be a savage irony in the fact that they are deluged with liquid – the flood is mead-provision in a grotesque sense, in that they got more liquid than they could cope with. At least the irony goes some way towards explaining why celebratory drink is connected with terror.

There is also a possibility that the ale or mead is a funeral drink: that providing strong drink is part of the preparation for a wake. In one Old Norse mythological poem, the god Odin anxiously quizzes a seeress about the fate in store for his beloved son Baldr. His worst fears are realized when he is informed that the goddess of the underworld, the aptly named Hel, has been preparing mead to welcome a new arrival. Finally, we should take note of another half-line in the poem about St Andrew: that Andrew's enemies experienced a *bitre beorþegu* (bitter provision of ale) referring to the flood sent by God. This may perhaps indicate that provision of strong drink might automatically – in context – indicate the opposite of the celebratory mead- or ale- or beer-drinking associated with happy times in the hall – rather as the phrase 'to get what is coming to you' always implies punishment or revenge.

Even more mysterious is the compound *facen-stafas* (literally, perhaps 'deceit-staves'), which the *Beowulf*-poet asserts are not – yet – evident in Heorot (although of course, the narrator's broad hints about treachery and violence in the future of the Danish royal house make it clear that there's a very limited period remaining in which this lack of treachery might be celebrated). Heorot, says the poet, was still a haven of amity; *facen-stafas* were not yet known. So what are these 'deceit-staves'? Although the word does not occur elsewhere in Old English poetry, it is clearly cognate with an Old Norse compound *feiknstafir.* In both languages, *stafas,* or *stafir,* are letters, or writing, and may originally have referred to a curse incised in runic lettering. But it seems from other compounds in *Beowulf* with the second element *-stafas* that the sense of staves, or letters, has faded. And in one Old Norse mythological poem, interestingly enough, Baldr's home, like Heorot, is a place where *feiknstafir* were not found: like Heorot, it was a place of harmony and fellow-feeling. But in another, later, context in Old Norse, *feiknstafir* are clearly envisaged as runic writing, wicked pagan texts as opposed to the heavenly scrolls read by angels.

I have dealt with this in such detail not to show how difficult a poem *Beowulf* is, but to give an idea of its poetical richness, even if we may never be able to access its depth and subtexts. But it's interesting, isn't it, that both of these mysterious compound hapaxes have a possible connexion with the Old Norse god Baldr, and that the first may carry a powerfully negative charge we would not necessarily expect, while the second is used in both Old English and Old Norse poetry to in the context of an Edenic haven untouched by wickedness.

By contrast, where the two building blocks of a compound – such as *morgen* (morning) and *ceald* (cold) in the compound I have already drawn attention to, *morgenceald* – are familiar and transparent in their senses, the basic meaning of the compound is clear enough, although as I have said, this compound word is evocative, and full of possibility, rather than having a straightforward and limited meaning, with one dictionary definition. Does *morgenceald* denote the naturalistic coldness of the first touch of a finger on metal? Might there be a hint of the grim poetic cliché 'cold steel'? And elsewhere in Old English verse, morning is a time of sorrow, of elegiac reflection, of the recall of past troubles. Could *morgenceald* suggest all of the above? Our problem here is not one of inferring some meaning: this compound is almost too *full* of meanings.

What we see in the poetic diction of *Beowulf* is a constantly absorbing blend of the familiar and the novel, the same words and phrases at times pointedly differentiating senses and contexts, and times drawing them together to bring out suggestive similarities – as, for instance, the way the element *wylm* ('surge', as in Modern English words compounds such as overwhelm) can be combined with words for sea, sorrow or fire, bringing together all the irresistible forces which humans cannot prevail against. The resultant texture of the poem is not, therefore, one of prolixity, but of a rich, seamless and tightly woven whole, patterned with echoes but never simply repetitions. The interconnectedness of the human and non-human world is continually expressed and emphasized through kennings and compound words, whether by shadowy, half glimpsed associations, or by sudden and shocking juxtapositions, and the poem's diction in this way underlines and expands its central themes and worldview, at the same time as tying together its far-flung times and places.

So far, this analysis of the poetic texture of *Beowulf* – its poetic diction and metre – has figured the poem as if it were a continuous whole, a steadily unrolling scroll of intricately patterned tapestry or the indivisible flow of a long stretch of water between two banks. But in fact, although there are, as I have said, no effective breaks or divisions in the poem, the flow of the narrative is not uninterrupted. Instead, it constantly changes pace and direction, the narrator skipping back and forth in time, and introducing new voices and different kinds of speaker. *Beowulf* is a kaleidoscopic patchwork of different stories from different times, places and voices, and, to continue the metaphor of the river, a flow continually looping back on itself, branching off into tributaries, and being joined sporadically by new streams from distant places and times. And to push the river image even further, its pace is always changing, at times slowing almost to a standstill, and at others, flowing rapidly and steadily. But the river image breaks down, when, as we shall see, the narrator skips over a stretch of storytime in only a few lines.

Narrative speed and the order of events

The pace of *Beowulf* changes often and sometimes dramatically. The narrator passes over some events very quickly, and lingers a little more over others. As we shall see, changes of pace are often bound up with the many stories within the main story, as the narrator turns from the history of Beowulf and his monster encounters to relate different episodes and events from other times and often far distant pasts. When these stories are presented as recitations, told by the fictional *scop* in Heorot, the pace of the poem suddenly slows, because this material takes as long to recite – and almost as long to read – as an actual recital in Heorot would have. The same effect is produced by the very many formal speeches in the poem, for instance, those delivered by Hrothgar, or Beowulf himself, or other, more minor, characters. Similarly, when characters articulate their inner feelings, their recollections of the past or misgivings about the future, they are presented as if they are speaking aloud. So between the narrator's own changes of pace, and the slowing effect of stretches of direct speech, whether recitals of story matter, formal addresses or dramatic monologues, the narration of *Beowulf* is very far from unvaried.

The poem begins, for example, with a steady, chronologically ordered account of the Danish dynasty – with, as we have seen, its foundation by the mysteriously arrived Scyld Scefing, and continued by his heirs, right up to the point at which we hear of Hrothgar's generation, and the horror of a new and dreadful inheritor of Heorot, the proud central symbol of the Danish kingdom: the monster Grendel.

Once Beowulf arrives in Heorot, the pace of the narrative slows dramatically. There are a series of speeches – for instance, the Danish coastguard interrogating the new arrivals, Beowulf introducing himself, Hrothgar's retainer reporting the Geats' arrival and Hrothgar welcoming them. As I have explained, reported speech – presented as if recited aloud – slows the pace of any narrative because it takes up as much time in the narrative as it would have taken up if actually spoken in a real-world setting. A simple illustration of this is to compare the summary statement 'Hrothgar welcomed Beowulf' with a formal speech of welcome. There is also an obvious effect of immediacy – we seem to hear a character speaking directly, unmediated by a narrator – so there is automatically an emphasis on what is being related. However, we should remember that the information in the reported speech is limited by that character's perspective and is possibly partial. There may also be a disruption to the chronological order of events, because as is the case here, although the speeches are reported in the order in which they would have happened in a real world – first the coastguard asks who the visitors are, and then Beowulf replies, for instance – some of what the characters say recall events of their past. Hrothgar, for example, remembers out loud his previous dealings with Beowulf's father. This method of bringing the poem's past into its present moment becomes more and more prominent as the poem goes on, and I shall discuss it in more detail shortly.

When Beowulf is aggressively challenged by Unferth about his youthful dealings in the contest at sea with Breca, and makes his spirited defence, the narrator, as I have already explained, is able to bring into his primary narrative – that is, Grendel's attacks on Heorot, and Beowulf's arrival – a story from much earlier on, without disturbing the chronology of events: the exchange itself happens at the 'right' time, but refers to events beyond the time of the main narrative. The episode with Unferth is also the first instance of an important theme in the poem: that different narrators – in this case, Unferth and Beowulf – may produce unsettlingly different accounts of the same events. We see this again when Beowulf recounts his adventures in the Danish kingdom to his lord Hygelac: as we have seen, he relates material which the narrator of *Beowulf* did not mention the first-time round: Grendel's sinister glove, for example, and Beowulf's grim predictions about Freawaru's marriage. It's as if we are getting the inside story of what happened, from Beowulf's own point of view (although of course both accounts are the poet's creation).

Beowulf's recap of his adventures at Hrothgar's court heralds a very dramatic change of pace in the poem. As we have seen, reported speech in any case slows down the pace of the narrative to near isochrony: a perfect equivalence between the time taken to deliver the speech in both the real and the story worlds. And further, in one sense it might be said that narrative time as measured by actions and events stops altogether when Beowulf recalls what happened in Heorot, because nothing else can happen while Beowulf is delivering his account about the past; the narrative cannot move on into its future. But having finished his speech, and presented Hygelac and Hygd with lavish gifts, Beowulf is himself rewarded by Hygelac, and all at once the narrator does a remarkable thing. Without any notice at all, the narrative future is brought crashing into its present moment: Hygelac, we are abruptly informed, is destined to be killed in battle, and his son Heardred is to be defeated by the Swedes. Beowulf inherits the kingdom of the Geats, and *He geheold tela | fiftig wintra* (he ruled it well for fifty years). More than half a century suddenly passes in the space of a handful of half-lines. This rapid transition marks a turning point in the poem. Most obviously, we are moved from Beowulf's youthful adventures in Heorot to the scene of his mature – even elderly – end of reign in Geatland. But the temporality of the narrative changes too. From the steady forward motion of the first half of the poem, whether recounting the early history of the Danish dynasty, or Beowulf's exciting adventures with Grendel and his mother, the perspective –

and, in step with this, the pace – of the narrative changes. The order in which events are presented becomes wonderfully intricate: as the narrative moves onward, the characters delve further and further back in time, and frame their recollections in speeches. Beowulf, after his fifty-year reign, and nearing the fight with the dragon and the consequent end of his life, recalls his far-off childhood and youth, and with it, the troubled history of his people, the Geats, and the enduring enmity of the Swedish Scylfings. Distant past and very imminent future – the two extremes of Beowulf's life – suddenly collide, because this old enmity is predicted to arise again – to be re-kindled, one might say – once Beowulf, the powerful leader, is dead. Beowulf himself recalls the aggression and brutality of the Swedes, who killed Hygelac's son, Heardred; this is what led to Beowulf, Hygelac's nephew, taking over the Geatish throne. Beowulf claims that the Swedes were at that time *frome fyrdhwate | freode ne woldon* (aggressive [and] warlike | they didn't want peace). And so when, a little later in the poem, a messenger, announcing Beowulf's death to the Geats, warns that the Swedes are now certain to make an attack on the Geats, we automatically suppose that these warlike Swedes have always been the aggressors, and will again be taking advantage of weakness in the kingdom of the Geats. Beowulf himself suggests that this is a likely tactic, by citing events from even further back in time, explicitly linking the death of Hrethel the Geat – another old king – with a Swedish attack and the consequent killing of Hrethel's son Hæthcyn, a whole generation before the killing of Heardred. Hæthcyn has accidentally killed his own brother, so he would seem a very damaged heir to the throne, and for this reason he and the whole Geatish people might be obvious victims of the Swedes' aggression. But the messenger's version of this enmity between Geats and Swedes tells a different story: according to his account, the Swedish attack which led to Hæthcyn's death was not unprovoked Swedish aggression, but was in fact undertaken in vengeance against the Geats for their own unprovoked acts of hostility on the border, initiated by Hæthcyn's overconfident belligerence. The messenger's version of events does not present the Geats as innocent victims of overbearing neighbours. Here we have the age-old 'who started it?' debate, as familiar to a contemporary audience, no doubt, as it is to us now, in the twenty-first century. And then, just as now, there are as many answers as there are voices.

Throughout the first half of the poem, action-packed narrative – Beowulf's encounters with Grendel, and his mother – is punctuated and framed by much slower paced stretches of direct speech, as Hrothgar, for instance, delivers his celebrated 'sermon' to Beowulf, or Beowulf, home in Geatland, recaps – with significant differences – his adventures at Heorot. Action and reflection alternate. But after the sudden and rapid shift from young to old Beowulf, which functions like a hinge between the two parts of the poem, there is only one action to be related: the dragon fight. The rest of the narrative is recollection, reflection and grim prophecy. These inset speeches are put into the mouths of the characters, and are necessarily limited by their knowledge and outlook and experiences. But the narrator – and ultimately the poet – has knowledge far exceeding that of the characters in the poem. I turn now to explore how 'our' narrator uses and displays this knowledge.

What the narrator knows

The first thing to note here is that the narrator himself assumes the role of a *scop*, or oral court poet, initially dangling the possibility that he is about to recite a stirring poem about the Spear-Danes' heroic deeds and purporting to address an audience familiar with this sort of material. The use of the pronoun 'we' in the very first line of the poem ('Listen! We have heard of the Spear-Danes' glory …') situates narrator and audience in the same time-frame – indeed, in the same space, as if in the same hall, perhaps. And so we can imagine ourselves to be in this fictional setting, playing the role of an audience just as the narrator plays the role of *scop*. There is a Chinese box structure to the poem: the narrator acting as a *scop* tells a story (*Beowulf*) in which another *scop* (in Heorot) tells stories. And all these stories are set in the past.

Most conventional narratives are recounted in the past tense, and many are explicitly about a particular stretch of time in the past, as in the familiar opening to favourite stories: 'Once upon a time … '. Authors – and authoritative narrators who are not themselves part of the story, like the narrator of *Beowulf* – can see the whole story from the outside, from beginning to end, in their mind's eye, and from this stance they can make hints to their audience about what is yet to happen in the story. I have to say that I am not wholly convinced by authors who claim that they don't know how their narratives will develop, or what will happen to their characters, but 'make it up as they go along'. It seems to me that an author, using a narrator to tell a story set in the past, must know how the story develops and indeed ends, even before beginning it. And further, the narrator, looking back on the whole era, can refer to events which happened even before the story in hand began, or to ones which will happen after it has finished. This past or future may be made up – part of the imagined heroic world of the whole poem – or historical, part of the actual setting, in time and geographical space, of the story. Sometimes, such allusions can be put in the mouths of characters in the poem, who recall past events or gloomily confide their fears for the future. But at other times, allusions to past and future are articulated in the narrative voice – the imaginary voice we hear delivering the story to us – and there is direct communication between narrator and audience, over the heads, as it were, of the characters in the story. In both of these ways, whether through the voices of characters in the story or in the narrative voice itself, the *Beowulf*-poet moves backwards and forwards in time from the present moment of the main narrative. Each of these voices has its own perspective on the action of the poem and the storyworld around it, but the narrator, for reasons I've just explained, knows more than the characters. Timebound as they are in the storyworld, they may be shown as able to recall or know something about the past. It is Hrothgar, for example, who contrasts Beowulf with the evil king Heremod – Heremod being a Danish, if distant, figure from the past, whose villainous reputation Hrothgar might plausibly have heard about. But the characters in *Beowulf* cannot know their own future, although they may predict and fear it. However, the narrator's perspective is that of an intelligence situated right outside, and apart from, the storyworld. This narrator controls the pace of the story, lingering on some episodes, and racing through others, creating tension, variety and focus, as we have seen. But further, the narrator's voice manages the course of events from a perspective of virtual omniscience, seeing the whole stretch of time relevant to his story, both in the real, historical world and the imagined storyworld. It is from this perspective that the narrator is able to comment on the future of the narrative, or show characters unaware of their fates, or place their parlous situations in the context of other such situations in the heroic, legendary and indeed biblical past.

Many commentators on *Beowulf* have remarked on what is often called the 'fatalism' of the poem – that is, the sense that characters and events are predetermined, that there is nothing the characters can do to avert their fates, that they cannot exercise free will. In fact, such supposed fatalism is simply a consequence of the narrative of *Beowulf* being set in the past – nothing could have happened differently because this is what *did* happen. This doesn't mean, by the way, that everything in *Beowulf* is historical actuality (though it may be that some events and characters – but not the monsters, obviously! – did actually exist). Rather, it means that a widely known fictional world can no more have its ending changed than history can – as I explained near the beginning of this book, it's a serious step to alter the main outlines of a Shakespeare play, for instance, whether or not the play represents actual history accurately. But what gives *Beowulf* such a powerful sense that the characters are unknowingly trapped by their unknown fates is the way the narrator continually expresses his external perspective on the events of the poem, intervening in the narrative to point out their ignorance of what is coming to them, just around the corner of time.

I have already commented on some of these interventions. At the beginning of the poem, for example, when Hrothgar has been credited with building his magnificent hall Heorot, the narrator describes its enormous size, and its wide gables, and without any notice remarks – as it were, to the audience or reader – that *heaðowylma bad | laðan liges | ne wæs hit lenge þa gen | þæt se ecghete | aðumsweoran | æfter wælniðe | wæcnan scolde* ([it] suffered hostile-surges | of malicious flame | nor was it to be far off | that blade-enmity | between son-in-law and father-in-law | after mortal hate | was to awaken).

The allusion is to future violence when Hrothgar marries off his daughter Freawaru to Ingeld, a prince of the Heathobards, with whom the Danes had long been feuding. The marriage was meant to cement a truce between the two peoples, but as we have seen, Beowulf himself predicts that the peace will not hold, and communal celebrations – perhaps even the wedding feast itself – will descend into violence. This is all in the narrative future of the poem, as far as the Danes are concerned, and they cannot know that this is what the future holds for them. But the narrator knows, even from the very beginning of the poem, and chooses to allude to this calamity at precisely the highest point of the Danish King Hrothgar's so far triumphant reign.

Certainly, this and other similar interventions cast the Danes as unknowing and fated, while the narrator and we as audience, or readers, know better. There's a lesson for all of us here too: that it's not wise to expect success to last, and that good fortune may easily give way to bad and is no guarantee of future happiness. There may even be a note of moral censure in the narrator's placing of this allusion to the future right next to the account of building Heorot in all its magnificence: that pride goes before a fall. And finally, the allusion is no casual aside. The hostile flames, whether consuming bodies or buildings, connect with other references to burnings in *Beowulf,* and the use here of that evocative verb *wæcnan* (to kindle, or awaken), recalls dead warriors who will now never awaken, dormant feuds which certainly will, funeral pyres which will be kindled, and grim new dawns. And finally, the Danes will be over*whelmed* – this time not by battle or sorrow, but by fire.

The other trouble lying in wait for the Danes is a bloody power struggle for the Danish throne between Hrothgar's sons and his nephew Hrothulf. The narrator's hints about this aspect of the future of the Danish dynasty are so cloaked that it's not totally certain what he's alluding to, and Scandinavian sources do not portray Hrothulf as a treacherous usurper, but as a great leader. Nevertheless, the narrator makes a pointed remark immediately following the Danish celebrations after the defeat of Grendel: that in Heorot *sæton suhtergefæderen | þa gyt wæs hiera sib ætgædere | æghwylc oðrum trywe* (uncle and nephew [Hrothgar and Hrothulf] sat | there was as yet still peace between them | each loyal to the other). In an even more oblique aside earlier in the poem, the narrator describes Hrothgar and Hrothulf drinking mead in Heorot, but undercuts the scene by remarking that *facenstafas* (a compound word of uncertain sense but associated with deceit or betrayal, as I discussed in the previous section) were certainly not – well, *not at that time,* at least – evident amongst the Danes. I can well imagine a live recitation of *Beowulf* in which the slyly knowing narrator leans forward towards the audience, confidentially speaking from behind his hand. We need to see these asides in the context of Wealhtheow's ostensibly confident – but more probably anxious – speech about Hrothulf's loyalty to Hrothgar's sons, and it's worth noting too that the first aside is coolly set between a mention of Wealhtheow pouring drink for the uncle and nephew who still trust one another, and an apparently casual mention of Unferth, who stands accused of committing the archetypal treachery by killing his own brothers.

Narrative interventions which hint at future calamities do imbue *Beowulf* with a sense of doom-laden inevitability. However, they do not necessarily tell us something we may not already know. Several times, for example, the narrator intervenes in his account of Beowulf's fight against the dragon to point out that Beowulf will not survive the encounter. But for one thing, we know that Beowulf is by now an old man, and that he has determined to face the dragon without the help of his warrior retinue. Death is certainly on the cards for him. And perhaps more significantly, the fact that Beowulf died defending his people against a dragon may well have been perfectly familiar to a medieval audience – as, indeed, it is to anyone, medieval or modern, who has heard or read *Beowulf* before. That Hrothgar's daughter's marriage will end in disaster was probably not news to a contemporary audience either, for as we have seen, the name of her husband, Ingeld, was invoked by the churchman Alcuin as a figure his monks ought not to be listening to stories about. In fact, some narratorial asides actually reassure an audience that a calamity is *not* about to happen – as when we are told that even though his companions do not expect Beowulf to survive the encounter with Grendel, the Lord (*dryhten*) was weaving a war-victory for him, as if God were one of the valkyries in Old Norse tradition, weaving the cloth of fate for one of Odin's warriors.

What, then, are the effects of the narrator's asides to an audience? I think one of the primary impressions is the sense that here we have an authoritative narrator in command of his material, confident and knowing about his subject matter. Danes and Geats may not know their future, but the narrator knows it – and their past, how they got to where they are and how they will end up. It is instructive to recall how the fictional *scop* in Heorot is described: 'a carrier of tales, | a traditional singer deeply schooled | in the lore of the past', to quote Seamus Heaney's translation of the relevant lines. It is significant that this description – which fits so well our own narrator – carries the implication that subject matter might be well known and traditional, and that success lay in knowing the material and being able to transmit it skilfully. There is a good deal of evidence that in medieval times the re-telling of old stories was more prestigious than the novelty of new ones. And it is significant too that the ideal *scop*, according to the next few lines, had to have mastery over words and rhythm when re-telling an old story: *word oþer fand | soðe gebunden* ([he] found new words | correctly linked in metre).

(iv) The *scop*

The narrator's superior knowledge is not of course limited to his overview of the past and the future of the primary narrative. This primary narrative is also embellished with allusions to characters and events from outside the main storyworld – learned asides which briefly halt the narrative but enrich the audience's understanding of the poem's background, or remind the audience of the narrator's learning. One example is the remark that the magnificent golden torque which Wealhtheow gave to Beowulf was the greatest treasure since the legendary necklace of the Brísings – a reference I mentioned in the earlier discussion of the *Beowulf*-poet's knowledge of Old Norse myth and legend. The repeated detail about Grendel's relationship with the Cain tradition falls into the same category of a narrative aside above the heads, as it were, of the characters in the poem, who of course cannot be expected to know biblical or apocryphal material. The narrator's pointed contrast between good Queen Hygd of the Geats, and wicked Queen Modthrytho is another example. But like his fictional audience, the fictional *scop* in Heorot cannot know about biblical, Christian traditions (so there is of course dramatic irony about the Christian echoes in his reported account of creation). Two longer stories, presented as recited by this 'deeply schooled' but timebound figure, are presented as narrative events in themselves, part of the fictional evocation of life (and death) in Heorot. I have explored the first of these – the story of how the legendary hero Sigemund killed a dragon – in my discussion of Old Norse (or perhaps more broadly Germanic) themes known and used by the poet; again, as with the Brísing necklace, we are benefitting from the poet's knowledge of such themes, whether delivered by 'our' narrator or by a fictional *scop* in the poem. These longer poems within the main poem used to be known as the 'digressions' in *Beowulf*, as if they bore little or no relation to the rest of the poem. But there is in fact a double relation between 'digression' and primary narrative. What seems at first sight to be a flattering comparison between Beowulf and the celebrated dragon-slaying hero Sigemund is very obviously connected to the substance of the poem, and this may be how the fictional audience in Heorot received the story. However, as we have seen, a closer look raises awkward questions about how admirable a hero Sigemund actually was, and about his relationship with his nephew Fitela. In fact, it prompts us to question the construction of heroism and fame in the poem as whole. In its narrative context – the aftermath of Beowulf's triumph over Grendel, and part of the Danish victory festivities – the subtext of this recitation must strike us as a very odd way to celebrate, and its placing immediately following Beowulf's victory is part of the poet-narrator's art.

The second example of a recitation within a recitation is the tragic story of Queen Hildeburh, who married Finn, King of the Frisians, and lost both son and brother when her own Danish people launched an attack on the Frisians. This story is told in the same context as the Sigemund account, as part of the Danes' victory celebrations for Beowulf. But although its surface relevance to the poem as a whole is not in doubt, being a story about Danish warfare, its underlying message, the grief and loss associated with tribal feuding, is another strange and challenging choice for celebratory entertainment. There is again a double perspective here: the unsettling subtext of both the Sigemund and the Hildeburh recitations is evident to an attentive real-world audience, whether to us, in the present day, or to a medieval one – but not, apparently, to the fictional audience of the Danes in Heorot. The Danes are described in the poem as enjoying and appreciating the story of Hildeburh – there is no suggestion that they were discomfited by its implications. But we as audience can see the darker implications of the episode, which the narrator of *Beowulf* carefully emphasizes.

The episode is introduced as being a story about the sons of Finn, and how Hnæf, Hildeburh's brother, was killed in Frisia. This ought to be enough in itself to give the Danes in Heorot pause for thought: it is the lamentable history of a Danish leader killed by his enemies. However, the *Beowulf*-poet goes further by explicitly framing this story as a pointless tragedy for Hildeburh, an innocent victim of the violence. Hildeburh herself is placed at the centre of the account, and events are even seen from her point of view. Although it is usually supposed that the story is part of the fictional *scop's* recitation (as the italics and subtly altered metre of the Heaney translation imply, for instance), in fact without any original punctuation in the manuscript, it's not entirely clear whether the account of what happened to Hildeburh is the direct speech of fictional *scop's* actual recitation, or a very partial re-telling of the story by 'our' narrator. Although Hnæf's death is an important part of the episode, to summarize the story as being *be Finnes eaferum* (about the sons of Finn) is baffling, since only one son is mentioned, and he is dead before the episode begins, that is, at the point at which Hildeburh becomes aware of her terrible loss. But as with the poem's opening lines, in which a story about the glory of the Spear-Danes is apparently heralded, the story of Finnsburh which follows is not what its introduction might lead us to expect.

The contrast between the ambience in Heorot and the *scop's* account of the violent and tragic events in Finn's Frisian hall could not be more pointed: in Heorot *þær wæs sang ond sweg | samod ætgædere* (singing and music | both together); the word for 'pleasure' is repeated in two compound words, *gomenwudu* (pleasure-wood, that is, the harp) and *healgamen* (hall-pleasure); and the audience are all seated *æfter medobence* (along [the] mead-bench). But as we have seen, there is no indication that the Danes are disturbed by the implication that a hall can be a place of grief and suffering as well as celebration. And after the bleak recitation, their pleasure – that word *gamen* again – is apparently undiminished, and the drink is passed around again to the sound of their revelry. But the narrator is not blind to their blithe imperviousness. As we have seen, he notes that when Wealhtheow comes to sit down after the drinks have been replenished, she sits between Hrothgar and his nephew, who are – *as yet* – still trusting allies. And there's that mention of Unferth, too, embodying the spirit of Cain, a human avatar of the monster who has just been dispatched, for Unferth too was a fratricide.

The subject matter of the Hildeburh story – a woman caught up in the enmity between the family she has married in to, and the family she was born in to – is familiar not only from *Beowulf* itself (as Hrothgar's daughter Freawaru is envisaged to be awaiting the very same fate, her marriage to be a doomed attempt to heal a feud between the Danes and the Heathobards) but also from various other sites in Germanic heroic literature. The celebrated Old Norse heroine Guðrún is shown being married off to Attila the Hun, who is so keen to get his hands on Guðrún's brothers' treasure that he invites both of them, Gunnarr and Högni, to his fortress in Mirkwood, where he murders them when they will not disclose the whereabouts of the treasure. As you may read in the eddic poems which relate Guðrún's tragic story, she in turn murders her husband, and Medea-like, kills her own sons. And in the oldest Old Norse poem which has come down to us, 'Ragnarsdrápa', one of the scenes painted on a ceremonial shield depicts the story of Hildeburh's near-namesake Hild, who is abducted by her lover Heðinn and, perhaps after a peace mission gone wrong, suffers bereavement when her father fights Heðinn to get her back.

Hildeburh's fate echoes the stories of these other women. Although Danish, she is married to Finn, a Frisian King, and her brother, Hnæf, leader of a Danish force, is suddenly attacked on a visit to Frisia. The full story remains a little bit obscure: Hnæf is killed, but it seems that the Danes have done enough damage to the Frisian forces to prevent decisive victory. An awkward compromise is reached: Finn offers Hengest, the warrior now apparently leading the Danish contingent, a share of his Frisian hall space, and each side promises to abide by a truce, the terms being that no-one in the hall will provoke anyone from the opposing side by making taunts about the compromise. The dead are cremated on a funeral pyre – Hildeburh's half-Frisian son alongside his uncle Hnæf – and the remaining Danes spend a tense winter with Finn in Frisia. But ironically, when spring at last arrives, allowing the Danes to escape this humiliating confinement, Hengest is provoked to launch a revenge attack on Finn. Finn is killed, and the victorious Danes return home, carrying all the usual spoils of war, including Hildeburh herself.

As well as the details of the story itself – the woman caught between warring tribes, and like the other female victims, doubly bereaved; a vengeful feud first suppressed and then awakened; a woman returned to her people, like the Swedish king Ongentheow's old queen after his victory over the Geats, recounted towards the end of the poem; even a vividly grisly cremation – the whole manner of telling it is completely consonant with the rest of *Beowulf.*

In terms of metre and poetic diction, Hildeburh's story in the original poem is completely indistinguishable from the rest of the narrative, and plays its part in the echoing of compound words and the repeated metaphors which characterize the poem. It is in the morning after the night fighting that Hildeburh suffers her overwhelming grief, chiming with the association of morning and misery we have seen elsewhere in the poem. The description of the funeral pyre prefigures the cremation of Beowulf himself at the end of the poem: the pyre is similarly constructed and decked with battle-armour. But when the flames do their horrifying work, the details recall the other kinds of death in the poem: *bengeato burston | þonne blod ætsprang* (wound-slashes burst open | then blood sprang out), recalling the moment when Grendel's arm was torn from his torso; and *lig ealle forswealg* (flame swallowed up everything), just as Grendel's mother devoured sleeping warriors in Heorot. This fire is summed up as *gæsta gifrost* (greediest of spirits), a phrase which recalls both monsters, with the flames naturally prefiguring the depredations of the fire-breathing dragon. The end result of the cremation is that *wæs hira blæd scacen* (their glory passed away) – that word *blæd* first used in *Beowulf* about all that was fine about the long-gone Danish kings at the very beginning of the poem. The cremation is presented as bleakly denying and apparently undoing the possibility of a lasting reputation celebrated in heroic poetry. If we were in any doubt about the cruel pointlessness of warfare, then Hildeburh's tragic command to have her son cremated alongside his Danish uncle makes the point with unequivocal finality. In Germanic tradition, there was a special bond between a man and his sister's son. Hnæf and his nephew are united only in death. There's even, perhaps, an echo of the Old Norse story of Sigurðr and Brynhildr, parted in life, but cremated on the same pyre.

In the spring, when the remaining Danes launch a successful counter-attack, and Finn is killed, Hildeburh is returned to her people. As with Ongentheow's elderly wife, we cannot help but wonder whether she would have been glad about her anticipated homecoming. It does not seem to have mattered enough for us to be told, and we never learn what happened to

Ongentheow's wife when the tables were turned on him and Hygelac's forces overcame his own.

Not the *Beowulf* poem

It remains a mystery why a story introduced as being about the sons of Finn and the fall of Hnæf should be so little about the sons, centring instead on the grief of their mother Hildeburh. One possible response is that the story as summarized was actually well known to the *Beowulf*-poet and his audience – it does, after all, end with the counter-attack from the Danes and victory over Finn, and so might easily have been part of the repertoire of both the fictional *scop* and the narrator of the poem. If it were indeed a familiar tale, then the *Beowulf*-poet is demonstrating something about narrative that we have seen elsewhere in the poem: that the same set of events can be told a very different way if related from a different perspective. It is as if the narrator of *Beowulf* were saying, 'The *scop* in Heorot told them a story we all know about the sons of Finn and the fall of Hnæf. But what do you think that story would be like if told from Hildeburh's point of view?'

And as it happens, we do – just – have another version of the Finnsburg story. Usually known as 'The Fight at Finnsburg', or 'The Finnsburg Fragment', these forty-odd lines of Old English poetry were already a fragment when the eighteenth-century scholar George Hickes transcribed them from a manuscript leaf now lost – in fact, it was probably lost not too long after Hickes transcribed the lines on it. It begins, and ends, midline, and we have no way of knowing how much of the original poem has survived, and how the narrative would have begun or ended. But even from these few lines, we can see that in spite of the obviously related subject matter, this must have been a very different poem from *Beowulf*. Indeed, the opening lines of the Fragment almost define themselves against *Beowulf*: *ne her draca ne fleogeð | ne her ðisse halle | hornas ne byrnað* (there's no flying dragon here | nor here [in] this hall | do gable-ends burn).

It's not easy to reconstruct the full story of what happened at Finnsburg from the Fragment, let alone relate it to the Finnsburg episode in *Beowulf*. It begins with the sudden, panicked realization that the light which one of Hnæf's look-outs has spotted is not a dragon, or a burning hall, or even dawn breaking, but an army advancing in moonlight. The beasts of battle, wolf and raven, or eagle, which we came across in *Beowulf*, are imagined as making their sinister presence felt with howls and shrieks, and there is the unmistakable sound of weapons clashing. We are plunged right into the present moment of the attack, very far from the almost meditative post-fighting mood of the Episode. It seems that the Danish defenders are inside a hall, for arrangements are quickly made for the doors to be manned. Hnæf urges on his warriors to fight bravely and is answered by proud promises of valour.

There is fierce fighting, and warriors fall. But the fighting is described as noble and honourable – there is no sense here of the waste of brave and often young lives. The younger warriors are commended for fulfilling so loyally the bargain of the lord-retainer relationship: their leader Hnæf gives them gifts, and they repay him with their lives. There is no pause in the breathless narrative for any rumination on the killing, on the part of the narrator or those involved. The fighting is said to go on for five days, and just before the Fragment breaks off, a commander, perhaps Finn, questions a wounded warrior about how those inside are bearing up. This may be the cue for the establishment of an uneasy truce, the stalemate we hear about in the *Beowulf* episode, with the first attack over, the dead waiting to be cremated and the tense winter of hall-sharing still to come.

Most scholars have identified the Fragment as part of a heroic lay, a brief dramatic poem about warfare and its imperatives: bravery, loyalty, fatalism and disdain for death. The narrator of the Fragment admits no qualms about what is happening, and in his persona as *scop*, he roundly applauds the way the warriors fulfil their own irresistible roles: *ne gefrægn ic næfre wurþlicor* (I have never heard [it done] more worthily). There is no comparison to be made with other conflicts or fighters, and no Christian perspective. The battle creates noise, clamour and death, but there are no lessons to be learned, at least as far as this Fragment goes. The survival of the Fragment is a tiny and at the same time major coincidence in the mysterious history of *Beowulf*. But nothing could show more clearly the distinctive qualities of *Beowulf*, a complex, learned, meditative elegy for the heroic past, rather than a loud and dramatic celebration of it.

3

Post-Medieval Meanings

Earliest audience

Beowulf has been read in many different ways. By 'read', I mean interpreted and understood, not, narrowly, either recited out loud or read silently and individually from a written copy. We can only guess at the ways in which the poem's first audiences received it, although it is most likely that it was delivered orally, as a recitation, and that it had a communal audience of listeners. Possibly the speaker recited the poem from memory, in an animated way, or perhaps could read it from a manuscript, although that would be physically cumbersome and would surely detract from the drama of the narrative. But maybe a literate cleric read it out to an audience in a great hall just like Heorot, a mixed audience of aristocrats, clerics, merchants, warriors and their families, and all those who served the hall, such as craftspeople and cooks, cleaners and cowherds. Or – speaking of cowherds – perhaps the monks were indulging in some dinner-time period drama, to which humbler members of the wider monastic community might also be welcome, as we saw from the story of Caedmon, the cowherd who fled the hall because he didn't have a party-piece to perform. An audience like this might well enjoy pretending that the monastery refectory was a sort of Heorot, and relish a reconstruction of just the kind of recitation they knew from other poems, or from cultural memory, if not actual experience. This would be a form of audience participation, as we see in some medieval drama, in which the real-world audience watching the play is directly addressed by figures such as Herod, and would be encouraged to respond accordingly, as if they were a biblical crowd.

It has sometimes been claimed that the length, complexity and poetic artistry of a poem like *Beowulf* tell against oral delivery, especially recitation from memory, and certainly rule out oral or impromptu composition. But it's nearly impossible to overestimate the feats which memory-trained people in a largely illiterate or only recently literate society might be able to perform, and the likelihood is that such ability is mostly underestimated, because of our own position in a society in which the memorialization of words and numbers is very (and increasingly) rarely called upon. The recitation of complex narratives, and the enjoyment and analysis of them by an audience, was probably no great trouble to people in the early Middle Ages. Two other practical points deserve mention. Firstly, it is possible that *Beowulf* was not so much recited as sung – perhaps to a musical accompaniment – or perhaps chanted in some way. And secondly, and finally, we don't have a clear or certain guide to how the language of the poem was pronounced. Nowadays, there is amongst scholars a generally accepted way of pronouncing Old English, but it's hard to say just how close that might be to how the poet heard it in his head, or how a performer recited it to an audience. And since we don't know which part of the country the poem was first composed in, we can't even imagine the effect of a local accent, although it seems likely that the basic language of the poem represented a sort of prestige dialect used throughout the Anglo-Saxon kingdoms for elite poetry.

Everything about the early medieval origins, performance and reception of *Beowulf* rests on speculation. Some have argued that the style of *Beowulf,* such as the narrator's use of the first person in phrases such as the opening one, 'We have heard … ', is a good indicator of an oral origin for the poem, but it has been clearly demonstrated that supposed stylistic markers of traditional, oral literature were copied by authors who were in fact translating texts from learned Latin originals. Presumably Anglo-Saxon clerics enjoyed heroic literature in some form, or Alcuin of York would not have had to rail against their interest in stories about Ingeld. It has been suggested that Alcuin's reference to Ingeld – 'What has Ingeld to do with Christ?' – is not to the figure of that name, but to a poem named after him, which would bring us closer to *Beowulf,* but there is no more evidence than this one tantalisingly brief allusion. The question that remains in my own mind is whether *Beowulf* is typical of the kind of literature

Alcuin was warning against or, by contrast, was itself a response to the church's condemnation of it: *Beowulf*, as we have seen, has rather a lot to do with Christ, even though he is never mentioned by name, and the moral tenor of the poem contrasts very markedly with the full-throated celebration of heroic warrior ethics we find in *The Fight at Finnsburg*.

Beowulf was copied into its sole surviving manuscript towards the end of what is conventionally regarded as the Anglo-Saxon period, early in the half century preceding the Norman Conquest in 1066. That someone believed it worth the considerable investment of having two scribes copy out a long poem on expensive vellum should tell us something about the regard in which it was held. But it's impossible to know whether it was written out for contemporary performance, or was an attempt to preserve a time-honoured but already almost out-of-date example of the literary heritage of the Anglo-Saxons, when the whole heroic tradition was nearing its end. Some mistakes in the manuscript are good evidence that it was a copy of an earlier written source, but there is no trace of any prior version.

The existing manuscript contains four other texts as well as *Beowulf*, and these texts ought to shed light on how those responsible for collecting them together regarded *Beowulf*. But they are at first sight bafflingly disparate works. They are all in Old English, but the first three are not poems at all, but prose texts. There's a fragment of a saint's life – *The Passion of St Christopher* – and a complete prose work, *The Wonders of the East*, about monsters in far-off lands, and packed with extraordinary illustrations of weird and wonderful creatures. It's translated from a Latin original and is the only illustrated text in the manuscript. It has been suggested that finding *Beowulf* in a manuscript alongside *The Wonders of the East* might mean that the poem was notable first and foremost for its monsters. The story of St Christopher also features a monster – St Christopher himself, who is a giant, in the sense of being prodigiously tall. In another Old English version of his life, he is depicted even more monstrously, as having a dog's head, although this aspect of him is missing from the fragment in the *Beowulf* manuscript.

The third prose text in the manuscript is *The Letter of Alexander to Aristotle*, also a version of a Latin text. As its title suggests, it purports to be an account by Alexander the Great himself, focusing on his travels in India, where he too encounters monstrous creatures. Next in the manuscript compilation comes *Beowulf* itself, and then the other poem, an Old English version of the biblical story of Judith and Holofernes. As with many early medieval saints' lives and biblical paraphrases, there's a good deal of violence and traditional heroism – even the beasts of battle, oddly out of place in a biblical desert instead of a chilly, wooded northern Europe, put in an appearance – and Judith succeeds in decapitating Holofernes, which has been held to be a link with *Beowulf*, although Holofernes is monstrous only in the moral sense. So these five texts – two on Christian subjects and three on secular ones – are perhaps not as absolutely disparate as might at first appear. But whatever prompted the inclusion of them all in one manuscript doesn't give us a clear idea of what *Beowulf* meant to an Anglo-Saxon audience at the end of the tenth or the beginning of the eleventh centuries. And before that, as we have seen, apart from tentative speculation about its possible influence on other Old English poems, there is no hard evidence of its existence whatsoever.

Early Modern audiences

This silence was to continue for another seven centuries. In the year 1700 CE and for a few years following, the antiquarian and librarian Humphrey Wanley was sending out letters to various scholars enquiring about a poem he had found concerning a hero called Beowulf, the Scyldings, and – in a query particularly directed to a Swedish scholar – 'some of your Suedish princes'. But no-one seems to have known anything about any such poem or its hero, and '*Beowulph*' got scarcely a mention from other eighteenth-century scholars in England, although Wanley had noted its existence in his catalogue of 'old Northern books' in 1705, which described their contents. This particular book was made from two different manuscripts which had been bound together: a manuscript of various Old English texts and then the manuscript which is now usually called the Nowell Codex, that is, the manuscript containing *Beowulf* and the other four texts I've discussed. It was called the Nowell Codex after the sixteenth-century scholar Laurence Nowell, who wrote his name and the date – 1563 – on the first page. Puzzlingly, several people had read this codex before Wanley sent out his enquiries, and had noted the existence of the other texts in it, and yet none of them mentioned *Beowulf*. But it is worth pausing to note how Wanley described the poem: 'a most noble treatise written in poetry', and, in the Index to his catalogue, 'the history of Beowlf [*sic*] king of the Danes, in Dano-Saxon verse'.

Confusion surrounding who and what the poem was about persisted for a long time. But those two references to Danishness in Wanley's catalogue meant that Scandinavian scholars, ransacking libraries and private manuscript collections for texts that could tell them about their own national origins, became interested, even if English readers did not (one Danish scholar openly expressed surprise that no-one in England had ever tried to edit the poem). And the idea that it was originally a Danish poem, and that either its language was an early form of Danish, or that it had been translated from Danish into Old English, also persisted. In its early life, then, *Beowulf* was an orphaned text, unclaimed by the English and adopted by Danes. When the time came for German scholars to follow their leaders in their politically dubious quest to establish a pan-Germanic culture, this supposedly Anglo-Danish poem was swiftly appropriated, and German scholarship dominated the reception of *Beowulf* throughout the nineteenth century.

So *Beowulf* was never really established as an English epic for readers more general than antiquarians and scholars. German scholars made enormous progress with elucidating the poem, especially with regard to language and metre, but also focused on all those difficult, and sometimes unanswerable, questions which I have purposefully sidestepped in this book: issues of date, authorship, provenance and sources. And of course, *Beowulf* never could be accessible to a wider audience until it began to be translated, and translation, as we shall see, brought and still brings its own difficulties.

Translations

The aim of the first translators of the poem was simply to give readers an idea of what the poem is like – as when selected short stretches of it were offered in translation – or what the whole poem is about, which, as we have seen, was not clarified for quite some time. The very first translation of the whole poem which made it accessible to English readers was in fact made by an Icelander – Grímur Jónsson Thorkelin – in 1815, and he translated individual half lines into literal Latin. It still didn't give a very good idea of the poem's storyline, though. Thorkelin had transcribed the poem from the original manuscript, but there were errors in the transcription, and he didn't really manage to make much sense of the Old English and therefore the narrative. He failed, for instance, to recognize most of the proper names in the poem. He was also one of those who believed that the poem was originally Danish, and had been translated into Old English. The influential Danish scholar N. F. S. Grundtvig was next to translate the whole poem, but he translated it into Danish, which was no help to most English scholars. At least he got the story right, having properly learnt Old English. However, he had ambitions for *Beowulf* beyond simply giving access to its basic storyline. Grundtvig's idea was to present the poem as a national epic, polished up and tidied up to conform with classical notions of literary unity. He has been called the first person ever to understand what *Beowulf* is about, and he very enthusiastically praised its artistry and inspiring spirit. But this was not by any means a literal translation. Grundtvig wanted to remake the poem in the very positive image he had of it. This, then, is the point at which we must look at what has constituted 'translation', and how different translations of *Beowulf* reflect the differing aims of its translators, and needs of readers.

I have already drawn attention to the kind of translation project whose object is simply to make the literal meaning of the poem accessible to those who cannot read it in the original. (Incidentally, a literal meaning – the bare facts of the storyline – may not be the only kind of meaning the poem has to offer. Readings of the poem as an allegory of something else have been put forward. Even Grundtvig was tempted to understand the poem as an allegory of Denmark bullied by its overbearing neighbour Germany, and German scholarship suggested that Grendel's depredation of Heorot was an allegory of the North Sea attacking a vulnerable coastline. In these days of climate change and rising sea levels, this sounds like a curiously contemporary allegory. More recent literary criticism has advanced all kinds of Freudian interpretations of Beowulf's wrestling match with Grendel's mother, and of the significance of all the failing or broken swords in the poem.)

The most literal kind of translation – a word for word rendering – is rarely feasible. In the Anglo-Saxon period, when religious texts, and especially the Bible, were being translated into English, translations absolutely had to be accurate, for fear of leading readers into doctrinal error, or even heresy. But Alfred the Great, one of the most celebrated patrons of the translation of key Christian texts into English, recognized that they could be rendered 'hwilum word be worde, hwilum andgit of andgiete' (sometimes word for word, [but] sometimes meaning for meaning). There is, and always was, a balance to be struck between literalness and fluency: a translation that is too literal will be helpful to learners, but awkward to read, while achieving fluency, or readability, almost always means sacrificing the usefulness of a literal translation, and perhaps even nuances of meaning which, in a religious context, might be crucial. The most literal possible kind of 'translation' – which hardly counts as translation at all – was the scholarly gloss, in which the Old English equivalent of a word in Latin (or vice versa) was squeezed in above the line, leaving Anglo-Saxon readers (or Latinists) to make what they could of the grammatical sense. Some modern editions of medieval poems have mimicked this kind of glossing, printing the text of a poem on the left-hand side of the page, and translations of individual words, and their grammatical function, on the right; this has been done for *Beowulf* and is invaluable for students trying to read the poem in the original, but doesn't really count as a translation.

To return to more or less literal prose translations: since *Beowulf* was adopted as a key text in the history of English Literature, and as a set text on many World Literature survey courses, there has been a steady stream of them; they too are cribs, really, although it's up to individual readers (or classes) whether they serve to completely replace the poem in the original language, or rather, to help the reader to attempt the Old English themselves. The problem with these more-or-less literal prose translations is that they strip the poem of its poetic qualities – diction, metaphor and metre – which have been central to this book. And it is important to recognize that these qualities are very much not ornamental: as we have seen, they bind together the oddly unbalanced storyline of the poem and draw the complex allusions to early Scandinavian history into the monster fights, which, in a prose narrative, assume undue prominence, and can seem unbelievably fantastic. As the American poet

Robert Frost famously, and acutely, said, 'poetry is what gets lost in translation'. A bare recounting of the poem's plot does *Beowulf* no favours at all, and yet this is how many of its readers will encounter it.

There is, finally, the issue of what tone, or register, to adopt in a prose translation. Here, the extremes are the formal and the colloquial. Formality suits the solemn tenor of the original poem (there's not a lot of humour in it!) but inclines towards the ponderous and even the pompous. There is also the danger of what we might call 'fake formality': the adoption of archaic language not only because this is an old poem, but also because archaisms may be thought to be venerable and grave. As I have already remarked, poetry is always susceptible to archaism, the language of time-honoured and established literary predecessors, but of course *Beowulf* was not (or at least, probably not!) ancient in its own time. Nevertheless, some translators have used archaic past tenses for their verbs ('spake' or 'did speak' for 'spoke') and a host of archaic nouns: 'byrnie' for 'mailcoat', for instance. But to be fair, *Beowulf* is full of obsolete words for items and ideas which are no longer current: þegn, thegn, thane and retainer span literary centuries but there is no exact modern equivalent since the whole heroic hierarchy no longer exists.

What has sometimes been called neutral language is likely to be just boring. Colloquial language may be more accessible, and user-friendly, but can seem silly (I mentioned the early twentieth-century translation which begins, jauntily, 'What Ho!'). It is also likely to become dated. One very recent translation of the poem uses a contemporary American idiom which has been praised as a bold, electrifying and energizing move, but may very well seem both anachronistic now and, paradoxically, old-fashioned in years to come. Translating the first word of the poem as 'Bro!' certainly conveys to us the immediacy, the comradeship and the male ethos of the heroic poem, but may not even be intelligible in time.

This last translation is not prose, but verse. The issues surrounding poetic translations of *Beowulf* include all the difficult balances outlined above, but bring in their train a whole lot of other difficult choices. 'Poetry', whatever that is, may not be lost, exactly, but what kind of poetry is replacing the Beowulfian variety? There's really no possibility of reflecting both the literal sense of the line and its original metre and alliteration: the difference between early and modern varieties of English just won't support both. Many of the most critically admired translations of *Beowulf* have used blank verse, recognizing this metre as Shakespearian, the classic high-status metre of English poetry. But blank verse recalls other celebrated examples of English poetry (and, indeed, many translations of classical texts into English), and it is quite foreign to Anglo-Saxon style. And rhyming couplet translations of the poem have been a complete disaster. Imposing an already-established poetic form on a translation of *Beowulf* never seems to work.

Before moving on to two specific examples of poetic translations which attempt to preserve the stylistic features of Old English poetry in general, and *Beowulf* in particular, I want briefly to address a final issue about the translators themselves: poetic translations of *Beowulf* by established poets. It is, for instance, often assumed that a translation into verse by another poet will automatically, as it were, ensure if not the preservation, at least the existence, of 'poetry' in the text, and that it is not lost in translation. But whose poetry is this? We routinely speak of 'Heaney's *Beowulf*' or 'William Morris's *Beowulf*', and it is clear that these poets' choices now dominate our reception of the original poem. This is probably the inevitable downside of poetic translations by poets.

The choices William Morris and Seamus Heaney made in their respective translations of the poem were very different, but both works reflect, in their different ways, the poetic conventions of Old English verse which have been outlined in this book.

I have already shown how the opening lines of *Beowulf* – like the opening lines of many long poems – are a bravura demonstration of the poetic devices available to the poet. So even though – or perhaps even because – these lines present challenges of interpretation and translation, I will take them as representative examples of the translation methods of Morris and Heaney.
William Morris was a highly experienced translator of medieval texts when he published his verse translation of *Beowulf*. He had translated, with the help of an Icelander, Eirkur Magnússon, over thirty Old Icelandic sagas, and a large quantity of Old Icelandic poetry. He had also written poems based on medieval sources and written works based on literature in other medieval languages. His aim with *Beowulf* – so far as we can judge from the resulting translation – was

to give a strong sense of the 'otherness' of the poem itself, and of Anglo-Saxon poetic style in general. In the technical terms used by translation theorists, Morris's *Beowulf* is a 'foreignized' rather than a 'domesticized' version of the original, that is, the reader is always aware that the text is a translation from a foreign literary tradition and language, and can never at any point forget this, because of the evident unfamiliarity of its language and style. Paradoxically, Morris's strangely medievalized translation brings us closer, if not to the original poem, in the way a literal prose translation might, then at least to the experience of reading the original, with its dense diction and distinctive rhythms. But it is hard to read, and very few scholars of either *Beowulf* or Morris have had much time for it. Here are the first eleven lines:

> What! we of the Spear Danes of yore days, so was it
> That we learn'd of the fair fame of the kings of the folks
> And the athelings a-faring in framing of valour.
> Oft then Scyld Sheaf-son from the hosts of the scathers,
> From kindred a many the mead-settles tore;
> It was then the earl fear'd them, sithence was he first
> Found bare and all-lacking; so solace he bided,
> Wax'd under the welkin in worship to thrive,
> Until it was so that the round-about sitters
> All over the whale-road must hearken his will
> And yield him the tribute. A good king was that.

I begin with the first three lines. The opening word 'What!' of course sounds like that mysterious *hwæt* in the original poem (and in fact, *hwæt* is the Old English form of it) but I'm not sure that the modern English word works here as an exclamation; it's now an interrogative word ('What's the matter?') or a sort of particle ('What a good poem!'). The literalness of 'yore days' nicely echoes the sound of 'Spear-Danes' but the force of 'so was it' is hard to understand. The use, throughout Morris's translation, of ''d' for the past tense of verbs (here, 'learn'd', 'fear'd', 'wax'd') is an anachronistic nod to eighteenth-century usage in English, in which the original '-ed' of a past tense would have been pronounced as a separate syllable unless the apostrophe indicated otherwise. It's a sort of faked medievalism – it conveys a sense of the medieval to a reader, but is not strictly true to the history of the language. Morris simply uses the form 'atheling' for the original Old English word *aþeling*, leaving the reader to puzzle out the identity of this rank, and – passing over the archaic but familiar enough verb form 'a-faring' – we see an interesting rendering of the Old English verb *fremian* (to push forward, or further), with Morris's archaic 'framing': in *Beowulf* the *aþelingas ellen fremedon* (princes furthered bravery), while Morris's athelings busied themselves 'in framing of valour'. Detailed analysis of Morris's choices in every half line calls for a little tutorial in the history of the English language.

Obviously the success or otherwise of each individual choice will depend on personal preference. I can see that 'scathers' (those who do harm, or scathe) is only just comprehensible given that 'scathe' is now a rather rare term, but I like the formal closeness to the original Old English word *sceaþa*. I like 'mead-settle' too, instead of the more familiar but rather clichéd 'mead-benches', and many of Morris's new compound words throughout his translation are pleasing. But as with the syntax of 'so it was', I acknowledge that some of his medievalisms fatally impede understanding. For instance, Morris's earl 'fear'd' his enemies, but this means 'made them afraid', 'put fear into them' – and not the very opposite. And sadly – though this is not really Morris's fault – 'round-about sitters' (literally translating *ymbsittendra*, those who are settled around) sound like an occupying force of eco-warriors protesting against a new road. Overall, his translation is much wordier than the sparse style of the original – there are twice as many words in the opening three lines as there are in the Old English, for instance. But reading – and especially, hearing – Morris's text, we can experience the patterns of half lines, and the insistent alliteration, and the variation in the number of syllables in each half line, with some half lines crowded with jostling words, and others with many fewer syllables, so that a slow and emphatic pace alternates with a distinctly urgent one. And Morris sometimes hits the spot: the emphatic conclusion 'A good king was that' is, for me, perfect.

The problem with an extremely foreignizing translation like Morris's *Beowulf* is that for full comprehension and enjoyment, the reader's knowledge of Old English has to be just about good enough to read the text in the original language. It's hard, then, to see the point of the translation at all, except as a diverting philological exercise. But this fundamental issue is not the only problem readers have had with Morris's work. The Scottish poet Edwin Morgan – who also produced a translation of *Beowulf* – was the most, er, scathing: he called Morris's *Beowulf* 'disastrously bad, uncouth to the point of weirdness, unfairly inaccurate, and often more obscure than the original'. He also mocked Morris's collaboration with the Anglo-Saxon scholar A. J. Wyatt, who produced a literal translation of the text which Morris then worked from, although the alliance of scholar and poet ought to have worked well.

The final point I want to make about Morris's *Beowulf* is a slightly curious one. Morris felt a keen need to create a national epic for English-speaking peoples, recognizing that nations need not only the usual paraphernalia of the state, but also a cultural identity, primarily, a shared vernacular language and a body of literature. However, Morris's choice for the subject of a national epic was not *Beowulf,* but the Old Norse story of the Volsung dynasty, the people of the dragon-slaying Sigurðr and the tragic love-triangle of the hero and two women, Guðrún and Brynhildr. Morris transformed this material into what some scholars regard as his masterpiece, the long poem *Sigurd the Volsung.* Morris hoped that this material would be for English-speaking readers the cultural and national equivalent of Homer's *Iliad.* But very few people read it nowadays. In fact, it now seems likely that many more will know *Beowulf,* at least in Seamus Heaney's translation. Why then did Morris pass over *Beowulf* for the role of national epic? Perhaps the tragic theme of the Volsung legend attracted him. Maybe he had become so obsessed by Old Norse literature that it was this that dominated his creative plans. Possibly, he felt that the Sigurd material had a wider – and therefore unifying – appeal. The tactful silence with which post-Victorian critics have treated Morris's *Beowulf* has meant that our question has attracted little critical interest, but I shall return to it shortly.

Seamus Heaney's translation could not be more different from Morris's, and has received near-universal critical acclaim quite unlike the reception of poor Morris's work. Here are his first eleven lines:

So. The Spear-Danes in days gone by
and the kings who ruled them had courage and greatness.
We have heard of those princes' heroic campaigns.

There was Shield Sheafson, scourge of many tribes,
a wrecker of mead-benches, rampaging among foes.
This terror of the hall-troops had come far.
A foundling to start with, he would flourish later on
as his powers waxed and his worth was proved.
In the end each clan on the outlying coasts
beyond the whale-road had to yield to him
and begin to pay tribute. That was one good king.

I have already remarked on how Heaney begins the poem with the solemn monosyllable 'So'. The absence of an exclamation mark has a remarkably steadying effect, preparing us for a recitation which is a ceremonial event, thought-provoking as well as simply exciting. Heaney has explained that the inspiration for this opening came from what he calls the 'weighty dignity' of the formal (and even informal) utterances of his Ulster relatives. This Ulster dimension is a very significant aspect of Heaney's translation. Occasionally, Ulster English is used in spite of the possibility that English speakers outside Ireland may not immediately understand its nuances: words such as 'kesh', 'bawn' or 'thole', used elsewhere in the translation, are not standard English at all, and Wealhtheow 'saluting' the warriors in Heorot has no militaristic overtones in Hiberno-English, but simply signifies a polite greeting, especially in the quasi-courtly romantic register of some Irish folk-songs: 'I took off my hat, and I did salute her'. By contrast, traditional Irish musical culture sometimes provides startlingly appropriate terminology for what happens in Heorot: the transformation of the warriors' experience in the great hall of Heorot from celebratory feasting to the terror of Grendel's attack is embedded in the way the hall timbers 'sing' as Beowulf and Grendel fight in an encounter Heaney calls a 'hall-session', and as we have seen, the Anglo-Saxon *scop* is vividly realized as 'a traditional singer deeply schooled | in the lore of the past'. This is still somewhat specialized knowledge for many English-speaking readers. However, these usages are a vital part of Heaney's strategy: they are coded signals to remind the reader of the shared, but very different, marginality of two cultural and linguistic departures from Standard English: Ulster English and Anglo-Saxon. But there is, as always, a price to pay in terms of the reader's comprehension. And Heaney's finale – 'That was one good king' – echoes Irish usage, but introduces a slightly uncomfortable note of American colloquial language.

So in a rather complicated way, we might see Heaney's politically motivated Irishisms as contributing to a sort of 'foreignizing' translation of the original text. But in terms of syntax, most of the diction, and English literary tradition, Heaney's *Beowulf* (to give the translation its deserved autonomy) seems reassuringly familiar to readers of English poetry. The plentiful use of compound words echoes the work of Gerard Manley Hopkins and John Keats as much as Anglo-Saxon poetic style. Perhaps the most striking feature of the translation as a whole is Heaney's transformation of a succession of untethered half lines into linear syntax – as in those first three lines, which Heaney represents as two separate sentences instead of the ambiguous and heavy double genitive of the original, 'of the Spear-Danes, of the people-kings'. The solemn approbatory truth of the first sentence is underlined by its transformation into a simple statement of fact; the authority of the first-person speaker governs both. The long-term effect of this transformation is what Heaney himself has described as 'a narrative line that sounded as if it meant business'. But in spite of the conventional syntax, a careful reading reveals that almost miraculously each long line still splits quite naturally into two halves, preserving the distinctive rhythms of the half line. Unlike in Morris's translation, there are very few archaisms (apart from those which are still current in Ulster English) and the alliteration is evident but much lighter, although it cleverly reflects how in Old English the alliteration falls on the stressed syllable of a word, and not on a prefix, so that as in the penultimate line, 'yield' alliterates with 'beyond'. Both translators preserve the kenning 'whale-road'.

Heaney's direct experience and knowledge of Old English literature derive primarily from his undergraduate studies at Queen's Belfast; he studied Old English poetry in the original language, and *Beowulf* was firmly situated at one end of a continuum of 'English Literature'. *Beowulf* itself has been preserved in a poetic *koine* which has been described as the standard literary language amongst Anglo-Saxon poets, and in both tone and content it exudes centrality, authority, a profoundly wide-ranging and secure humanity. But *Beowulf* is not now regarded as the foundation stone of the canon; its ever-increasing marginality is perhaps inevitable given that fluency in Standard English – or even facility with Shakespeare or Chaucer – is not enough to read the poem in the original. Ironically, one of the arguments *against* the marginalization of *Beowulf* in university syllabuses is the fact that modern poets such as Heaney once experienced it as part of the canon. *Beowulf*'s shift from centre to margin is a precise mirror image of Heaney's own position: though proudly conscious of writing and speaking from what is perceived by literary London as a linguistic and political margin, Heaney himself centralized that margin, foregrounding the literature, languages and politics of Ulster. Heaney's translation of *Beowulf* is a dizzying amalgam of opposites: very distant meets very recent; centralized margin meets marginalized centre.

This very nearly brings me to the final section of this chapter and of the whole book: the reception of *Beowulf* and its meanings for a modern audience. There are three kinds of violence in *Beowulf*: amongst family members; between warring tribes; and between men and monsters. There are also three monsters: Grendel; his avenging mother; and the dragon. These three monsters are surreal manifestations of the spirit of familiar, squalid human violence. Grendel is part of the legacy of Cain, who initiated the most intimate familial violence, fratricide – the mythic equivalent of neighbourly murder. His mother exemplifies the truism that violence begets violence, a fact disturbingly elevated to an ideal of vengeance in some societies. And the dragon represents a sort of solitary isolationism, nursing gold rather than sharing it; inward looking rather than socially interactive; possessive, defensive and dug in, but given to sudden provocative and flamboyant displays of its power. By contrast, Beowulf and King Hrothgar are peacemaking statesmen, nurturing neighbourly affection and repaying debts of gratitude. But as Hrothgar will find, when he marries off his daughter to the leader of his old enemies, peacemaking is a thankless task.

It is clear that there are a number of resonant correspondences with the recent history of Northern Ireland in Heaney's *Beowulf*. The terminology of the Troubles – tit-for-tat killings, the peace process, mixed marriages, tribal warfare, the legacy of history – is what we reach for to recount the story of *Beowulf*. But Heaney never uses this terminology in his translation. Although well aware of the danger of what he has called 'the slightly cardboard effect that the word "monster" tends to introduce', Heaney has avoided allegorizing the poem into a costume drama version of the Ulster situation. It is up to us as readers to read this into the poem – or not. I turn now to look at what *Beowulf* has been taken to mean by those who have encountered it nowadays: not translators, scholars and students, but film makers, video game inventors and writers of all kinds.

Contemporary meanings

Although translations of *Beowulf* – or indeed any literary text – may vary hugely in terms of form, style, register and fidelity to the original, it remains the case that they can all be regarded as a sort of commentary on the original text, so that even the most faithful ones inevitably reflect a particular understanding of what the poem means to the translator. This is even more true of fictional works which might be called spin-offs of *Beowulf* – original works based on Beowulfian themes and narrative elements. There haven't in fact been very many of them – a point I will return to later – but rather than list them, or summarize their (often woeful) plots, I will just look at four representative examples, with an eye to showing how they reveal what *Beowulf* may have meant to their authors, and how they may actually enhance our own readings of the poem.

Perhaps the most celebrated *Beowulf* spin-off is John Gardner's novel *Grendel* (1971), in which the first part of the poem – up to the death of Grendel – is recounted from the monster's own perspective. Gardner pulls off the imaginative feat of getting inside Grendel's head, not only describing the world of Heorot and Hrothgar from the point of view of an outsider, but recreating the whole animalistic response of a creature outside of human culture altogether. Presenting the action of the poem from an unexpected perspective is one of the strategies of the poet of *Beowulf* himself: relating the story of the Fight at Finnsburg from the grieving Hildeburh's point of view, for instance, or showing us Beowulf's take on Hrothgar's doomed plan to heal the feud between the Danes and the Heathobards by marrying off Freawaru to Ingeld. But we never learn what Grendel is thinking, or what motivates his murderous hostility to the Danes, and his only utterance in the poem is a wordless howl. Gardner's *Grendel* offers not just an alternative perspective, but a wholly new one and, in the process, highlights the terrifying otherness of Grendel in the poem.

In spite of its sensationalist title, Michael Crichton's *Eaters of the Dead* (1976) is a clever and thoughtful re-working of *Beowulf*, again from an outsider's perspective. One of the most celebrated (or notorious) witnesses to Viking funeral practices was an Arab Muslim diplomat, Ibn Fadlan, who described a tenth-century ship burial of a Scandinavian chieftain on the banks of the Volga – the new homeland of the Scandinavian adventurers and settlers who gave Russia its name: the Rus. In a way startlingly reminiscent of a contemporary anthropologist, Ibn Fadlan gives a detailed account of the Rus he observes; he watches and documents the funeral rites, and asks questions of his (presumably) Scandinavian intermediary, contrasting their customs and beliefs with his own (Muslim) norms. Ibn Fadlan is an outsider, and a highly intelligent and cultured person, whose narrow-eyed account of the Rus is justly celebrated, although not necessarily accurate.

Crichton picks up on the figure of Ibn Fadlan as the first-person narrator of *Eaters of the Dead*: he travels back to Scandinavia with the Vikings, and becomes involved in Beowulf's adventures, all the while maintaining his anthropological observations. The novel plays with historicity and authenticity, presenting the account of Beowulf's monster fights as an extension of Ibn Fadlan's actual memoir, as if the novel were a scholarly edition, even footnoting his text. The fundamental premise of the novel – the insertion of a new fictional observer into a pre-existing situation, whether that situation is history or fiction – is a classic technique of historical novels, and in fact, it is almost certainly the fundamental premise of *Beowulf* itself, which seems to insert a fictional figure, the hero, Beowulf, of whom there is no trace elsewhere in history or legend, who has no descendants, and whose name does not fit into the alliterative sequence of his Geatish heritage, into actual Danish history.

The Legacy of Heorot (1987), by Larry Niven, Jerry Pournelle and Steven Barnes, is, in spite of its title, much less closely based on *Beowulf*. But in a way, what seems to have struck its authors most about the poem is for that very reason all the clearer. It's a science fiction novel, although many of the names are mock-medieval, such as that of the hero, Cadmann Weyland. The equivalent of the isolated world of Heorot is a futuristic colony of space travellers on a far-distant and uninhabited planet. They upset the apparently stable and supportive ecology of their new home – a nod to contemporary concerns – and find that they and their livestock are being predated on by a creature which comes under cover of darkness. Again, we see that the monster dominates the action, but there is an intriguing twist in this novel which reflects the horror of maternal vengeance in the same way as *Beowulf*. For those who know *Beowulf*, the most significant connexion between the poem and this novel is that although the novel focuses on the futuristic equivalents of Grendel and his mother, there is no dragon. But at the very end (spoiler alert!) one of the characters recalls that Beowulf was killed by a dragon. Maybe, the narrative voice concludes, there won't be a dragon in this version of the story. But there is a sequel to *The Legacy of Heorot*. To paraphrase the dramatic ending of J. R. R. Tolkien's influential essay on the monsters in *Beowulf*, there is always a dragon waiting in the wings.

Maria Dahvana Headley's 2018 retelling of *Beowulf*, whose title, *The Mere Wife*, decisively shifts the focus of the poem from the hero to the anti-heroine, is set in a fantasy twenty-first-century America, and its ingenious updating of the *Beowulf* story raises distinctly contemporary issues. The initial setting is not Heorot, but Herot Hall, an exclusive gated community built by the family of Roger Herot as a suburban paradise. The police officer hero figure is Ben Woolf, and the equivalent of Grendel and his fiercely protective single mother live outside the gates of Herot, feared by its prosperous but oppressed inmates, and on the far fringes of society. There is even a dragon, in the shape of an abandoned train in a disused tunnel, nursing its deserted stations. *The Mere Wife* uses the scaffolding of the *Beowulf* story to explore issues of contemporary relevance: inequality, the social alienation of poor or deprived communities, the restricted lives of suburban housewives and even police violence. These very topical concerns don't of course tell us much about *Beowulf*, but the suggestion that Herot Hall has been built on the colonized ancestral lands of the outsiders, whilst tapping in to a strongly felt and topical issue in the real world, encourages us to look back a little more closely at the relationship between Grendel and his mother on the one hand, and the assertive splendour of Heorot's construction in what seems to be a wilderness on the other. Who are the newcomers here?

All four of these texts are to some degree explicit in their references to *Beowulf*, so that there can be no doubt that they are inspired by the original poem. But sometimes it's more a question of us seeing present-day actuality mirrored in the events of the poem, and identifying parallels in contemporary works. We may recognize in the depiction of the monsters in *Beowulf* the kinds and causes of violence familiar to us in the modern world – Grendel, resentful at being excluded from the prosperity of Heorot; his mother, embodying the principle of revenge; the dragon, guarding its wealth and position, and lashing out powerfully when provoked. As we have seen, Heaney's Ulster-inflected translation of the poem may make us reflect on these correspondences, but it's far from clear that Heaney consciously built them in to his translation, or chose the poem for translation because of them. Similarly, it has been somewhat light-heartedly proposed that the film *Jaws,* based on a novel of the same name in which a monstrous shark terrorizes a prosperous, paradisal but perhaps complacent community – Amityville! – and is overcome in a heroic encounter, draws on *Beowulf* for the underlying shape of its narrative. Of course, this is highly unlikely. But far more interesting than direct influence in any of these instances is the possibility that there are archetypal forms and issues of how humans deal with existential threats, and that *Beowulf* shares in this common framing of them.

The mention of the film *Jaws* reminds me that before moving on from this exploration of how *Beowulf* has been reworked and re-purposed in so many different forms, we must consider visual versions of the poem – primarily, films and video games. In fact, the film of *Jaws* neatly exemplifies one of the main problems of translating the poem into visual media. Critics of the film praised the opening sequences in which the great shark was either completely unseen or only partially visible as a threatening black fin breaking the surface of the ocean (clearly visible evidence, in another striking parallel with *Beowulf,* appearing at first only in the form of half-eaten mutilated corpses of its victims). But critics, and audiences too, were less happy with the shots of what purported to be the monster itself, a less than convincing studio-constructed model. Films of *Beowulf* have been dogged by this difficulty: as we have seen, the poem relies for much of its effect on the threat of the half-perceived, on an imaginary landscape. And the poem is not only about what actually happens, in the present moment of the narrative, but also about what might happen, or what has happened, and about parallels between these hypothetical or far-distant events and other legends, myths and stories. We are back to the old distinction, so crucial in the poem, between action and reflection. And most fundamentally, even the action of *Beowulf* is recounted in poetry. It takes a major transformation – far larger of course than the transformation from one kind of written text to another – to turn a poem, even a narrative poem, into a film. Films such as Robert Zemeckis's *Beowulf* have had to make serious changes to the poem, and there is no point in dismissing these changes – such as dramatically beefing up a sexual relationship between Beowulf and Grendel's mother, or clearing away much of the historical and dynastic complexity in the poem – as crude travesties of the original.

Video games based on literary texts present similar challenges, but there are in addition some tricky technical obstacles, such as the need to package the material into levels, or stages, that a gamer can work through. But any visual re-working of *Beowulf* can at least draw on – and sometimes, amplify – a familiar medievalist iconography, a set of images which conjures up for us the medieval setting of the work, even though these images may not be based on any actuality at all. The dragon in Zemeckis's film is a good example: everyone knows what a dragon looks like, although no-one has seen one, and everyone's idea of a dragon is an amalgam of the dragons they've read about, or seen depicted in art, with, perhaps, some imaginative flourishes added by the director. The same goes for details such as the dress of the characters, or the style of the buildings, and as we have seen, the poet of *Beowulf* does not routinely provide such details. But one giant anachronism must – with very few exceptions – be left untouched: the language spoken by the characters in medievalist film. And after all, who would want to watch actors struggle with a necessarily inauthentic recreation of Old English, even (or especially) with subtitles? Cinematic experiments of this kind, such as Mel Gibson's *Apocalypto* (dialogue in re-created Mayan) or *The Passion of the Christ* (the dialogue in Hebrew, Latin and reconstructed Aramaic), have been regarded as oddities rather than trailblazers.

Popular conceptions of what life and literature were like in the early Middle Ages are very rarely historically authentic. When we are dealing with mock-ups of dragons, or armour, or mead cups, this doesn't much matter from the point of view of the cinema audience. The more imaginative, the better, within certain limits. But the themes, tropes and ambience of Northern European medieval literature have been repurposed to much darker and more pernicious ends in some sectors of popular culture. From the earliest raciologists in the eighteenth and nineteenth centuries, who contended, absurdly, that the supposed moral and physical superiority of white Europeans had been honed by the bracing northern climate, through to the adoption of medieval images and mythology – especially Norse mythology – by the Nazis, right up to the tattoos, fancy dress and medievalist ideologies of recent extreme right and white supremacist groups in Europe and America, the Middle Ages has provided a starting point and a rich store of ideas and images which they have distorted and abused for their own ends. To explain and document all this would form an ample basis for a whole other book – but its main currents all stem from raciology – the theory of race, a now discredited category with little scientific basis, used primarily as a political tool for dividing humans into supposedly distinct groups. It has been repeatedly shown – and, indeed, seen – that distinguishing racial categories invariably results in making value judgements about the supposed categories – put simply, contending that some races are not only different from, but also superior to others. Those 'races' supposed, rightly or mostly wrongly, to be indigenous to a particular geographical space – for instance, white Northern Europeans – are especially privileged by race theory, and this is where Anglo-Saxon and Old Norse literature comes in, because it is presented as the precious inheritance of the superior white races of Northern Europe.

More generally, the European Middle Ages is often seen through a haze of toxic nostalgia, and believed, mistakenly, to be a place in time before feminism or gender fluidity, a pre-industrial Eden with none of the ills of the modern world, and crucially, before racial mixing. For some Nazi ideologues, even more misguidedly, it was even a time before the supposedly deleterious and weakening effects of Christianity on the people of pan-Germania. But although it's easy to track the development of extreme right and white supremacist ideas from this distorted and inaccurate image of the Middle Ages, the significant thing from the point of view of this book is that

Beowulf itself has never achieved the dubious status of a flagship of alt-right nationalists. J. R. R. Tolkien saw *Beowulf* as a candidate for national epic status, maintaining that the poem 'is written in a language that ... has still kinship with our own, it was made in this land, and moves in our northern world beneath our northern sky, and for those who are native to that tongue and land, it must ever call with profound appeal'. But *Beowulf* has not achieved that status, and in fact, such sentiments as Tolkien expresses are viewed with suspicion nowadays. Perhaps, paradoxically, the absence of *Beowulf* from the nationalist arena tells us most clearly where the essence of the poem lies.

For *Beowulf* is not a celebration of the heroic ideal, but an elegy for it. It is not a relic of Germanic paganism, but a surprisingly sympathetic depiction of an imagined pre-Christian society by a Christian scholar and poet. It is not unreflectingly action-packed, but repeatedly undercuts exciting encounters with thoughtful and often grave reflection. It is not clearly localized – unlike the unmistakeable Englishness of Morris's setting for *Sigurd the Volsung* – but is set, as I have said, in a landscape of the mind. It famously begins and ends with a funeral, the afterlife of the hero Beowulf and the whole heroic world figured in the smoke which rises from his ashes and up to heaven. The poet's verbal artistry is evident from beginning to end. It is a magnificent literary achievement.

Further Reading on Beowulf

There are a great many translations of *Beowulf*, and choosing from amongst them is to some extent a matter of personal preference. However, Seamus Heaney's *Beowulf: A New Translation* (London, 1999) stands apart from the others, managing to convey the poem's gravity without pomposity, and giving the reader some sense of its poetic artistry and subtlety. To my mind, Roy Liuzza's version *Beowulf: A New Verse Translation* (Peterborough, 2000, 2nd edn. 2013) runs it a close second. E. Talbot Donaldson's prose translation (London, 1967, and also included in the first volume of the Norton Anthology of English Literature) is readable and reliable as a crib. Maria Dahvana Headley's *Beowulf: A New Translation* (New York, 2020) is a highly colloquial twenty-first-century rendering of the poem, and has the added bonus of being a feminist response to a poem whose translators and scholars have been overwhelmingly male.

For those who want to attempt to get to grips with the poem in the original Old English, the most accessible edition is George Jack's *Beowulf: A Student Edition* (Oxford, 1994), with an excellent introduction and commentary, and a glossary down the side of each page, matching the poem line by line. The most detailed and weighty edition is *Klaeber's Beowulf (Fourth Edition),* edited, 'with Introduction, Commentary, Appendices, Glossary and Bibliography', by R. D. Fulk, Robert E. Bjork and John D. Niles (Toronto, 2014), which combines the thoroughness of pioneering early scholarship with more recent responses, and has a wealth of textual and contextual information in its critical apparatus.

A Beowulf Handbook (Exeter, 1977), edited by Robert E. Bjork and John D. Niles, contains invaluable summaries and chronological bibliographies of scholarship on the poem in themed sections which allow readers to follow up the scholarly debates – on date, provenance, authorship and so on – which I have largely avoided in this book. Many single-volume studies of the poem are aimed at professional students of Old English literature (the reason why I was motivated to write this book!) but the following short list contains a few of the most accessible, enlightening and thought-provoking ones. Arthur Brodeur's *The Art of Beowulf* (Berkeley, 1969) is an illuminating analysis of the poem's verbal artistry, and Fred C. Robinson's *Beowulf and the Appositive Style* (Knoxville, Tennessee, 1985) briefly but tellingly brings to light the appositions, oppositions and juxtapositions which characterize the poem's distinctive style, structure and scope. Edward B. Irving Jr., in his preface to *A Reading of Beowulf* (Utah, 1999) explains that he has in mind a non-specialist as well as academic audience, and the book is in many ways a model of traditional literary criticism. By contrast, James W. Earl's *Thinking about Beowulf* (Stanford, 1994) engages with contemporary critical theories about literary texts, and applies them to *Beowulf*. Finally, Francis Leneghan persuasively brings the poem's historical elements back to the centre of the poem in *The Dynastic Drama of Beowulf* (Woodbridge, 2020).

The time-honoured classic study of Anglo-Saxon England is Sir Frank Stenton's weighty *Anglo-Saxon England* (Oxford, 1943, etc.), but Henrietta Leyser's much briefer *A Short History of the Anglo-Saxons* (London, 2017) is wonderfully readable and scholarly. And finally, the essays in *Beowulf in Contemporary Culture*, edited by David Clark (Cambridge, 2020), illustrate the various forms *Beowulf* has taken in recent years, in a range of different media, and consider the place of the poem in present-day cultural and historical contexts.

Index